THE LOVE OF MY BULLY

EVERNIGHT PUBLISHING ®

www.evernightpublishing.com

THE LOVE OF MY BULLY

DEDICATION

To taking a chance, to finding the dream. This book holds a special place for me, I hope you all enjoy Drake and Pru's story as much as I did writing it.

THE LOVE OF MY BULLY

THE LOVE OF MY BULLY

Sam Crescent

Copyright © 2020

Prologue
Hatred from the beginning

Prudence, age five

"Look at you. You're so fat, you make the chair crack."

Prudence squealed as someone pushed her off her chair, and she fell to the floor. All the other kids in the class laughed. She tried to stop the tears flowing, but it was hard to do.

Her hands hurt and so did her side.

Looking up, she saw Drake Connor smiling down at her.

"You need to learn to stay in the dirt where you belong."

She tried to get up but he held her in place. His hand, so much larger than her own, kept her near the floor.

She whimpered, not wanting to be afraid, and yet, he had gotten beneath her skin and now she couldn't move.

"Drake, stop it now," Mrs. Winston, their teacher, said, shouting to be heard over the laughter.

Prudence let out a scream as he pulled her hair. "Let go!"

She dropped down, trying to stop him from pulling her hair out, but it didn't work. He kept on pulling and tugging until she had tears in her eyes.

"No Mommy to help you now, is there? No Daddy for you. You're nothing."

The very blissful tears she promised herself she wouldn't cry came. She did want her mommy, really bad. She would protect her. Drake's parents, from what little she knew, never did come. They were never there. He was always on his own unless his friends were around him.

"Everyone here hates you. They don't want to be your friends."

She didn't know how much more she could take before his weight was suddenly pulled off her.

He sneered at her and she didn't like how much he hated her. She wasn't used to being hated at all. Her parents had just moved to this small town, and she couldn't even remember what it was called. The name sounded like a bike or something.

Finally able to stand, she sniffed and waited as the teacher led Drake back to his chair. She didn't yell at him or tell him off, just made him sit back in his chair. Prudence knew deep down this was wrong.

He was mean to her and no one told him off.

They accepted it.

"Now, class, open your reading books and let's all take a moment to just relax."

She stared at the kid who had bullied her.

Drake smirked.

Why didn't the teacher tell him off or give him a

warning? Resting her chin on her hands, she stared at the open book, wondering what it all meant.

"Psst. Don't keep looking at him."

She turned to the young boy at her table. He wore glasses and he scrunched up his nose.

"Why?"

"Drake's mean. Stay out of his way or you'll be sorry. He doesn't like new kids, especially not poor new kids."

Prudence stared down at her worn clothing. Her parents had needed to downsize after her father lost his job. She didn't know what went wrong, only there was a lot of yelling at home. Her mother was often crying because of the unfairness of it all. They had gone from having nice things and a nice home to something really small. There was no yard and their neighbors played loud music and smoked all the time.

They hadn't gone shopping in a long time. Her mother liked to sew, and many of her clothes had been turned into either skirts or shorts, or even shirts. She would stand still for her mother so she could use her needles. She'd learned the hard way not to fidget. The needles she used hurt when they were stuck into her flesh.

"I'm Prudence."

"Sean."

She shook the boy's hand. "Are you friends with him?"

"No. My family isn't good enough."

"He sounds horrible," she said, wanting to make a friend.

"He is. Stay out of his way and don't respond to him. He always hates people who get in his way."

Mrs. Winston shushed them and Prudence quickly looked down at her book. She didn't want to see

Drake anyway. Her back still hurt and so did the base of her neck where he pulled her hair. Back at her old preschool, she never got shoved or hurt.

She didn't know what it was about her that he hated but she had no intention of ever going near him. Boys like that were bad news. Her mother was always telling her to stay away from mean boys. They were no good. Half the time her mother was giving advice, she rarely listened. None of it made any kind of sense to her, but she understood what she meant now. She was talking about boys like Drake.

By the time lunch came, she was so nervous because of her fight with Drake. Would he bring it out into lunch? Would any of the teachers be there to help? It was sunny and Mrs. Winston had told them all to go outside and eat. Benches were lined up in the playground for this occasion. She grabbed her lunchbox, holding it against her chest. Every time she looked over at Drake, he glared at her.

Swallowing past the lump in her throat, she stepped outside.

Everyone had a spot. They were all already friends. She had no one here.

"You can sit with me," Sean said. He stood beside her, a briefcase in his hand.

"Really?"

"Drake hates me. He doesn't come near me. He thinks I've got cooties. If you're okay with my cooties, we can eat together."

She smiled. "I don't mind cooties." She didn't want to sit on her own and she really didn't want to be anywhere near that bully.

Sean held out his hand and she took it, thankful for him even willing to be her friend. Making new friends was never going to be easy. Her mother said she didn't need to be someone different for others to like her. That she had to learn to be herself.

Again, she didn't have a clue what she was talking about, but her mother knew stuff.

They sat down at the table, and she saw others were laughing and pointing as Sean opened up his briefcase and took out his sandwich. So his briefcase was in fact his lunchbox, very strange. She didn't question it, and no one else said anything, so it must be something he did regularly.

"Fishy face!"

"Look, they got cooties."

"Gross."

Sean opened his sandwich and Prudence wrinkled her nose. "What you got?"

"Sardines. Mom always puts them on because my dad loves them but I hate them. Yuck."

"They call you fishy face."

"They're morons."

"You said a bad word."

"They always say worse." Sean shrugged.

Prudence opened her lunchbox. She had a cheese spread sandwich. After she offered him half of her sandwich, he took it with a smile.

"Where do you live?" Sean asked.

Her first lunchbreak, she told him everything. Where she used to live, the house they had moved into. Everything. She didn't leave a single thing out, and in return, Sean told her all about himself and life at Mountain Peak Valley.

That was the town she moved to. The town where her parents hoped to start a new life, and one she didn't want a part of. At least she had one friend, even if he did have a weird briefcase.

****

Prudence was late to come out of class again. She got caught passing a note to Sean, asking if he wanted to come to her house tonight. They'd been best friends since she moved to town and he always played with her. Their parents got along as well. They didn't live too far apart either, a couple of streets away, and her mother let her walk there, so long as she saw her cross the road. She was six now, not a baby. She didn't need constant babysitting.

Finally skipping out of class, she came to a stop when she saw all the kids gathered in a circle. She looked toward the swings where she and Sean usually stood during break.

He wasn't there.

She didn't like the way the other kids were yelling, laughing, and cheering. What was going on? Where was Sean? What had she missed?

Sean was always waiting for her. Nothing ever kept them apart, not even sickness.

She moved away from the swings and made her way toward the group who was watching whatever was in the middle of the circle. The moment she caught sight of Drake hitting Sean, she pushed her way through, determined to get to him.

"Move!"

"Get out of the way!" she cried out as someone shoved an elbow into her side, but that didn't stop her. Clearing the wall of people, she saw Drake straddling Sean, hitting him while Sean tried to ward him off.

No one was stopping the fight.

Her heart raced. She had to stop Drake from smacking Sean. She didn't know what had started the fight and she didn't care either. "Get off him," she screamed.

"Fuck you, fatso." Drake hit Sean even harder.

Not caring about her own safety, she charged toward Drake. The force of her impact knocked him on the ground. She was faster than him and where he'd been straddling Sean, she now was astride him.

"Get off," he said.

She thought about her first day of school. Of all the name-calling and crap he'd thrown her way. She was done with him, with it all.

There had been many nights when she hit her pillow, wishing it was Drake and getting no satisfaction out of it. He had hurt her friend for the last time.

Drawing her fist back, she punched him hard. She landed a blow to his face. Once, twice, and then he pushed her. The circle of friends had gotten bigger and she let out a cry as Drake moved over her. He sat on top of her. He brought his fist back and hit her again, not caring about the strength he used.

She looked back to see Sean was on the ground. He'd pulled his knees up against his chest. But she was strong, so before Drake could make another move, she hit him right between the legs. It did the trick, jerking him off her.

With blood running down her face, she wiped her fingers under her nose and then down her dress. Her long, brown hair had come out of the band her mother put in her hair that morning.

"You saving your pussy of a boyfriend."

She glared at him. "You leave him alone."

"He deserves to be hit. He's trash, just like you."

"The only trash I see is you."

Suddenly, teachers approached the group. All the other kids moved out of the way. She kept her gaze on Drake, not wanting him out of her sight. If she didn't keep an eye on him, he was going to hurt her. She had no doubt.

"What's going on here?"

The sound of the principal's voice had her shaking. She was terrified of him. He was always shouting, and he always took Drake's side, never hers. She hated him. In the year she'd been coming to school, she had seen how Drake was treated so much better. She'd also noticed that Drake was picked up by a limousine, and rarely was he left behind at school, whereas she and Sean always had to wait for their parents.

"Nothing is happening here," Drake said. "Nothing."

"Prudence?" the principal asked.

"Nothing." She whispered the word.

"Sean?"

She turned back to her friend and begged him with her eyes to stay silent. She couldn't have her mother coming back to the school again. She'd be so angry. Her mother hated coming down to the school because it meant taking time off of work, and then her parents would argue. They fought all the time about money. Prudence always tried to avoid it. Drake seemed to always know what to do to rile her up.

"Nothing," Sean said.

He'd be annoyed with her now because she made him lie. Sean didn't like lying. He said it only served to get them all in trouble.

The principal finally walked away and she turned toward Drake, who'd stepped into her path. "You betta watch yourself, trash."

"We just lied for you," Sean said, getting to his feet.

Prudence studied her friend. He grabbed his side as if he was in pain. She went to him, hating to see him in pain, and trying to offer him assistance. She looked up at Drake, and his glare was firmly in place.

"You think I'd get in trouble? My dad owns this town and one day, I will too. You two fucking losers need to see the fucking truth in that." Drake scowled at her one more time before finally walking away.

"He swore."

"So. Like he says, no one cares. Not about us. They only care about making it easy for him." She wiped at her face. Blood came from her nose and she winced. "Why were you fighting?"

"I was waiting in our spot. He didn't like it and said I needed to have my face pounded in."

"He dragged you?"

"He's got some serious issues. What did the teacher have to say?"

"Nothing." She turned to him. Sean hated confrontations and she didn't want to upset him any more than she already had. "Let's go play." She took his hand, leading him to the swings.

Drake was a bad seed. It was what her mother said to her, but she also told her not to get into any more fights. She didn't get it. Drake had hated her from the start, but there was nothing she could do to change that.

****

"You will sit with your partners and draw what you want for the future. Think about it. I know it's hard and you all want to be rock stars, but there is way more to life than that."

Prudence pushed her long hair off her face and stared down at the picture. At eight years old, what did she know about what she wanted in life? She didn't want to look to her *partner*. Ever since third grade had started, the teacher had put her and Drake together.

The bully who liked to hurt her hadn't stopped his taunts. Only now, he was closer to her to get away with it.

She gritted her teeth as he stomped on her foot.

"What do you want to be when you grow up, Trash?"

"Richer than you." It was a stupid answer. After her mother had found out Drake's family owned half of the town, she'd been ordered not to make any waves. She wasn't allowed to hurt Drake in any way. She knew it was because her parents were worried about losing their jobs. Drake's parents owned the town. They worked for the Connors and her parents had told her plenty of times to avoid him. They couldn't afford for Drake's parents to fire them, or worse, push them out of town.

Seriously, though, how could she keep on doing this? It wasn't fair.

His foot let up and she pulled her shoe behind the chair.

"Yeah, right. You're never going to be richer than me. I own your ass, Stewart. You'll always be beneath me."

She glared at him but didn't say anything. In fact, she found the more times she was silent, the more pissed-off he became. Staring down at her piece of paper, she picked up the crayon and began to draw.

"What are you doing?"

"The work. I know what I'm going to be and I know what you're going to be as well."

"You're going to be one of those food-eating contestants."

This time, Prudence smiled. "And you're going to be a sad man with no friends and no one." She didn't know why she kept talking to him or even entertaining him with words. Drake never listened to her and he always did what he wanted to do. He was a cruel boy.

No matter what anyone said, they didn't know the

truth. The teachers always pretended to look the other way and Sean, well, he couldn't fight Drake.

She wasn't afraid of him.

Bullies were cowards, or at least, most of the time, they were. Drake never picked on anyone else. She hadn't seen him hurt anyone or treat anyone the way he did her.

"I won't be alone. You're going to be my pet for life. Trash like you only need money and I've got a whole lot of it. You'll belong to me."

When he kicked her this time, she held on to the table as her chair jerked. Pain sliced up her leg and she tried not to let him see how much hurt he'd caused her. Revealing any kind of weakness in front of him wasn't good.

"Why do you hate me so much? I've never done anything to you." From the first day until now, Drake had hated her. Whenever he saw her, he made sure his revulsion of her was clear. Even his friends hated her, and if he wasn't around, they made sure she knew he wasn't too far. They were all ready to do his bidding.

Her mother never listened and her father was always working. The teachers told her he was just playing rough. She knew only one thing. Every single person she had told was afraid of him and she didn't understand why.

****

Pushing her feet back, she held on to the metal chains of the swing and looked out across the park. Mountain Peak Valley had one of the best children's parks around and Sean was supposed to meet her here any minute. They were going to head off and explore the woods. He wanted to see if he could accurately pick the right mushrooms to eat. Not that they would actually eat them. They were way too dangerous, but Sean liked to think he could do anything. At ten years old, he already thought he knew more than most adults.

There was no challenge he couldn't meet.

Gripping the chains, she let go of her feet and started to swing. After lifting her legs up, she brushed them down, then drew them back up before going back down. Higher and higher, she soared, staring up at the sky. Blocking out everything, including the memory of her parents' latest argument.

Her father was furious because her mother had bought too much alcohol for the party. They were always fighting about money. It was their favorite hobby. She missed their time in the city when everything seemed to be going so well. Her parents hadn't fought half as much. Closing her eyes, she tried to ignore the twisting in her gut but knew deep down it was no use. There was no getting away from the terror that clawed at her.

Her mother had screamed divorce and Prudence knew what that meant. She only hoped they would figure out what their problems were before they gave up on each other. She didn't want to have to live with both of her parents in different houses.

"What are you fucking doing here?"

She lifted her head, opening her eyes to see Drake at the park. He wasn't alone either. He had his friends with him. They smirked at her, standing at his back.

"You own the park now?"

"When are you going to learn that I own everything around here?"

Staring at him, she began to swing again. This wasn't his park. It wasn't anyone's park. Everyone and anyone could come here and have some fun. She wasn't going to be controlled by his bullying ways. This park was free.

When Sean got here, they were going to head out

anyway.

One of Drake's friends, Carl Long, sniggered. "She's asking for it, Drake."

In response to the taunting, Drake moved forward. She tensed up, not really knowing what to do as he suddenly grabbed her leg and pulled hard. His move was dangerous and she let out a scream, seeing no choice but to let go of the swing. They both collapsed on the dirt. She hit her head and reached out to rub the suddenly sore spot.

Drake held her arms, pressing them above her head, keeping her trapped.

She wriggled and noticed his friends went for the swing so it had no chance of hitting Drake in the face. "Let me go."

"You know, Trash, you're really starting to piss me off. You don't know when to stay to your own side of the tracks. No one wants you here." Hatred swam in his eyes.

"You're on my side of the tracks, rich boy."

She heard the gate opening and closing. Lifting up, Drake suddenly pressed an arm across her throat. The threat was there even though he didn't push too hard.

She would never understand why he hated her so much and if she was truthful, she didn't care. He was an asshole and she'd been putting up with him and his bullying ways for five years now. She wouldn't run away screaming. She wouldn't do anything.

"You're not the boss of me. You're not wanted here, Drake. Leave." She tried to lift up but he was stronger than her. No matter how hard she tried to fight him, Drake always seemed to be the one with the upper hand. It was growing tiresome.

Collapsing back on the ground, she waited.

He smirked. "Giving in already, Trash?"

"My name is Prudence."

"Get off her," Sean said.

They both turned to see her friend a couple of feet away from them. Both boys were growing tall and filling out. Sean kept showing her his muscles and making her touch them.

"Well, well, well. Are you two boyfriend and girlfriend?"

Drake's friends smirked but Sean merely stood, watching. His hands were clenched into fists. Even though Sean had been working out and training, she didn't know if he was any match for the bully.

With Drake distracted, she used his weight against him, pushing him off her to break free. Within seconds, she stood beside her best friend, scowling at her enemies.

"You're in our part of town, Connor," Sean said.

She'd never heard him sound so deadly before. She reached out to Sean, taking his arm in her own, holding him tight against her.

Drake smirked at the action. "You seen this bullshit? As if I want to be here."

"Then go," she said.

She was used to Drake's bad language. Out of all the guys at school, he always seemed the oldest.

Drake turned his cold stare to her. "You think you can tell me what to do?" He took a step toward her.

She felt Sean shake a little. Neither of them would be able to take on Drake and his friends.

"Let's go," she said. "He's not worth it."

Prudence didn't even make it a step before Sean was suddenly pulled out of her hands. To her horror, she watched as Drake's friends slammed him to the ground and proceeded to kick and hit him.

She went to him, but Drake held her against the

metal bars of the swing. One of his arms was across her throat, cutting off her air. With his other hand, he pulled on her hair. It wasn't up in a band so he only caught a few strands, but it was enough to make her scream for help.

Still, he wouldn't let her go. Tears filled her eyes as the pain exploded on her head.

"Leave him alone. Please."

"I like to hear you beg. Beg me, Trash. Beg me to stop your friend's beating."

She saw he wasn't kidding. This wasn't a joke to Drake. He truly despised her. He pressed harder across her throat and she tried not to panic. It was no use though.

Gripping his arm, she couldn't stop him from hurting her. The evil in his eyes took her breath away. "Please, don't hurt him."

"I can't hear you."

She cried out as he pulled on her hair. "Please, let him go. Please, please, please." She kept repeating it, getting louder as he continued to yank at her hair. He'd lifted the arm across her throat but she had no doubt who held the control here, and it wasn't her, not even close. Drake was always in control.

He smirked. "Boys, stop."

His friends dropped Sean, who was now bleeding. He curled up into a ball, crying softly.

She tried to pull away from Drake, only, he wouldn't let her go. She had to wait until he was ready for her to go.

"You better be careful about opening your mouth at the wrong times, Trash. It's going to get you killed." With that, Drake pressed a little harder against her throat before finally letting up. He left the park with his friends.

Pru reached down to help Sean up.

"Stop it. I'm fine," he said, pulling out of her arms.

"Sean, please. I didn't mean for any of this to happen."

"Why did you agree to meet in the fucking park?" Sean got to his feet and he wiped at the blood running down beneath his nose.

"How would I know he'd be here? He's never here. This is our place." She didn't know why Sean was so pissed at her.

"I'm heading home." He started to walk off and she felt like the world's shittiest friend.

"Sean, please. I know you're angry."

He suddenly stopped and turned toward her. "Yeah, I'm angry. When he's around, why do you have to stay and fight? This could be you, Pru. You ever think about that? He could hurt you."

"I don't ask for any of this."

"Dammit, I know. I'm tired of his shit." He bunched his eyebrows, staring off as if he was trying to figure something out.

Without waiting for him to reject her, she walked right up to him and wrapped her arms around him. "One day, he'll move on. He'll get bored of all this, and we'll never hear from him again."

She kept on waiting to see if Sean forgave her.

He didn't put his arms around her at first. Seconds ticked by, and just as she was about to give up, he finally held her. "I shouldn't have shouted."

"I forgive you."

"I would have pounded his face," he said.

She smiled. "I know."

"Friends."

"Forever."

Taking hold of his hand, they walked out of the

gates and toward his home. Sean's mother was shocked by his injuries. When she heard who did it, she didn't tell them to go and deal with them. No, she placed Sean on a chair and attended to his cuts and bruises.

Drake and anyone he was friends with were always protected.

One day, he wouldn't have all this power anymore, and she wouldn't have to be afraid.

Chapter One
One more year to go

"Come on, you guys. Don't be total losers," Ree Addie said.

Sean was already rolling his eyes.

Ree had joined their twosome three years ago when she moved to Mountain Peak Valley from New York. It had been a huge adjustment for her as she was used to city life, and they were all small-town peeps.

"We're not total losers just because we don't want to party," Sean said.

"Whose party is it?" Prudence asked.

Ree pressed her lips together and neither she nor Sean needed any other clues as to whose it was. Drake Connor's party.

"Hell, no," Sean said. "What the hell do you see in him?"

"Nothing."

Prudence didn't say anything because Ree had confided in her that Drake didn't give her the time of day. She personally didn't get the infatuation her friend had with Drake, but then, she'd rather avoid the kind of attention she still got from him. Ree though was a bit of a flake. She and Sean were no fools. If Ree was given a better offer of friendship, they wouldn't hear from her. Still, Prudence didn't have it in her to break off the friendship. The last thing she would want was to see Ree eating alone.

"You've got to see something, otherwise, you wouldn't come to us asking to go to his party."

"I just thought it would be cool. You know? Next year we're seniors and we're out for the summer. Come on, it could be good."

Sean slammed his locker closed. "No. I'm not

going."

"Me neither," Prudence said.

"Why not?"

"Are you, like, blind to all the shit he pulls on Prudence?" Sean asked, stopping in the middle of the hallway.

While Prudence's growth spurt stopped in sixth grade, Sean had continued to grow. He was one of the tallest guys in school. If he'd been athletically inclined, she had no doubt the basketball team would have loved to have him. Only, Sean screamed at balls flying toward him, and loathed any kind of sport, so it was a no-go.

"If she didn't goad him, it wouldn't be a problem!" Ree sighed, looking all around the corridor.

Prudence chuckled as Sean looked ready to vomit. "She really does have a crush on that slimeball, doesn't she?" he asked.

"I'm afraid so. It looks like she won't listen to reason." Prudence shrugged. Ree was a good friend … most of the time. Her infatuation with Drake made her kind of suck though. Again, Pru wouldn't stop talking to her even though she really wanted to date the guy who made her life a misery. She and Drake had never gotten along and she doubted they ever would.

It wasn't doubt, it was a fact. She couldn't stand the prick. He truly believed he was something special, and she hated how he assumed everyone would do whatever the hell he wanted just because he said so.

Not this girl.

No matter how many times he pushed her into a locker, or hit her, or whatever his new torment was. She'd opened her locker to spiders crawling out. There had been a putrid and acrid liquid poured all over her stuff, or he simply threw it at her on the way out of school.

Teachers looked the other way and well, she stopped retaliating. She didn't know when it happened, possibly not long after she had gotten her first period, but she just grew up. Where Drake was an asshole who would make her curse, scream, and do anything to get one up on him. He no longer registered on her radar. She didn't walk around school fearing for her life. She simply ignored all the bullshit. She either cleaned up the mess he caused or dealt with each problem as it came to her. Each time not showing him it bothered her. She didn't know if that was what bothered him more, her complete lack of giving a shit.

"It'll be fun. Please, don't make me go on my own. It wouldn't be fair. You guys are my besties and I do all the same stuff with you. When we hang out, we listen to music, watch movies, you know, that kind of thing."

She didn't. The only time Ree ever remembered they were friends was in classes they shared. Ree hated sitting alone, and despite Ree's obsession with Drake, Pru didn't see a reason to not sit with her.

"We've got a date with pizza," Sean said, putting his arm around Prudence's shoulder. "We can't crash at no rich boy's party."

"Prudence, please, I know you won't let me do this alone."

"I'm sorry. Sean and I do this every single year. It's tradition. A way to ring in the summer." She wrapped her arm around her friend and Ree glared at the both of them.

"Neither of you are fair at all. I just want one night to go to this party and all summer we can hang out." Ree stomped her foot.

Laughter from across the hall caught Prudence's attention and she saw Drake with his group of friends and girls who liked to hang around him.

"Instead of having a temper tantrum like a child, go and talk to him. He's right over there." Prudence nodded her head in his general direction.

Ree turned and when she looked back at them, there was a huge smile on her face. "Oh, my, you're so right. I have nothing to worry about."

Without waiting a second to think it over, Ree left them alone and headed toward Drake.

"You think this is a good idea?" Sean asked.

"I don't know. He's never been pissed at her. It could work. I don't know if I feel sorry for her or not."

"I don't. Whatever he does, she has it coming." Sean didn't lower his arm and they stood in the same place, waiting for Ree to make her decision.

"Don't be like that."

Prudence watched as Ree hesitated a few feet from Drake. He hadn't even noticed her approach yet. He was laughing at something one of his friends said.

"Why not? She's always talking about him and making excuses. Why are we even friends with her?"

Prudence nudged his arm. "We're the only ones who could put up with her brash city ways and attitude."

"No, you put up with it because you understood her. Me, I don't get her. She's seen what a dick he can be to you. Why would she think for a second we'd even want to hang out with him? You've heard all the rumors about his family. When someone makes waves, they disappear. Do you remember that Colin guy a couple of years back? They wanted to buy his property and land for some kind of development, and he wouldn't sell? Then all of a sudden, he's wanted for some kind of drug smuggling. He was arrested, the key thrown away, and the land is up for sale. I tell you, they're bad news. The further away we are from him, the better, and there's no way in hell I'm changing my mind."

She placed her head on his shoulder. Sean had always hated Drake from the time at the playground where he was beat up. She always felt responsible for it. Drake hated her and because Sean opted to be her friend, Drake always made sure he paid for it. Of course, Drake's parents were another problem altogether. She had never personally met them, but the rumors were rife around them. No one would stand up to them, not in their small town. They owned half of the factories and businesses, and there were rumors that extended to them blackmailing cops or buying them to do their dirty work. Whenever someone got in their way or didn't bow down to their power, something nasty would magically happen that would cause the person to leave, go to prison, or to sell up.

It often made her wonder if that was why Drake was as bad as he was. He was a bully, but deep down she knew there was more to him than she cared to find out. Then, she'd find herself not really caring because he'd say or do something that really pissed her off, and she wouldn't care what he went through or why.

She wasn't a bad person, though. Until she met Drake, she'd never once started a fight or gotten in trouble. At least in the past year, she'd learned to rise above and now she always held the upper hand, much to Drake's irritation.

Watching Ree, she couldn't help but feel sorry for the other girl. She was so desperate to be with Drake.

Ree took a step closer and Prudence tensed up as Drake and his boys all looked toward her.

"She really shouldn't have done this," she said.

Sean shrugged. "We warned her and now we've got to stand and wait here to see what evil dick has to say."

She giggled. "Evil dick?"

"You bet."

"You're crazy."

"True. I never claimed to be anything but." Sean pulled her in close, kissing the top of her head.

"Stop, stop. Don't be stupid." She burst out laughing.

This was why she adored Sean. No matter what, they always had each other's back. They both stayed still, watching as Ree finally began to giggle and flirt with Drake.

He didn't look impressed and the girls who hung out with them. They looked like they wanted to claw her eyes out.

"I don't see the attraction. He's a class-A asshole."

"True, but maybe that's a thing for chicks nowadays."

"You're a chick," Sean said. "I don't see you hanging off his every word."

"I'm clearly immune to his asshole ways." She sighed as Drake glared at Ree. She wasn't close enough to hear what he had to say, but Ree turned on her heel and walked over to them.

"Oh, no, he's being a douche again," Sean said.

She knew Sean wasn't a big fan of Ree, but she liked the girl. Ree reminded her a little of what it was like when she was younger and in the city. Ree hadn't left the city that long ago and often talked about her time in high school.

Ree had tears in her eyes.

"You okay?" Prudence asked.

"What the fuck do you care, bitch?" Ree pushed her arm away and before she could stop her, Ree was already running down the corridor and out of the school.

"Fucking bitch," Sean said.

"Don't. Don't even go there."

"I'm sorry. I don't know how you put up with it."

"She's got a crush and I like her."

"Come on, let's get out of here. I want to go for some pizza."

Prudence rolled her eyes. "I've got to pee. You take my bags and I'll meet you out there in a second?"

"Sure thing, baby."

She chuckled as she left him alone. Sean was always making teasing, cute comments. They were sweet and always made her laugh.

Before making her way inside the bathroom, she hummed to herself, moving out of the way as three girls left. She entered a stall and stared at the graffiti on the wall.

I fucked Drake in the locker room.
My boyfriend has a big dick.

Those were just two of the nicer things scribbled on the bathroom door. She wiped herself, flushed the toilet, and moved to the sink.

Out of the corner of her eye, she saw movement and cried out as she was suddenly pressed against the counter. Each sink had a small section of counter on either side of it.

"What kind of game are you playing?" Drake asked.

"You're in the girls' bathroom. You're the one playing games. Not me." She tried to straighten but Drake was just too strong. She stayed down, gritting her teeth. Was this another game of his where he tried to make her respond to him?

The only thing she knew to do was not give him the satisfaction of seeing her scared. She stopped fighting him, letting him have his way. He growled before lifting her up and spinning her around.

Some of her hair flew into her face. She had it in a low bun but with his attack, a few strands had loosened. Staring at him, she waited for his next accusation. It had been a couple of days since they'd last had a standoff. Gripping the edge of the counter, she watched him, very much aware they were alone.

Neither of them broke eye contact, waiting for the other to give in and admit defeat. She wasn't going to back down and from the look of it, neither was Drake.

"Why don't you let Ree go to your party?" she asked.

"I didn't say she couldn't go to my party. Why is she paying attention to me, huh?" he asked. "What are you playing at?"

She lifted her hands and he caught them, holding her wrists. "Wow, you really have issues with trust, don't you?"

"What are you fucking playing at?"

"Nothing!" She spoke the word slowly so he'd get the fucking clue. "You really think you matter enough to me to even give you the time of day?"

He stepped close to her. The menace in his gaze terrified her. She stared at him, waiting for whatever bullshit he was going to do. They were both seventeen years old, and they'd been fighting like this for so long now.

Drake could hit her, call her names, say and do whatever the hell he wanted to. He often did anyway, but she wasn't going to let him hurt her anymore. They were just words and the pain from his touch would disappear, as would the bruises.

She'd given him a fair few over the years as well. She wasn't proud of it, but she'd only been sticking up for herself. Every time she hit him, or hurt him back, the euphoria never stayed with her. In fact, she would go home flooded with guilt, knowing she'd hurt someone else. Pain never solved anything.

Did he ever feel guilt over what he'd done to her? Or was he happy to inflict all kinds of pain?

"What is it you're after, Pru?" he asked, standing so close.

She frowned. "I'm not after anything."

His hand sank into her hair, making her gasp. If he pulled or yanked on her hair, it was going to hurt. She felt the tiny hairs on the back of her neck begin to stretch and it made her eyes water. He tilted her head back and got right up in her face.

"Please," she said, hating how she sounded. She promised herself she'd never beg for anything from him, and knowing she'd just done that filled her with anger. "Let me go."

"That's the fire I'm used to. You think I don't know what you're doing?"

"I'm doing nothing. You're being an asshole." He was starting to rise a response out of her and she hated him for it. "What do you think you're doing, huh? You're giving yourself away right now. I've done nothing. Ree likes you. You want to know what I've got to do with that? Absolutely nothing, because it's not my problem she has sick taste in men." She reached out to grab his hand, wrapping her fingers around his wrist. "Let me go." She didn't squeeze his hand, simply laid hers against his wrist. With her fingers directly over his pulse, she felt how fast it beat.

Was he excited about their confrontation?

"If Ree comes to my party tonight, I'm going to fuck her brains out, record everything I do to her, and then I'm going to post it up on my page for the entire world to see," he said.

"You … bastard," she said. "I don't know what she sees in you, but she actually likes you. And you're willing to throw that away because of what? Because you hate me? I'm not going."

"Then I suggest you come, because otherwise, your friend is going to get a whole lot of air time, believe me. And let's just say I like it dirty with my woman pliant and ready to take cock. I'll have her willing cunt on the screen for all to see. You never know. Once I've had my fill, she might be useful to a couple of porn studios."

Prudence cried out as he tugged on her hair.

"Or I could play with you."

The pain in the back of her head made tears fill her eyes, and they slowly begin to fall. Drake simply watched her and leaned in close. His tongue pressed to her cheek. She cringed as he slowly drew his tongue up, licking her tears.

"What the hell are you doing?" She pushed against his chest.

"Don't you want this? Isn't it what you've been dreaming about?" he asked.

"Ew. No, I would never dream of you in that way. Get off me. Ree wants you. I don't. How could I ever want you? You're a horrible person." She couldn't believe he would even think that. They hated each other.

He shoved her hard and she cried out as she hit the counter, falling to her ass. She would have a bruise on her hip from the impact. Tears continued to escape her eyes, and she tried not to panic as he gripped her neck, tilting her head back to look at him.

"Let me go."

"Oh, I'll let you go when I'm good and fucking ready." He squeezed her neck tightly as he cupped her jaw. "I'm going to fuck Ree tonight and when I'm done, everyone is going to know just how easy she is."

"Leave her alone. I don't know why, but she likes you. You're a fucking monster." Grabbing his fingers, she bent them, pulling him away from her, and got to her feet. She saw the happiness in his eyes. The crazy look as if he was getting off on her fight.

"What are you willing to give me?" he asked.

"What?" This guy was giving her whiplash and she didn't know what the hell he was talking about now. Why would she give him anything? He stroked a finger down her cheek and she swatted at his hand. "Stop it."

"What will you give me to leave your friend alone?"

"Damn it, Drake. Why can't you just see she likes you? Can't you be a decent guy and just let her … fall for you?" She wanted to cringe at her own words. Why was she even talking about this? Was she crazy?

Drake, in response, threw back his head and burst out laughing. She didn't appreciate his reaction in the least.

"You know what, forget it. You're not worth it." She made to pass but again, he stopped her, stepping in front of her. "What the hell? I've done nothing to you. You're acting a little freaky coming into the girl's bathroom." She would say and do anything to get him to leave her alone.

He stepped toward her and even as she tried not to, she took a step back, which only served to make her hate herself for her own weakness. With every step he took, she kept trying to escape, but soon, the bathroom wall was behind her and she had nowhere to go. His hands slammed against the wall, trapping her against him.

"Will you stop?" she asked, needing her space.

"What's wrong, Pru? Am I scaring you?"

She didn't like how he wasn't calling her names. What game was he playing at? She preferred it when he called her names like Trash, Fatty, Ugly, all the taunts she was used to and didn't care about. They all melded into one. Hearing her name on his lips, it felt wrong.

"What are you after?" she asked, throwing his question back at him. He'd followed her into the bathroom for no reason.

"I want to know if I'm scaring you. Are you afraid, little girl?"

She wasn't afraid. She was fed up, angry, and just wanted to go home. Putting her hands on his chest, she glared at him. "I'm not afraid of assholes. What are you going to do now? Kick me? Hit me? What else you got, Drake?"

Shut the fuck up! What are you doing? Why are you even trying to irritate him?

She was beyond bored and irritated. She wanted him to stop his bullshit and to leave her the fuck alone. After this summer, they had one year left and when it was over, she intended to go to college and never look back. They both wanted out of this bullshit town.

Just as she was about to shove him back, Drake did no more than wrap his fingers around her neck, taking her completely by surprise as he began to put pressure on her windpipe. This was the closest he'd ever gotten to being scary. Even as she tried to calm her nerves, it didn't help.

She was so fucking afraid right now. So scared. The venom in his gaze was easy to read, and she wanted to scream at him, to beg him to stop. She kept her lips firmly closed, waiting for him to have his fun so he could just leave.

"You think you know me, Pru. I suggest you be very careful. You're afraid now, and if you're not, you will be. I will see fear in your eyes again. Keep on pushing me."

She sank her nails into his wrist. "You're the one who came here. Not me. I have no wish to push you or to do anything." It was the truth. Drake kept pushing her and she didn't know why. He was really pissing her off, and yes, it was scaring her a lot. Choking her went above bullying. It was more threatening, more long-term, especially if she couldn't get away from him. No one would believe her if she told on him. "Get out of my way." With one forceful shove, Drake stumbled back.

Pleased she caught him off-guard, she stepped over him, not paying him any more attention. She hated how her heart raced and the lick of fear traced down her spine. She didn't want to be anywhere near Drake, not now, not ever. There really was something seriously wrong with him.

No one stopped her as she rushed out of the high school. For the entire summer, she didn't need to come back here, and that was how she wanted it to be.

Sean was already waiting in the car.

Ree wasn't in sight. For now, Prudence was more than happy with that. After sliding into the passenger seat, she buckled her seatbelt and leaned back in the chair.

"You okay?" Sean asked.

"Yeah, of course. Why wouldn't I be?" She didn't need to tell him about her latest encounter. Clearing her throat, she sat up, playing with the radio and turning on a channel with loud music.

"You seem a little ... flustered."

"Big words, Sean. I'm good. Come on. Let's kick off his summer without the twenty questions. You think we can do that?"

"Yeah, we can." Sean let out a loud whoop as he

pulled out of the parking lot. Staring in the rearview mirror, she saw Drake as he exited the school. She didn't look him in the eye. His narrowed glare scared her.

Tapping her fingers on the doorframe, she let the wind run through her hair and she tried to relax.

School was out.

Life would be good.

More than good.

It would be spectacular because she had Sean. Her parents spent most of their time working. She didn't mind. The less time they all spent together, the less arguments they had. This would be a good summer as it would be her last one spent near home. Next year, after graduation, she intended to leave town and start a whole new life away from this place. Make new memories and dreams. None that even had the vaguest hint of this town attached to it.

Smiling to herself, she basked in the peace that she knew wouldn't last.

Chapter Two
It's just a party

Glaring, Drake watched Prudence drive off with her idiot of a friend. It wasn't like she had hurt him. It would take a lot more than a shove to even affect him. No, what pissed him off was Prudence thinking she could get away with it. She thought she was better than him. He saw it in her eyes, and had to witness it from the moment she turned up in town. Her parents were always around her. Coming to the school because he'd made her bleed, taking care of her. She was weak, pathetic. No one should need their parents to fight their battles.

If he really wanted to, all he would have to do is give his parents their names, and Prudence wouldn't have such a comfy life. The right words at the bank would squeeze them dry. His parents knew how to make problems go away, but for some reason, he never did tell them about her.

"What's got you looking pissed?" Marco asked, taking a bite out of his apple as he approached.

With him were Nick and Carl, his lifelong friends. Part of him believed they were only his friends because they were afraid of him. He didn't blame them. They knew what he and his family were capable of.

In his world, he got whatever he wanted because money spoke volumes, and with so many people beneath them, they could do whatever they wanted. He'd seen his father do this all of his life. All you had to do was have the balls to see it all through.

"Man, you're staring at Prudence again. What did the slut do?" Carl asked.

They knew about his hatred for the girl who had come to Mountain Peak Valley. She wasn't afraid, flashing those green eyes at him. She always saved her glares for him the most, and it pissed him off.

What also pissed him off was Sean's determination to stay friends with her. No matter what he did to the prick, Sean was always there, sniffing around her, helping her out. One day, Prudence wouldn't have anyone to turn to.

He walked toward his car, ignoring his friends as they demanded to know what was going on. He wasn't in the mood to tell them. They would only come up with lame excuses that he really didn't need to hear. After climbing into his car, he turned the engine over and his friends quickly jumped into the car. One by one, they didn't say a word as he drove out of the school grounds. He ignored the chicks begging for his attention as he drove by. They were all the same. Most of them loved to be tag-teamed by him and his buddies.

Prudence wasn't one of them, though.

She didn't come squealing to him for attention like her latest friend, Ree. Her blonde friend was constantly trying to get his attention and it irritated him.

Pulling up across the street from Prudence's house, he watched as Sean climbed out of the car, heading to the trunk.

Prudence was laughing at something he said, tucking her long hair behind her ear. He hated to see her so happy. From the moment she arrived in his life over ten years ago, he couldn't stand her with her sweet smile and calm attitude. Lately, though, nothing he did got a rise out of her. He loved it when she hit back at him.

Sean slammed the trunk closed and Prudence took his bag from him. He didn't like how close the two of them were.

"I hate to break it to you, Drake, but you're coming off as a little stalkery right now, and not even with a chick who will bang you. No offense, but I wouldn't spend all this time with Prudence Stewart. She's a first-class bitch and she hates your guts," Marco said.

Drake ignored his friends and simply watched her. He didn't even know what it was about her. He loved to see her hurting. To watch her eyes fill with tears, but it would only ever last a split second before the girl with a spine was back.

Since they were kids, Prudence never took any of his shit. Even at school, she would hit back harder. Slap him, kick him, yell, scream, and cuss. Teachers were fucking useless since they never listened to her. He was Drake Connor. His father and mother weren't the kind of people you wanted against you. They helped to fund the schools, to bring more positive focus to the academia as well as their football team. Being rich in a small town had its benefits, and well, Drake was used to enjoying every single one of them. Including having teachers look the other way. He glared at the girl who refused to back down, who refused to be afraid.

In the past couple of months, she'd changed. There were no more tears. He couldn't get a single rise out of her, no matter what he did. She would either take what he dished out, or she'd flat-out ignore him.

No comebacks.

No insults.

No violence.

Nothing.

He was used to this kind of treatment from Sean but not from Prudence. Her best friend was a grade-A pussy.

"Dude, this is getting really fucking creepy," Marco said.

"You got a problem with it, get the fuck out of my car. I don't have time for you, asshole."

"Dude, what is your problem?" Nick asked.

Pressing his foot to the gas, he ignored his friends, taking off down the street, nearly hitting a kid on a bike as he did so. He slammed his foot on the brake.

His friends burst out laughing as they always did.

Dismissing them, he sped up, wanting to go as far and fast as he could and never look back.

They were all howling and laughing, loving what he was doing. When he cleared the town, he smirked as he pulled the car onto the opposite side of the road just as a truck was coming toward him.

"Drake, don't be a dick," Carl said.

"Come on, Drake, get off the road," Nick said.

"This isn't funny," Marco said.

While they were all moaning and shitting themselves, he relished the fear, the tightness inside him as the truck got closer, blaring its horn.

When he faced death, it was when he felt so fucking alive. This wasn't a test. This was him challenging another driver. Daring them to hit him, to take out his little car. Car against truck, it wouldn't survive.

What would death feel like?

Could he handle the pain?

His parents would be so pissed at him for causing trouble, but he liked it, lived for it. This was what got his blood pumping. The thrill and excitement of the unknown driving him ever closer.

Finally, he pulled off the road and drove right past the truck. Up ahead was a small parking zone. No other cars were there, and as he parked the car, he burst out laughing.

"Did you fucking see that?" he asked. His hands were shaking but he kept them on the steering wheel.

"You're a fucking asshole," Marco said.

Each one had something to say about their near brush with death. They could all fuck off as far as he was concerned. He wasn't going to kill them. Death was something he was going to take for himself.

"You want to get out and walk, you fucking can. I won't miss you," Drake said.

None of his friends climbed out of the car. They never would. They were afraid of him, just like everyone else.

Pulling back onto the road, he spun around, heading back to town. He didn't stop at Prudence's house though. He went straight for home. Parking right outside the house, he saw his father's car in the driveway. He climbed out, not waiting for his friends, but entered his home in time to hear his mother and father shouting.

"You're a poor excuse for a man. I don't know why I put up with you."

There was a resounding slap, followed by his father's voice. "You put up with me because I'm the only one here who'll keep your ugly ass. You like my money and you like being my bitch. You like how you're the fucking queen here. So shut your fucking mouth."

Drake rolled his eyes. He'd gotten used to his parents' violent outbursts. It was nothing new and he certainly wasn't going to run screaming about it to the therapist. He had used it on the previous school therapist but that was to garner sympathy so he could bang her, which he had done, and then she'd gone.

Drake moved out to the pool to see it had been cleaned per his instructions. His parents would leave in an hour or so and then he could have his party.

"What is going on with you, man?" Marco asked, coming to stand beside him. "You're quiet and you're angry all the time. What gives?"

Nothing was wrong with him. He simply didn't

give a shit, but if he said that, people seemed to think there was something wrong with him.

"Are we the kind of guys that sit around and talk now? You grow a pussy since you been banging that chick Charlene?" Drake stared at Marco, waiting to see what his friend would do.

Like always, Marco gritted his teeth and stared down at the floor.

He'd fucked Charlene months ago. Mainly because she'd begged him to. He knew she'd gone through all four of them, with Marco being the last one. His friend clearly thought there was something *special* between them but the truth was he didn't mean shit to her. Marco was just a dick and Charlene just a cunt, but he was the bad guy to point it out.

Sitting back, he stared up at the ceiling, waiting for his parents to leave. All he needed was the final slam of the door. His parents didn't give a shit if he had parties or even fucked over the entire house, just so long as by Sunday night it was clean.

He paid a lot of money to a cleaning company to come on Saturday to make sure the place looked as good as new. Rubbing at his eyes, he waited. They were taking fucking longer than usual and starting to piss him off.

Pinching the bridge of his nose, he closed his eyes and counted in his head. By the time he got to thirty, he heard the slam of the door.

Smiling, he looked toward his boys. They were all fucking sheep. They kept on looking at him for guidance and shit. He didn't even know why they were his friends half the time. Actually, that wasn't true. It was because they were paid to keep an eye on him. He'd seen the evidence of that in his father's study. He'd caught sight of the bank accounts his father placed money in every single month. Not to mention the fact they were always hanging around with him. He'd even tried to test each of them to see if he could push them away. So far, nothing had worked. They all had stuck around to see how far he'd go.

"Time to call the calvary, boys. Let's get this party started." While his friends dealt with getting their school peers to his house, he called the guys who could bring him the booze without question. Money talked a hell of a lot more than threats.

Within an hour, his place was heaving. People were everywhere. Chicks were naked, jumping all around and begging to be fucked. Drinks adorned every single counter, and a couple of kids were already smoking dope or dealing out coke.

He didn't touch any of the drugs. Swigging on his beer, he looked around the party, waiting for one person, Prudence. He hadn't caught sight of Ree yet, but that bitch was simply waiting to be taken into a corner and fucked.

Moving his way through the crowds, he glared at the girls who thought they had a chance with him. He fucked who he wanted to and anyone else could wait in line or fuck off.

He caught sight of Marco snorting a couple of lines. Just because they hated how far he was willing to push with death didn't mean they didn't have their own vices. All three of his friends were pathetic, weak, fucking morons. None of them were a challenge to him.

One picture taken at just the right angle and they were all fucking fools. Each and every single one of them. He got a clear shot of Marco, making sure to capture the lines and the sweet look of release on his face.

He was pleased with the way the night was going. The cops wouldn't come because they were all too fucking afraid of his family and what they could do.

Standing by the side of the pool, he watched the girls as they fought opposite the boys, throwing a ball back and forth. Half of the girls had their tits hanging out of their tops.

Swigging from his beer, he moved on, bored with the party already. Everything was carrying on how every other party did. Heading back into the house, he got a little aroused when he caught sight of two chicks starting a fight. It didn't last long, though, before they were kissing and heading upstairs. Each of the rooms had a video camera and he always opted on what footage to keep and what to get rid of.

Just as he was about to give up with the lack of excitement, he spotted her. Ree. The girl who was best friends with a certain girl he didn't like. Prudence. She was nowhere in sight and it pissed him off.

Now if Ree's friend had arrived, he would've been able to have some fun, but now, he was angry.

After finishing off his beer, he threw it into the trash and walked over to Ree. The moment she caught sight of him, her eyes seemed to sparkle, and he hated that shit. He was no one's savior. "Where's your friend?"

"What?" she asked.

"The bitch you hang out with. Where is she?"

"Oh, Prudence didn't want to come. She doesn't like parties at all."

"Then you better get your fucking ugly ass out of here. I don't want you here unless she's here. Do I make myself clear?" He grabbed the back of her neck and shoved her out the door, not even caring if he hurt her.

People would learn to do as they were told. He was getting tired of being taken for an idiot. Slamming the door closed, he ignored the round of applause that greeted him. She wasn't the first person to be thrown out of his home, and she wouldn't be the last.

He needed another beer.

Now, either Prudence would arrive to help her friend, or he wouldn't see Ree again. Either option was … enjoyable to him.

Chapter Three
It's not fair

"You know I hate horror movies, don't you?"

"Yeah, but come on, this one isn't so bad," Sean said.

Prudence grabbed a handful of popcorn then shoved some into her mouth, chewing as the gore factor increased. She wrinkled her nose and wished there was some way to avoid what was going on. Sean had won at rock, paper, scissors, and now on her first night of school vacation, she was terrified.

"Ugh," she said. "This is so gross. I'm going to go and grab us sodas." She climbed off the bed, leaving Sean to continue watching his horror.

Her parents didn't have a problem with Sean staying the night. He was strictly friend-zoned and she had made sure her parents were aware of that. She loved Sean. He was her best friend, but she didn't think of him as someone she'd want to … date.

Sean had also never made a pass at her. Not that she wanted that. It would be too awkward and then she'd have to consider what to do as they were supposed to be best friends.

She was grabbing two sodas out of the fridge when her cell phone went off. She'd left it downstairs. The house was all closed and locked up.

Seeing Ree's name on the screen, she rolled her eyes. "What can I do for you?"

The first thing she could make out was the sniffling.

"Ree?"

"Prudence."

"What's going on, Ree?" She didn't like to see Ree upset and also the feeling something bad was going to happen.

"He … he won't let me into the party and I don't get it. He wants you to come or I'm not allowed to come."

Prudence closed her eyes. "Have you ever for a second even thought that maybe Drake is not worth this bullshit?"

"I like him, Pru. I want to be his girlfriend."

She rubbed at her temples, really not getting the attraction. Drake was a dick. "Then go and see him at the party or whatnot."

"But he kicked me out," Ree said. "I mean it, Pru, he's not letting me in until you come and it sucks. I'm so bored. Please, come and help me."

"Ree, I'm not going to the party. Sean and I are enjoying a movie. You were invited to come."

"As if I want to spend all of my time watching movies. Wow, you guys are so pathetic. Why do I even hang out with you in the first place?" Ree hung up the phone.

"Because no one else would hang around with your bitchy ass anyway." She slammed her phone on the counter and growled as the screen cracked from the impact.

"Ree?"

Prudence gasped as Sean entered the room. "The one and only."

"I thought I'd come and see what was taking the sodas so long to arrive."

"You paused the movie?"

"I paused it."

"When will this nightmare end?" She held out a soda to Sean and he took it.

"Are you wanting to go to the party?" Sean asked.

"No. I'm wanting to stay at home and watch the horror movie. Eat my weight in popcorn and pass out from a sugar rush. Our standard end-of-school ritual."

Sean held his soda up and she clinked hers with his. "But our ritual has to change for Ree."

"Does it really? I mean, does it make me a bad friend for not wanting to drive over there and let her go into a party? It's Drake's party."

"I know."

She leaned against the counter, crossing one leg in front of the other. She opened her can of soda, taking a large gulp as she looked past Sean's shoulder.

"You know he'll hurt you if you go to his place," Sean said.

"I totally know that." She rolled her eyes. "Ugh, I fucking hate this."

"Just leave it alone. So, she can't get into one party. Boohoo. If you ask me, Ree's too used to getting what she wants."

"If I drive over there, I can literally escort her into the bastard's den and leave. I can, like, deposit her, like a letter."

Sean laughed. "You're really considering this. Entering the lion's den. What if his parents are home? You've been lucky to have survived this long going against Drake."

"I know. His parents sound scary. She's still our friend and I don't want to be a total bitch to her. I know you don't agree with everything she's done, but come on, she at least deserves to have some fun."

"You do know she calls us names regularly and pretty much hates us."

"Oh, I know, believe me, I know." She sighed. Even as she knew what a total bitch Ree could be, that didn't mean she should be the same, regardless of what her friend did to her. She wasn't made that way.

Sean groaned. "Seriously? You're going to ruin years of our tradition because she wants to screw one guy?"

"It's not about the guy. You know I hate Drake and can't stand him. I do everything I can to avoid that piece of shit. No, this is about more than that. Ree may hate us, and I accept that, but it doesn't mean we have to be terrible people because of it, does it? We're better than that. Otherwise, we're the same as the people we hate."

Sean shook his head. "Nah, I don't buy that. You see, it's different because we're not assholes and everyone else is a fucking prick. That's not on us."

"Come on, don't be like that," she said.

"We can't keep on hanging out with her. You've got to realize that girl is toxic. No, even more than toxic."

"You don't mean it."

"I do. I'm not like you, Prudence. I'm not a good guy. I don't see the good in everyone."

"Neither do I."

"No? Then why are you even considering going to Drake's party when you know he hates your guts, and you're going to get hurt in the process? None of it makes any sense. I'm sorry, but you're making a mistake going there tonight. Ree may be our friend, but if she was a real, true friend, an honest-to-God great friend, she'd be with us right now rather than wanting you to hurt yourself by going and dealing with whatever bullshit they've got going on." He held his hands up in the air. "I'm sorry, but it's true. You shouldn't go there tonight."

"If I don't, Ree will do something stupid."

"That's on her."

"I can't do that. I can't just pretend like

everything is okay."

Sean let out a frustrated growl. "For fuck's sake, Pru. It's not up to you to save other people. Ree's a full-grown chick. She can do whatever the hell she wants."

"What about you? On the first day of school, Drake hated me, but rather than ignore me like the rest of the others did, you befriended me. What about that? You want me to just forget that? You were nice to me and I refuse to stoop to anyone else's level."

"I liked you. Drake's a dick. Always has been and always will be. This thing with Ree, if you go tonight, you're going to regret it."

"Then come with me," she said. She watched him hesitate and knew she could at least try to convince him. "Look, all it will take is me literally walking in, dropping Ree off, and coming straight out. Nothing out of the ordinary. You can even keep the car running. Come on, please. Please." She pressed her hands together, hoping her begging would at least encourage him to consider it.

Sean sighed, staring at her. "You know I don't like this."

"I know, but come on. It's just one time and you don't even have to go in to see them. I'll do it. I'll do all the work." It wasn't like she wanted to go to a party, anyway. She had no interest in being around Drake.

Even the thought of leaving her home was so oddly irritating to her. Part of her wanted to scream and shout at Ree for being a complete and total bitch and for not seeing the true side to the asshole she wanted to date.

Why date someone who won't even allow you to enter his party? She didn't get it. The guy clearly wanted nothing to do with her friend, and yet, here she was, begging Sean to drive over there so she could help her.

"I can see you're working this out for yourself," he said. "You think this is going to be the last party Ree wants to attend. Drake knows you're friends with her. He's aware that your soft spot is your friends. You were once the big-city girl yourself and now, you're just you, and he knows how to exploit it. This isn't going to be good for you."

"I know."

"But you still want to go and help our *friend*?"

"Don't say it like that."

"I'm saying it how it is, and you're not listening. Ree will do this every single time because she wants what she does. She's not a very good friend and you know it."

She knew. "You've got a condition to us going and helping her, don't you?"

"Yes."

"What is it?"

"You need to stop. This one time and then that's it. No more. No more helping Ree. She has to go as our friend."

"Sean, come on, you don't mean that."

"I do. You think it's easy for me when I see her laughing at the bullshit he does? No, it's not. I'm your best friend. Your only friend and I don't find what he does funny, Pru. I find him repulsive and I want nothing to do with him. Not a single thing. If you want us to go to this thing, we're doing it for Ree, and that's it. You've also got to make her aware this is the last time we're helping her." He folded his arms, and she knew he meant business. This wasn't a silly, petty demand. This was him putting his foot down, and there was no way for her to stop it. "What's it going to be? I care about you. You know this."

"I do, and I'm going to agree."

"You are?"

"Yes. I'll help Ree this one time and then that's

it. I won't go back on my word. I promise. Whatever she needs from here on out, or at least after today, she'll be on her own." Sean was her best friend and she knew deep down, he had her best interests at heart."

"I'm proud of you."

She glanced down at her clothes. "I think I need to go and throw on some more clothes, though. I'm not entering Drake's house in just my pajamas." She wrinkled her nose to which Sean laughed.

Prudence preferred it when he laughed. She hated the idea of hurting him.

After putting her soda can down on the counter, she made her way upstairs and quickly threw on a pair of pants and a sweater. She didn't bother to deal with her hair, or even to put on any socks. It wasn't like she had any intention of sticking around. Far from it. If it wasn't for Ree, she wouldn't even be doing this.

Sean was at the door waiting for her with keys already in his hand. "You really don't want to go."

She glanced down at her pants. She often wore then to deal with the trash. "Well, now I get to deal with the trash," she said, flicking her hair off her shoulder.

"Come on, let's get this show on the road."

****

Sean didn't need directions to Drake's house. Anyone who was anyone knew where he lived. His house was the biggest in town, and of course the one most people wished they lived in.

Not Prudence.

From the first time she saw the house as a kid, it always looked … sad. She hated the house and staring up at it now, she felt sick to her stomach, and not because she was about to see Drake either.

No, this house was a nightmare. It was too garish. It screamed luxury and prosperity and looked down on everyone else.

Sean pointed at the side of the road. Cars were everywhere and there was no way Sean would get close to the door or be able to leave if he came with her.

"We could leave her," he said.

She was so tempted. "No, we came all this way. Don't worry about it. I'll deal with this and then we're back to our night. There's no way his parents are home so it's not like I have to worry about having my ass thrown in jail or chased out of town." She unbuckled her seatbelt, the nerves finally starting to get to her. This was a mistake. She had no doubt something bad was going to happen, or maybe nothing would. It wasn't like she was going to crash this party. Drake had told Ree to get her to bring her inside.

The moment she closed the door, Ree looked up.

Her friend with wild blonde hair gave a little squeal and rushed toward her. It was like the past couple of hours hadn't happened.

She would never understand Ree or her need to be accepted by assholes like Drake.

"Hey," she said, offering Ree a smile.

Ree threw her arms around her neck, holding her close. "I knew you'd come. I'm so pleased you did. This is going to be awesome."

Prudence grabbed Ree's hands, making her friend stop. "I'm not coming to spend the night, Ree. I'm letting you in and then I'm leaving."

"But you can't leave. What if Drake wants you to stay?"

"I'm my own person. I don't give a shit if he wants me to stay. I'm not going to."

"Oh, come on. Don't be a party pooper."

Prudence wasn't going to be pulled in. "Come on, just lead the way and get this done."

Ree wouldn't stop talking. "He is like the best guy in the world. I know he comes off all hard and mean, but that's just the way guys are. They have to protect themselves, and I know Drake is a good guy where it counts."

Prudence rolled her eyes, pleased Ree hadn't seen her. The only thing Drake cared about was himself, but she wasn't going to argue with her. Walking between the cars, she didn't let go of Ree's arm once.

"Hey, Sean came. He can come too. I'm sure he would love to come and party," Ree said.

"Not happening." She didn't want to be here, so there was no way she was dragging Sean in any deeper than he already was.

"Wait, wait," Ree said the moment they got to the door. "We can't go in the front door."

"Are you kidding me?"

"No, we're going to have to go in the back entrance." Ree put a hand to her face. "Oh, my, that is so funny, because a back entrance, is, you know."

"I get it." It wasn't funny though. "I'm not sneaking around the back."

"You're going to get us into so much trouble." Ree kept on giggling. "I wonder why he wanted you to come. Oh, no, what if he wants to be mean to you again? I didn't think about it. At least you'll be the talk of the party if he is. It will be so funny what he does but know I didn't mean for it to be this way. I'm such a bad friend."

Gritting her teeth, she tried not to growl at her friend or to get angry. With every second that passed, it was getting harder and harder to not say something.

"I know Drake's an asshole but his parties are the best, and I really want to be in there. You understand, don't you? Or don't you? I know you're a loser. You and Sean are happy to stay in the loser camp but I've got plans and I need Drake. We have to go around the back. There's no way he's going to want to see you like this."

Prudence had heard enough. Sean was right, as usual. Ree didn't deserve their friendship. "You know what, I'm done. After tonight, you're on your own. I'm sick and tired of you treating me and Sean like we're some kind of lesser beings. You get what you want, and then you don't come near us again. And another thing, I'm not going around the back, Ree. I'm going through this front door, and that's final." She opened the front door to Drake's home, her heart pounding. She felt sick to her stomach.

The door closed behind her and several people noticed her. All it took was one look, and she watched as they ran out of the main hallway, probably about to alert Drake to her presence.

"See, we should have gone around the back," Ree said.

"Not happening." Still holding onto her friend, she charged through the group of people, wanting them out of her way. She wasn't going to run away or be scared. Drake was just a baby in a guy's body.

Moving through his large home, she didn't take the time to enjoy it. The place seemed cold and empty, even with all the people inside. It didn't take her long to find Drake. He sat with his friends in what looked like a game room.

Someone was talking to him and she pulled Ree toward her. "Connor," she said, drawing his attention to her. His blue eyes glared right back at her, but she didn't give a fuck.

This was her vacation time as well, and she didn't want to be here at this party.

"So, you finally decided to show up."

She pointed at Ree, wanting to hurt him instead,

to wipe the smug look off his face. "I didn't finally decide anything. I don't want to be here, but Ree is here. So all of your requirements have been fulfilled." She let Ree go and made to take a step back. Her exit was covered, though, and she refused to back down. There was no way she'd ever show any kind of weakness in front of this guy.

Drake laughed but ignored Ree, who grinned at him with hope.

"Where's your boyfriend?" Drake asked.

"Sean's not her boyfriend. They're just friends," Ree said.

She didn't avert her gaze from Drake, and neither did he from her.

"What more do you want, Drake? Blood? A urine sample?" She wanted to shock him, to make him look weak in front of his friends. Instead, he smirked as if he knew what game she was playing. She didn't even have a clue what game she played, only that she had to survive. She was in Drake's territory now. There was no one on her side here.

Drake watched her, and it made her feel really unsettled, especially to have this kind of attention from him. It was the first time in a long while that she'd felt like this.

This wasn't high school, or the park.

She was in his home, and in a way, she was at his mercy. And she didn't like it, not even a little bit.

"Why don't you just let her go?" Ree asked. "She's going to go and watch boring movies anyway. We don't need her to have some fun."

Ree moved up to Drake, reaching out to touch him, but he did nothing more than push her aside as if she was trash.

"Why do that?" Prudence asked. She went to

reach for her friend to give her a helping hand but Drake was in front of her, stopping her. "What is your problem?"

"She was more than willing to have you come here, to deal with me, and you're still going to help her."

"It's what friends do."

He laughed. "You really need to think about who you keep as a friend."

"Are you fucking kidding me?" she asked. "I'm done with this." She had enough of dealing with this crazy drama for the year. She would have to put up with Drake for another year once school started, but that didn't mean she needed to bother with him for the summer too.

Just as she was about to leave, he captured her hand, stopping her from going anywhere.

Staring down at where he held her, she gritted her teeth and glared at him. Why couldn't he just leave it alone? Why did he have to always make something bad? She didn't get it and doubted she ever would.

"I've got an idea."

"For what?"

"You do something for me, and I'll let you leave."

Prudence laughed. "You can't be serious."

"I don't see anyone letting you leave. So how about we have a little fun?"

She wasn't the least bit interested in having his kind of fun. "I'm done. You got what you asked for." She turned on her heel, ready to leave, only no one would allow her to pass.

This was what she hated most about doing this. Once she was inside Drake's territory, he was the one in charge, not her. "Get out of my way," she said through clenched teeth.

No one moved.

Drake chuckled and tutted. "You see, Trash, you're nothing here. No one gives a fuck about you here. You could even call Sean, but I'd have my boys kick his ass and toss him into the pool naked. He'd be humiliated."

She didn't want him to win. This was a power struggle, but one she was determined to win.

How?

Turning to face him, she folded her arms beneath her breasts and stared at him. "Okay, big guy. You want to play a game, let's play." She could play whatever game he wanted. He didn't frighten her, and she had no intention of backing down.

Ree moved up beside Drake again. "Let's go and party."

He did no more than push her away once again.

"Well, Drake, what is it going to be?" she asked. She didn't know why she was goading him. The last thing she wanted was to be anywhere near him, and yet, she couldn't stop herself.

She truly was screwed.

Chapter Four
Time to play

Drake watched her, seeing the attitude shining back at him. This was the Prudence he knew. The one that didn't back down, the challenge in her eyes. This was better than he imagined. "I say we play a game. It's pretty simple. Truth or Dare."

"Truth or Dare? Seriously? You want to play that game?"

He smirked. "Why not? Have you ever played it before?"

"Everyone has played that game at least once in their life and I'm no exception."

"Then what is the big deal?" he asked.

"I don't have a big deal. You want to play Truth or Dare, we'll play it. How many turns?" She dropped her hands and took a step closer.

Drake knew he had a captive audience. Everyone was waiting to see what he'd do. They were all fucking cowards and he didn't care about a single one of them. What he liked was to make people do what he wanted. He was the one with all the power, and because they were no better than blood-sucking idiots, he liked to control them. Every single person here would do what he wanted and all he needed to do was click his fingers.

"We play until I say we finish," he said.

"There's nothing to stop me walking right outside that door."

"Go ahead. See if you can try. Not one person here is going to let you leave. They do, they'll never come to one of my parties again, and guess what, my parties are the fucking best."

He watched her hand clench into a fist. It had been years since she last hit him back or gave him a real good punch. He didn't know why he even craved this kind of reaction from her. Anyone else, he'd fucking kill them, plain and simple.

With Prudence, he liked to play with her, to tease her, to see just how far he could push before she'd even think to push back.

"Are we playing here? Who is playing?"

He smiled. "You and me. No one else, right fucking here." He pointed at the ground.

She lowered herself into a sitting position, crossing her legs. He wondered if she and Sean had anything special going on tonight. She wasn't dressed to impress. She was never dressed for anyone but herself and he liked that. It was probably the only thing he did like about her.

"This is a game for twelve-year-old kids, Drake. You can't come up with anything else?"

He sat opposite her, ignoring all the bullshit coming out of her mouth. Drake didn't care about anyone else, just her, and being right here in this moment. "You scared, Trash?"

"I'm not afraid of you, Drake. You know that. This isn't the first time we've been doing this together and it won't be the last." She stared at him. "How does this go?"

"Simple. Truth or dare?"

She rolled her eyes. "Fine. Er, Truth." She held onto her knees, staring at him.

"You ever fucked anyone, Trash?" he asked.

"No."

"You're still a virgin."

"My turn. Truth or dare?" she asked.

"I'll go dare."

"Kiss your own ass," she said.

The crowd erupted into laughter. He did no more

than kiss the tip of his fingers and place them against his butt. "Done. Truth or dare?"

"Truth."

"You're not going to go with a dare?"

"Drake, just ask me a question so I can get out of this," she said.

"You ever sucked a guy's cock?"

"Wow, okay, this is just fucking ridiculous. No, I've never fucked anyone. No, I've never messed around with anyone. Yes, I'm a virgin. Are we done now? Can I go?" she asked.

"Not yet."

"Truth or dare?" she asked again.

"Truth."

"Why do you hate me so much?" she asked.

This took him by surprise and he remained silent, very much aware of everyone watching them. He couldn't stand to have their attention and he certainly didn't want it.

"Well! Are you not going to answer me, hotshot?"

"I never said I did," he said.

"Oh, come on, you totally fucking hate me!"

"Does that bother you? Thinking I hate you?"

She glared at him and he loved the challenge in her eyes. "No, it doesn't."

"Then why waste a question?"

"What I don't get is if you don't hate me, why oh, why, do you treat me like shit?" she asked.

"'Cause trash is always treated the way it's supposed to be." There was a loud chorus of whoops around the room. "Truth or dare?"

"Dare."

Now they were getting somewhere.

He didn't want to scare her off too soon.

"Drink a shot. Someone grab her a shot."

"That's it. One shot?"

"Why not?"

He was handed a shot, which he immediately gave to her, waiting for her to drink it. The booze at his parties were always the good stuff, and he watched as she knocked it back, trying not to cough as it burned the back of her throat.

"That's right, that's the good stuff."

She handed him the glass while shaking her head at the same time. "That's horrible." She covered her mouth to cough. "Truth or dare?"

"Dare."

"Ugh." She looked around the room and then he saw the wicked smile that played across her lips. "Kiss Ree," she said.

"That's it? You're going to waste your dare on a silly kiss with your friend?"

"What's the matter, Drake? Chicken?" she asked.

"Oh, you don't even know who you're messing with." Grabbing Ree, he pulled her down to him. She was always close by anyway, always hanging around for whatever crumb of attention he could give her. Gripping her hair tightly, he slammed his lips against her, kissing Ree while at the same time looking at Prudence for any reaction. Her brow was raised but she seemed completely unmoved by him kissing her friend.

Ree stroked his face and he quickly pushed her away. He didn't like to be touched unless he was the one doing it.

"Truth or dare?" he asked, sitting on the floor, watching her.

"I'm going to go with truth."

"You ever fantasize about me?"

"No, ew, gross. Are we done now?" Prudence

asked, getting to her feet. "I'm done playing silly games. I'm not like this. I don't party, and I don't mess around. Sean's waiting for me."

"With the snap of my fingers, I'll have my guys beat the shit out of him. Is that what you want?"

"You're an asshole," she said.

"I didn't claim to be anything more. Question is, are you going to just sit around and bullshit with me, or are you going to play fair?"

"Why don't you just tell me what you want so we can both get over this?" she asked.

"Everyone out," he said, shouting to be heard over the music. When no one moved, he broke eye contact with her, forcing everyone to get the fuck out of the game room. The moment the door was closed, he got up and flicked the lock. His parents, for some reason, always insisted on having locks on doors, but he didn't mind that. "We're all alone." He took a seat opposite her.

"I don't like this. You don't like me."

"What makes you think I don't like you?"

"For years now, you've been calling me trash and hurting me. I don't know how you can see that as being anything other than hatred, to be honest."

He smiled. "Like I said, I don't hate you."

"You have a funny way of showing it."

"I dare you to strip."

"This is ridiculous."

"Do I look like I'm joking around? I mean business, Pru. Strip. Or do you want Sean to pay the price?" He was more than happy to make Sean pay for her insolence.

She had come into his domain and now she thought she could be the one in charge. Not happening. Not on his watch. This was his turf and there wasn't anyone who could make him stop.

He held his cell phone up, ready. "You want to test me, Prudence?"

"Why are you doing this?"

"Because I can and because it's fun. You really think you're the one with the power here? You shouldn't have come, Prudence. Now, take those clothes off or Sean will pay the price again for your bullshit. Isn't he always paying in some way because you can't handle all this crap?" He held his phone between his fingers. "Decisions. It's so hard to make the right decision, isn't it?"

"Fuck you."

"Oh, fuck me. What's the matter? Don't like when you're beat?" he asked.

"I know what the hell I'm doing," she said.

He was surprised as she took her jacket off. She paused on the strap of her pants. "What are you going to do? Make me walk back through the party with no clothes on? Make me a mockery so when we get back to school, they can all laugh and joke at the fat girl who was naked at your party?"

He smiled. "That actually sounds like a lot of fun, but to be honest, I want you naked because I feel people tell the truth without their clothes on. Besides, where's the fun in playing a game completely dressed?"

She still hesitated at the buckle of her pants. They did look so cute on her, and he couldn't recall her wearing them in school. She cursed his name and started to wriggle out of her clothes.

With only her bra and panties on, he couldn't help but admire her. Her body was a lot bigger than most of the girls he knew but it certainly didn't distract from her natural beauty. She never wore makeup or tried to gain his attention. She really was a real enigma to him.

She sat down on the floor but he tutted.

"Not going to happen. I said strip. I meant all of it, or are you too stupid to follow even basic orders?"

"You know, you're really starting to piss me off, Drake. I don't have to do this. What you're doing right now is fucking illegal."

He held his cell phone as a reminder of his reach. His family didn't have to worry about legalities. They owned the police. They owned everyone. "You seem to keep forgetting who's in charge here. I'm the one who will decide if your precious boyfriend gets left alone or we drag his ass in. You really think Sean has what it takes to defend himself?"

"Why are you wasting your time with me? Ree wants to be with you. I don't have a clue why she does, but she's right outside, waiting for you. Why can't you just accept it?"

Drake smiled. "I can accept that. By the end of the night, I'll probably use her, and like most bitches, she'll get discarded along with the rest."

She snorted. "You really are a piece of work, you know that?"

He shrugged. "I don't care what you think. I never have cared about what you or anyone else thinks. You need to learn to pick better friends, Pru. Ones that aren't so willing to throw you into the fire."

She shook her head. "I'm not taking my underwear off."

"Okay, well, then, I think something else is in order." He stood up, grabbing her arms and pulling her to her feet. She tensed in his arms and he saw the flash of fear. He hadn't seen her react to him for a long time and he missed it. He missed seeing how worried and afraid she would get. He smiled. "Not so immune to me as you like to make me think."

"Leave me alone."

"I don't want to."

She held on to him tightly, refusing to let him go. "You don't have to do any of this. There's always a way out. Why do you have to make everything so fucking difficult?"

"It comes naturally to me. Don't you get it? Being predictable is boring and no fun. You're not predictable. Well, apart from when it comes to your friends. You always know how far to push and how to piss me off." He smiled. "I don't mind. I like playing this game with you, and I know you like playing it with me."

She shook her head. "You're delusional. Let me go."

"No." He quickly spun her around, flicked the catch of her bra, and removed it from her body before forcing her back to face him. "You're so stubborn, Pru. They're just a pair of tits!" He let her go, watching her fall on her ass, and he didn't even bother to help her up. "Come on, hurry up."

He saw the anger now in her face.

Before he could stop or restrain her, she attacked him, throwing him onto his ass. She straddled his waist, and he caught her wrists before she could sink her nails into his face. He didn't want to mess up his pretty little face. It was part of him, after all, and he liked the way he looked and had no intention of changing it.

"I fucking hate you."

Drake was shocked by how strong she was. There was real power in her and she looked so fucking fierce it made his dick ache for more of her. She was stunning, but this was his home, his domain, and she'd come into his place, not the other way around.

Sure, he'd forced Ree to call her, but that didn't mean she had to come and it certainly didn't mean she had to bring Sean. He knew what to do to piss her off. To really fuck with her head. Sean was her weakness. She always, in some way, felt responsible for the little fucker. She needed to learn the only way to fight him was to cut all those ugly fuckers out of her life, and then she'd win.

Without Sean, he wouldn't have been able to keep her here. Sean made her weak, and in order to be strong, she would need to learn to make some pretty fucking brave decisions.

Using all of his strength, he turned her, rolling her to the floor beneath him. It took him several attempts to get her hands above her head, but once he did, he finally was in control. "You need to learn to stop fighting me so much."

She cried out, releasing a growl. "I'll never stop fighting you. You think you've won. You're not even close to winning."

"I've got you pinned underneath me and you're nearly naked. Just think of all the amazing things I could do to you right now." He didn't let go of her wrists but to prove just how vulnerable she was, he thrust his cock against her. He was fucking hard. Fighting with Prudence always aroused him. He didn't even know why, only that he couldn't help himself. He liked to fuck with her, to mess with her mind.

She stopped struggling and he didn't want her to just stop. As he stared down at her, the silence seemed to ring out in the room. In the distance, he heard the music from the party. Everyone was all around, and yet, he couldn't give a single fuck about what was going on in other rooms. All of his focus was on the now, waiting to see what she'd do next, what would happen.

"Get off me," she said.

"No."

"Why do you have to keep on pushing? Why don't you just leave things alone?" She began to wriggle against his hold but he was stronger. She was at his mercy, not the other way around. It didn't take her long to get tired and start to scream at him to let her go. He watched her, feeling like an intruder.

There was so much passion in her actions, so much desperation, and he wanted to harness it. To fill the void that was inside him. Instead, he merely watched, waiting for her to lose control.

Tears welled in her eyes and he was fascinated as they cascaded down her face. Her body shook, as did her tits.

She was a bigger girl, had thicker hips and thighs. He'd bullied her because of her weight but he'd never really given a fuck about how heavy she was. Staring at her now, he felt a stirring in his cock.

Tilting his head to the side, he already knew what her lips tasted like, sweet. He wanted to taste her again and to have her completely at his mercy. No girl had ever made him feel this way. Never had him so consumed with her that he wanted to find out exactly what made her tick. "Are you giving up yet?" he asked.

"I've got nothing more to do. Why are you doing this to me? I've never done anything to you and I can't handle this anymore. Please, just stop."

He sat back, off her body, staring across at her, seeing her so lost and so broken. This wasn't what he wanted. Resting his hands on his knees, he waited, expecting the usual anger he normally felt curling inside him. Most often when he was with her, he was more than happy to lash out and hurt her. He liked her tears but he preferred her pain more. Especially when she hit him back, when she forced him to deal with him.

Rubbing circles on her knees, he was a little perplexed about what to do. This wasn't normal for him, and he didn't like it.

She sat up, her tits shaking as she did.

Her nakedness seemed right to him. What was going on between them was more than modesty. He didn't need for her to be covered to respect her.

"Drake?"

He didn't want her to speak, not right now. Leaning forward, he was so close that he felt her breath fan across his face. Her eyes were incredibly wide and if he moved a little closer and she rapidly blinked her eyes, it would look like butterflies.

She tried to pull away but he couldn't have that. He didn't want her leaving him so quickly. Cupping her face, he held her, not giving her room to leave.

She tried to struggle away but he wouldn't let her go. She was at his mercy, which was exactly where she was meant to be. If she lifted her hands off the floor, she'd hurt herself.

Her lips looked so inviting. Plump and ready to be kissed.

Chapter Five
She shouldn't be here

Nearly naked and alone with Drake was not on Prudence's to-do list. Nor was being held by him with no way to escape. Her heart pounded and she wanted to run to Sean and have him drive out of the party without a second glance.

She held on to Drake, hoping he'd stop being a dick and finally let her free.

He didn't let her go. He kept on staring at her lips, and even now, it was impossible not to look at his. He was so close. When he told her to get naked, she'd expected him to bully her about her weight.

She was almost naked in front of him, and he could throw every single one of those hated words at her, and yet, nothing. It was like he didn't see her naked. Yet, when he pressed his cock against her, she felt how hard he was. He liked being this close to her and that scared her. She didn't want to be close to him, or to anyone. "You won't hurt Sean," she said.

He smiled. "I will. I'll do it for fun."

"Leave him alone."

"Will you fight for all your friends with that much spirit, Pru?"

"You'll never know because you are not my friend."

He pulled her a little closer so their bodies were now flush together. They shouldn't be this close. She'd never been with a guy. There were a few times she'd slept beside Sean, but that wasn't anything sexual.

Drake made it even more so with the way he rubbed his body against hers, so she had no doubt about his arousal.

"Why do you have to be such a dick?" she asked.

"It comes naturally."

She let out a gasp as he suddenly cupped her face and slammed his lips down on hers. The kiss took her completely by surprise. At first, she didn't do anything, then she realized who was kissing her and the fact this shouldn't be happening.

As she fought against him, Drake grabbed her hands, pressing them above her head, stopping her from resisting him.

The kiss went on and on, and after a short while, maybe even only a couple of seconds, it started to feel … nice.

She didn't try to bite him and as he slid his tongue across her lips. Instead, she opened her mouth, kissing him back.

This was wrong on every single level. Kissing him was a giant mistake. Totally irrational, and yet, she did it. His cock hardened even more, pressing between her thighs, but she wasn't afraid. This guy had been the one person she'd hated more than anything in the entire world, and yet, his kiss heated her blood.

Drake broke the kiss first. He stared down at her. Neither of them spoke. Her heart galloped inside her chest.

Every part of what they were doing was wrong. She shouldn't be in his home. The only reason she was here was because of him and Ree.

Sean was waiting for her outside.

Drake licked his lips.

She didn't have any words.

The kiss wasn't horrible. It wasn't anything.

Biting her lip, she waited, hoping to wake up from the worst dream she could ever have.

There was a bang on the door, making them both jump. "Come on, Drake. Let's get this party started. It drags without you."

She didn't know which friend it was nor did she care.

Drake still held her down, even as she tilted her head, looking toward the door.

"I need to go," she said. All the fight had left her.

Much to her surprise, Drake sat back, giving her the chance to get up. At first, she didn't move, almost afraid to do anything. Staring at him, she waited for him to strike out, but he didn't budge.

Sliding away from him, she put some distance between them. All the while, she was acutely aware of the tingling of her lips from the kiss they'd shared. They had kissed and she couldn't even pretend to have forced him into it. The first touch of their lips, she could say she didn't participate. The second she started to respond, all matter of force went out of the window.

With Drake giving her space, she rushed toward her clothes and quickly pulled them on, needing the extra layer of protection.

This, between them, was a huge mistake, and one she wouldn't be repeating.

When she'd pulled her pants on, she turned toward Drake. He still sat in the same position, watching her. She couldn't move as he stared at her, and she felt a fluttering in her stomach. She wasn't nervous, though.

"I'm going to go." She nibbled her lip as she turned on her heel, making her way to the door.

Drake didn't make a sound. He didn't stop her.

With her hand on the door handle, she wanted nothing more than to run as far away from him as possible, to never look back.

Still, she rounded herself, turning to glance back at him. He watched her.

Why was he suddenly paying such close attention

to her, and why wasn't she running away from him?

This was a mistake, a big, giant, fat mistake.

Letting go of the door, she walked up to him. He didn't back down, didn't move a muscle. Just stayed perfectly still, and it irritated her. Standing in front of him, surrounded by his wealth, she clenched her hands into fists before stepping back and going to the door.

"You know what? You're a pig. You could have let Ree come in here and party with you. Instead, you treated her like shit." She walked right back to him, even though she wanted to leave.

She didn't understand why she didn't leave him right now. He'd given her an out and yet, here she was, still waiting for more.

He got to his feet. That cocky grin of his was still firmly in place and she wanted to smack him. To stop him from looking so confident.

"You know, you're starting to sound a little jealous," he said.

"I'm not jealous. Let's remember who got who naked here, Drake. Not only that, you were the one who wanted me here. Not the other way around. This isn't my house. This isn't my party. Ree didn't want to get into my pants. She wanted yours and you demanded she bring me." She slapped a hand to her chest. "So I could say you're the one who wanted me."

He didn't dispute it and as she took a step toward him, she didn't have the faintest clue what was going on inside her head. This was crazy.

Just turn and leave.

Don't stick around.

She stepped closer to him, feeling his breath against her face.

"Are you jealous of Sean, Drake? Does he make you nervous?" She didn't know why she was saying these things. Drake hated Sean. There was no love lost between the two. She didn't back down, though. Staring him in the eye, she waited for a response.

"That little shit doesn't make me nervous. He's scared of his own fucking shadow, Pru. You should really think about who you hang out with. A whore and a coward."

She went to hit him, but Drake caught her arm, tutting as he did. "Is violence really the answer?"

Prudence hated him so much at that moment. She despised violence. Each time she retaliated to Drake in the past, it always left her sick to her stomach. Even though he was the bully, she loathed stooping down to his level, and she had done that so many times. This year had been different, until this moment.

Still, as she glanced at his lips, remembering the feel of them on hers, she wanted to kiss him.

No, hell no, she didn't want to do that.

She tried to pull out of his hold but he refused to let her go.

"What's the matter, Pru? What's on your mind?"

She gritted her teeth and pulled away from him, determined to not let him win. "Nothing."

Taking a step back, she had every intention of leaving, only Drake once again stopped her. He grabbed her arm, halting her progress away from him. Her heart raced and once again, her gaze was drawn to his lips. Why was she suddenly so fascinated by his lips? They weren't that great.

Drake was her first kiss. Before moments ago, she had never kissed a boy. It was somewhat ironic that the guy she hated more than anyone else also happened to be the guy who kissed her.

What she hated even more, she wanted to kiss him again.

No.

This wasn't going to happen.

She didn't take a step back. She stayed still, and then she decided to fucking screw it and cupped his face, slamming her lips back down on his, sealing her fate. She kissed him. Not just a small kiss either. A full-blown kiss. When his tongue teased across her lips, she opened to him and moaned as he filled her mouth.

Drake cupped her back, holding her close as he kissed her. Every single part of her was begging to run, asking her to leave.

She couldn't do it. There was no way she could leave without this kiss. His hands moved down, going to her ass before sliding up to sink inside her hair. He was her enemy. Someone she didn't want to be near and yet, this kiss was the best thing she'd ever experienced.

She was only seventeen, but this was worth so much more than her pride right now. Drake shouldn't be kissing her.

Pulling away from the kiss, they both panted. Neither of them said anything. This was a mistake, she knew it. "I've got to go."

This time, she pulled out of his arms with ease, and when she got to the door, she didn't look back. She didn't say anything. Opening the door, she knew people were staring at her, but she ignored them all. Ree rushed to her side but she pretended not to notice her friend. Ree wasn't a friend, not even a little bit. She was only ever after what she could get, and from now on, it wouldn't be from her.

Leaving the house, she saw Sean hadn't moved an inch. How long had she been gone?

"You okay?" Sean asked. "You're shaking."

"I'm fine."

"You're not bleeding or broken. I take it nothing

happened."

"No, nothing happened." The lie slipped off her tongue and she hated herself for it. Rather than explain herself, she buckled her seatbelt. "Let's get out of here."

She couldn't look up at Drake's house.

"You sure you're okay? You look a little weird."

"You mean because I've just come out of my enemy's house and I'm a little freaked out?"

"Wow, Jesus, Pru. I was only asking because I'm worried about you."

"You don't need to be worried. Ree got what she wanted and now we can return to doing what we do best, which is hanging out and having fun." She wanted to forget the kiss she'd just shared with Drake. Nothing good could ever come from allowing herself to think it was any good.

Biting her lip, she sank down into the seat, feeling his lips still on hers. She had to get over this, otherwise, she'd drive herself crazy.

When they got back to her place, Sean went to the bedroom to set up the movie again as she promised to deal with the popcorn.

After grabbing the kernels out of the cupboard, along with the butter and sugar, she warmed up a saucepan and got to work. She preferred to make her own popcorn rather than buy it out of a packet. She just liked making it from scratch and after her time with Drake, she really needed to get control of her senses.

It had been one simple kiss. Nothing serious had happened and nothing bad had either. One little kiss that meant nothing.

Ree was at the party, so she had done what was needed of her. Now, she just had to forget about the kiss.

Her first-ever one.

Why couldn't she get that out of her head?

Lots of girls had their first kisses with meaningless guys. It meant nothing.

Drake was just that, nothing and meaningless. She was overthinking everything right now, and she had to stop before she went crazy.

She poured the kernels into the oil, working on sheer memory alone, without really seeing what she was doing. Her mind wasn't on the popcorn but on the boy she hated. Closing her eyes, she let out a hiss as she touched the side of the pan. She placed the lid in place as the kernels began to pop.

Licking her lips, she remembered the taste of him. She had to get him out of her mind before she went insane.

Melting the butter, she listened to the last of the kernels as they finished popping.

"Everything is all set up. How much longer are you going to be?"

"Nearly done."

She felt Sean's gaze on her as she worked. She didn't know what to say to him. Talking about what happened at the party wouldn't exactly improve things.

Once she had mixed the popcorn, she poured it all into a serving bowl before shoving a mouthful inside. The butter and sugar tasted good. It was much better than Drake's kiss or his lips.

Sean stood in front of her, frowning.

"What?" she asked.

"I don't know. You seem … different?"

"Nothing happened, Sean. You don't have to worry about it."

"You'd tell me?"

She forced a smile to her lips. "Of course. Why wouldn't I tell you about it? I tell you about everything else. It was just a boring party and Drake wanted to play a boring game. Nothing happened. It was perfectly fine. You would have been totally bored." She slapped his shoulder with the hand that didn't have sugar and grease. "Now, could we drop this and pretend it didn't happen? We can go back to our night without any drama or chaos, or anything."

"If that's what you want."

"Yeah, it really is." She was through with guy talk for the night. "Can we just pretend tonight didn't happen?"

"Nothing happened. Let's go and watch a movie."

This was why she loved Sean so much. He never made things complicated.

Chapter Six
It was just a stupid fucking kiss

Drake tossed the ball into the air before catching it. He did this several more times, and no matter what he did, he couldn't get Prudence out of his mind. Shit! When had he started to think of her as Prudence? She was trash. The girl from the wrong side of the tracks who shouldn't even be in his thoughts, especially after he fucked her friend last night. Ree had been all about making noise and it had driven him crazy.

He'd wanted to strangle her to get her to shut the fuck up. Ree was like a little puppy dog that didn't get the hint. He wasn't interested in her. She was way too easy for him. Her adoration and neediness were complete turn-offs.

Gripping the ball, he launched it across the room, sending it into the drink cabinet. The glass smashed and he got to his feet. He didn't do shit like cleaning. There were maids who were paid to clean. Grabbing his jacket and car keys, he headed out of his home. There were a couple of kids playing near the gate. The moment he clicked the button for it to open, they scurried away.

His father didn't like kids walking around outside of his house and would often take any balls that were accidentally kicked over the fence or had found their way onto his property and pop them. No parents dared stand up to him as they had all the money and power, and everyone else didn't.

Pulling out of his driveway, he noticed the scared kids watching him. All of his life, kids had been scared of him. Even his supposedly best friends were. Not that he cared. He was so used to watching others cower in fear that if they didn't do it, it made him nervous.

Prudence.

From the first moment she entered their school, she had smiled at him. Fucking smiled. No one had ever smiled at him. Not even his parents. He was an obligation. Something they had to create together in order for someone to inherit the family fortune. The men who had the first-born son of the next generation inherited a fortune, and well, his father got in there, but then he did fuck everything that walked until one woman came forward with a son that would be born before his uncle's.

Competition was always rife within his family. You had to be the best at everything. Even his mom, who got the crown of glory for getting knocked up first, had to fit into a certain role.

Again, all his life he was used to playing by a certain set of rules and well, now all of that was changing and he didn't fucking like it. No, it wasn't changing at all. One person out of an entire fucking town was testing him. The moment she moved here, she'd been testing him and it grated on his last fucking nerve as well.

Prudence was nothing and yet, kissing her last night had been the last thing he intended to do but he'd done it. Why?

He didn't have a clue why.

Driving out of town, he pressed his foot to the gas, ignoring all the speed warnings. He needed to fucking breathe and the only way to do that was to drive like crazy. Pulling onto the main road, even with oncoming cars, he overtook vehicles that were going too slow for him, not caring as they honked their horns at him. Nothing was going to stop him from getting what he wanted.

He laughed as he pushed on through. Coming to a diner, he made a quick stop. He jerked his car with the force of his braking but slid into the space easily. One thing he was good at was driving his car. No one else was better than him.

No matter the risks he took while he drove, he'd never been in a single accident. He didn't think it was down to his good driving either, it was down to sheer luck.

He grabbed a breakfast burrito and a coffee to go.

Lingering in the diner's parking lot wasn't his idea of fun, so he left, finding a quiet space near a falling-down garage. He stared at the crumbling building that had probably once been a really busy place. There were no signs and most of the windows had been smashed. It looked like there had even been a fire and coming out of the roof there appeared to be a small tree. To most, this was just an eyesore, but he could easily see it being rebuilt and once again being a thriving business.

Too many people were happy to write something off if it looked like it was going to take too much money or too much time. When something was worth the time or effort, Drake didn't mind dealing with it.

For him, people were never worth either precious commodity. They always had their own agenda, constantly working for something else, which he never failed to find fucking irritating. It was one of the reasons he liked to push people, to see what he could get them to do and how far they were willing to go before they called him on his bullshit.

Prudence, for example. If Sean hadn't been there, she wouldn't have gotten naked for him. Drake didn't like how much the little pussy had control of Prudence. He rarely was there for her when she needed it. If he got into a fight with the little shit, there was no way he'd be able to protect her. Most of the time, Prudence always got involved and it annoyed him how she was still friends with him.

She deserved better.

They were both fighters. They were both better than everyone else, and he didn't fucking see why they had to put up with the kind of shit that was thrown their way.

Finishing off his food, he tossed the wrappers into the trash bin that looked like it hadn't been emptied in years. That was another thing he hated. Once someone lost interest in something broken, they always turned their back on it. Why bother putting any energy in the first place if you were just going to give up when things got hard?

He didn't get it. Never would either.

After climbing back into his car, he pulled away from the garage. He felt calmer than he had before he left. The need to do something crazy had disappeared and now he could think.

Still, his thoughts returned to Prudence, the kiss they'd shared, and the fuck he'd given Ree. She was like a vulture constantly hanging around. He even noticed the way she laughed whenever he bullied Prudence.

He drove back into town, past the first sightings of the town hall, the church tower, and even the neon sign of the local diner with a couple of the letters missing. This town was his home and yet he wanted nothing to do with any of it. The people were all fake and anyone who put up with him was only doing so because of his name. His father was the one in charge of this town, and he merely a puppet as well. What his father wanted, he always got.

He came to a stop at the traffic lights in town. It was rare for a line of cars of any kind, even during the height of tourist season. He knew the town loved being available and easy to get around in. He'd even seen it posted on leaflets and incorporated in slogans.

Coming out of the library, he saw none other than the little bitch herself. Her hair was pulled back into a ponytail and he had a sudden urge to pull on it. To force her to look at him.

The lights hadn't changed yet, but he was done waiting. Pulling out, he turned his car down the one-way street and up onto the curb, stopping Prudence from walking. He didn't run her over—there were limits to what he would do. Climbing out of the car, he saw her push a curl of hair off her face and glare at him.

"Seriously? You may think you're some kind of mad car racer, but you could have killed me."

"I was nowhere near you."

"I don't have time for this." She went to move away but he caught her arm, forcing her against the car and trapping her there. The only way she could move now was if she pushed him out of the way. "What the hell, Drake? Didn't you get enough last night?"

"I didn't get nearly enough of what I wanted."

"Ugh, what the heck is this?" She pointed at him and growled. "You hate me. We hate each other, and now you're chasing me down in the street. This can't be good for your reputation and it's certainly not good for mine."

"What? You got a lot of people invested in your future, Prudence?"

"Stop doing that!"

"Doing what?" he asked, laughing. He loved to see that he could unnerve her. Her cheeks were bright red and she looked flush.

"Calling me by my given name. Go back to calling me Trash or something else just as cruel."

"Nah, I think I like this name a whole lot more." He stepped close so his body was against hers.

"Drake, I mean it. Stop."

"Or what? What exactly are you going to do to me?" He saw her gaze go to his lips and he smirked. She wasn't going to do anything because she wanted him. She could fight him all she wanted, but he saw the interest in her eyes. There was no denying where her thoughts had disappeared to, and he liked it, wanted it, and he was going to have it.

Reaching out, he twirled a loose strand of hair between his fingers. She didn't immediately pull away.

He stared down at her as she tilted her head back to look at him. "Why did you stop me here?" she asked, the first to break the silence between them.

"I don't know."

"Are you used to not having a clue what you want or don't want?"

"Do you always know what you want?" He was genuinely curious.

"No, but I want to know why you're being like this. Why you're here with me when you should be somewhere else."

"Where else should I be?"

"Anywhere that isn't here with me?"

Her attitude didn't deter him. It would take a lot more than her being pissed off for him to leave or to let her go. "You don't sound too sure about that."

"Don't you have some other person to piss off?"

"Nah, I like pissing you off. It's fun."

"I don't like you."

He laughed. "Do you think I give a fuck if you like me or not? I don't care, plain and simple."

She put her hands on his chest and he loved it. She had willingly touched him and there was no taking that back. "Drake, please?"

"What?" He stared at her full lips. They were nice

and plump. He'd never noticed just how perfect they were. He wanted to feel them again. They were incredible last night. He could imagine them wrapped around his cock. Not that Prudence would ever suck him off. She would more than likely bite his dick off than suck it.

"I don't know what you're doing and, frankly, I don't care for it. Leave me alone, please."

"Nah, I've got all day."

"I don't and I've got places to be."

"Ah, you've got to be with your little gay friend."

"Sean's not gay."

"I know for a fact Ree's not." He watched her tense up and he liked that. Any reaction he got from Prudence was a win.

"What did you do?"

"Only what she begged me to." He pressed his body against hers. "You know how much she's been wanting me, and well, she got what she wanted last night."

Prudence's jaw clenched and she glanced away.

Gripping her face, he forced her to look at him. Her reactions were all for him.

"Get off me."

Her words were muffled with the way he held her but he understood every single thing she said, and he wasn't going to let it go. Staring into her eyes, he didn't see any fear. There was always hatred shining back at him, and he didn't mind that. Rather, he relished it, but now he saw something else he liked.

He released his hold on her but didn't entirely let her go. Stroking the tips of his fingers across her cheek, he slid them into her hair.

"What are you doing?"

"Why aren't you running away?"

"What?" she asked.

"I don't have you anymore."

"You're in my way."

"Or you want to stay here a lot more than you make out."

"You're insane."

"Maybe? Or maybe you like me keeping you here a little too much."

She shook her head and yet, she still hadn't pushed him away. She could've been long gone now. It wasn't like he was going to chase her down the street in the middle of the day. He wasn't *that* crazy.

Those lips though, they were driving him crazy and he couldn't stop thinking about them. Not even a little bit. It hadn't even been a whole twenty-four hours but he wanted to taste them again.

Why don't you?

You know you want to.

Look at her, she wants it just as much.

Without taking a second to hesitate, he slammed his lips down on hers, taking her lips once again. He hoped they wouldn't be as good as he remembered or feel fucking incredible.

He was wrong.

What the hell was it about her? She wasn't anything special. Just a girl, not even one who came from any wealth. Prudence was exactly what he'd been calling her, nothing. So, why couldn't he stop kissing her? Biting on her lip, he heard her moan, and it was nearly his fucking undoing. He wasn't used to this.

"Push me away!" He broke from the kiss long enough to speak.

She put her hands on his chest but she didn't push him away. Her hands gripped his shirt, holding him tightly to her.

He held her, wanting to get as close to her as humanly possible. The kiss was incredible. The fire. The passion. All of it blew his mind, and his cock was so hard. He wanted nothing more than to take her to the nearest surface, spread her open, and fuck her senseless.

Suddenly, she pushed him away.

"No. No. No. No. No!" she yelled, finally breaking free of his hold and taking him off guard.

She wasn't trapped between himself and the car.

He watched her.

Her lips looked slightly swollen from his kisses and she shook her head. "This isn't happening. I don't like you and you don't like me. That's how it's going to stay."

He smirked.

"Stop it!"

He saw she was quickly losing her temper. "I hate to be the one to break this to you, Prudence, but you don't need to like someone in order to kiss them."

"I don't care what others want or need. This is about me. what I want. What I need, and it's certainly not you."

"Keep telling yourself that."

"You're an asshole, Drake."

"And you're nothing but trash, Pru." He continued to stare at her as she glared right back.

"You remember that the next time you stop me. I'm trash. I'm nothing. I'm scum. Once you get all of that through your thick skull, drive right on by because I want nothing to do with you."

Drake watched her go, knowing there was no way he'd ever forget she was trash, but that didn't mean he couldn't start seeing her as something else. The taste of her lips still lingered on his, and he wasn't going to stop. She'd given him a hint of … something. He didn't know what it was, but he knew he wanted more of it, so much more.

Chapter Seven
Why was he everywhere?

During summer vacation, Prudence was used to working, studying, spending time with Sean, and relaxing. That was how she always spent her summers. This time was usually Drake-free. She often heard he went away on the family yacht or was skiing in some cold, distant place.

Not this time. No matter where she went, Drake was there.

Part of her wondered if he was stalking her. That couldn't be possible. Two people who hated each other didn't suddenly find a reason to be everywhere that other person was. Even when she hung out with Sean at the park, or went walking in the woods, Drake was there, either alone or with friends. The same at her new workplace. She'd gotten a brand-new job at the mall in a clothing store. It wasn't the most ideal place to work, but she didn't mind serving customers and stocking shelves. Every now and then a customer would ask her opinion on an item and she hated that. Fashion wasn't her forte but she did her best. That was all she did throughout her life, her best.

So by the second week of being completely aware of Drake, she'd had enough. Finishing off her burger, she threw the leftovers of her shake in the trash as she was full and stormed over to his table at the food court.

"What the hell is your problem?" she asked.

"My problem?" He leaned back in his chair, looking like he owned the place. Knowing her luck, he probably did. His parents owned most of the town and it was why he got away with everything, which only served to piss her off.

"Why are you always around?"

"I hate to break it to you, sweetheart, I live here."

"You live in the mall?"

He chuckled. "You know I don't. You've seen my house, you know where I live."

"Why are you here?" she asked. There was no way he was going to get smart with her. She would've noticed him a lot sooner than now if he was always hanging around with her. That wasn't the case! She wasn't imagining this. Drake appeared every-freaking-where, and she was done with it.

He looked around. "Last time I checked, this is a free country. I can sit and eat lunch wherever I want."

"And you just happen to pick one of the spots near where I work."

"Well, well, well, Pru. I'd say you were becoming a little … paranoid."

"Cut the crap, Drake. You and I both know that we rarely see each other during the summer."

"So you noticed that?"

She rolled her eyes. "I'm not doing this with you." She was about to walk away but he grabbed her arm, stopping her from moving.

"Don't go."

"Let go of my arm or I'll scream."

"Scream and you'll notify the cops. They kind of know who I am and it won't end well for you."

"For me, even though I've done nothing wrong."

"All the security cameras around will see you approaching me. I'm just an innocent stranger."

She scoffed. "Innocent? There's nothing innocent about you."

"Yet, as I sit here minding my own business, you're the one who has come to interrupt my peace and tranquility."

She stared at him. He looked so smug as if he had

won this round, and he had. "You knew I'd come here."

"I knew you couldn't resist confrontation."

"You haven't gotten your kicks out of me this year. What? You hate how I've let everything go? Is that it?"

He smiled. "If I don't bother you, why are you here?"

Glaring at him, she wanted to walk away, but instead, she found herself sitting down, opposite him.

"Well, well, well, do you want to dabble in the dark, Pru? Is that what this is about?"

She didn't say anything, watching him instead. She tried to read what his intentions were and yet, she came up with nothing. There was no way to understand what he was doing and she was just wasting time. "I've got to go."

"Then go."

She stood up but his words made her sit back down again.

He laughed. "Always so undecided."

"I don't get you."

"What's there to get?" He sat up. "Am I so confusing to you?"

"Why?"

"Why what?"

"You're infuriating."

She stood up.

"You know, I'm going to be spending a lot more time around town."

She looked at him, waiting for him to elaborate. Again, he refused.

She lowered herself down into her seat. She had time.

"You certainly know when to be a good girl, don't you?" he asked.

"Get to the point."

"I think you're becoming obsessed with me."

She burst out laughing. "That's what you think this is? You think this is obsession?"

"You don't think it is?"

"No, I know it's not obsession."

"You've thought about our kisses?"

Prudence looked at his lips and hated herself for being so weak. "No."

"I had no idea you could be a little liar."

"I don't think about your kisses or about anything when it comes to you. Leave me alone, Drake. I don't like you stalking me." She got up out of her seat and without looking back, made her way back to work. She tried to ignore everything he'd said and what he believed. She didn't have a crush on him, not even a tiny one.

The kiss they shared—it meant nothing because it wasn't a real kiss. Not to her, at least. He'd put her in a position where she'd had no choice but to kiss him. It didn't matter to her if it was her first or last kiss she ever shared. It wasn't exactly memorable.

She restocked the clothes and tried to ignore everything outside of the shop.

She failed. A quick glance let her know Drake was still there. He wasn't eating this time. He sat on a bench directly out of the shop, drinking a soda. He winked at her, holding up his drink as if in offering.

She turned her back and was sure she heard him laugh. Why couldn't he leave her alone? Summer vacation was the one time of the year she didn't have to think about him. Moving away from the doorway, she served customers, and by the time six o'clock rolled around, she was more than ready to go home.

It meant having to pass Drake, who still sat in the same spot. Without looking back over her shoulder, she started to walk, hoping to avoid talking to him at all.

Once again, she failed.

"What's the rush?" he asked.

"I want to go home."

"I know you didn't get here by car and you walked, so why don't I drive us?" He grabbed her arm.

"Will you stop?" she asked as she tried to push him away. But he wouldn't release her. "Now you look like a crazed maniac."

"Please, the cameras probably saw how fucking needy you were and would anyone would give me a break."

"You're an asshole."

"Name-calling. I thought you were above that, Pru."

"I would be if you'd just leave me alone." There was no point in fighting. She stopped trying to resist and allowed him to lead her to his car.

He opened the passenger door and she climbed in, folding her arms as he slammed the door closed.

She was in his car.

The car of her enemy.

This wasn't even funny anymore.

"Why aren't you away or off partying?" she asked as he got behind the wheel.

"I've got better things to do with my time."

She grabbed her cell phone.

"Who are you calling?" he asked.

"I'm texting Sean. He'll meet me at my house."

Drake grabbed her cell phone and threw it out of the car.

"Hey! What the hell?" She tried to get out to pick up her phone. Drake did no more than open his door, turn, and stomp on her phone. The sound of splintering glass angered her.

"There, all done. You don't need that damn phone or your nerd."

She clenched her hand into a fist and punch his arm. It wasn't very hard, but she just couldn't take anymore. The moment she did it, she didn't feel any satisfaction. Violence never, at any point in her life, thrilled her. If anything, it made her feel sick to her stomach to know she'd been pushed that far.

Drake caught her wrist in his hand. Hers was still clenched.

"Now, now, is that any way to treat the guy who's going to be driving you?"

"Why are you like this?"

"I'm a lucky guy and I get what I want."

He smiled at her, and she tried to pull her hand away. "You can't drive if you keep a hold of my hand."

"I've got no problem driving one-handed, princess."

"Leave me alone," she said.

"No can do. I happen to really like holding your hand."

She growled as he lifted her hand and licked across her knuckles. "Gross, get off."

"Not going to happen, little virgin."

He did it again and Prudence realized what she was doing wrong. She was responding to him rather than just ignoring him. Taking a deep breath, she closed her eyes, counted to ten, and then just let everything go. This was how she'd coped with the past year at high school. Just ignoring him, and as she opened her eyes and smiled at him, she waited.

This was boring.

"You think I don't see right through you?" he asked, letting go of her head.

She stayed silent. Another thing Drake hated was

complete and utter silence. She didn't mind the quiet. After hours of being left home alone, she got used to it. Quiet was her safe place.

He chuckled. "I got your number, Pru. I don't mind. I happen to like the quiet as well."

He started driving again and she stared out of the window, not really seeing where they were going. She also wasn't paying attention to their surroundings, trying harder than usual to ignore the guy beside her. She didn't want him to know she was greatly affected by him, but there was no denying it.

Drake had gotten under her skin.

She was determined not to ask him a single question, not to even care where they were going. It didn't matter. People had seen them leaving together. He had even boasted of security watching them, so if she were to disappear, unless he blackmailed a whole lot of people, he couldn't kill her.

Or could he?

Drake's family held a lot of power in town and she had no doubt they could probably get away with anything. Even covering up a murder.

She stared out of her window, not recognizing anything. It was on the tip of her tongue to ask where they were going but she was too stubborn.

"You're going to have to pay for a new phone," she said.

She wanted to call Sean more than anything to let him know she was safe or at least, alone in a car with Drake and it was all her fault. She shouldn't have approached him at lunch or given him the time of day.

"I'll buy you a new phone. No worries about that, sweetheart."

"Don't call me that."

"You don't like me calling you sweet names?"

"I'm trash to you, remember?"

"Yeah, well, I like to live dangerously."

"Stop talking to me." She folded her arms across her breasts, hating this feeling. She didn't even understand it and that alone scared her. For as long as she could remember, Drake was her enemy.

Kissing him had been a mistake. Approaching him today had been an even bigger one.

She closed her eyes and counted to ten very slowly, hoping when she opened her eyes, she'd recognize something.

After ten, she couldn't make anything out.

You're going to get killed if you don't ask.

I don't want to ask him. He's an asshole.

An asshole who could totally kill me.

Rubbing at her temple, Prudence knew she couldn't not ask him. This was just way too dangerous. "Drake, where are we going?"

"I was wondering when you were going to ask that." He laughed. "Do you have any idea what could happen to you if you were to take a ride from a stranger? That shit is dangerous."

"I know you."

"Yeah, and? You think you're safe with me?"

She glanced over at him and decided to take a chance. "Yes. I do. You won't hurt me."

Again, he barked out a laugh. "Wow. Shit, you can even surprise me."

"You think just because we've had our fights and you've bullied me, you think I don't see past all the bullshit you're spouting?" she asked. "You could have hurt me a lot worse ages ago. You never have. You've always held back. I've seen you fight before. It was what made me realize that you're never going to hurt me. Your threats are completely useless but that's okay. I don't mind. You can pretend to be a bad guy all you want." She shrugged her shoulder. "I've got all the time in the world."

She leaned back against the chair, staring out of the window.

For the longest time, Drake didn't do anything. He didn't say anything, just kept on driving at a rather slow pace.

She chanced a glance over at him, and she couldn't read his expression. "Drake?"

He slammed his foot down on the gas. They went from driving normally to suddenly speeding along.

"Drake, what the hell are you doing?"

"Giving you a fun time. It's what you want, right? Some fun, some excitement. I bet that asshole doesn't give you any. I sure hope you know what you're doing!"

Chapter Eight
She drives me fucking crazy

Drake wanted nothing more than to hurt Prudence. He hadn't done anything to hurt her so far and yet, here she was throwing out all kinds of accusations. She was no different than him, and all she did was hide behind her little friend.

"Leave Sean out of this."

"He's a fucking pussy. I bet he doesn't even make you laugh."

"What do you have against him, huh? You guys have hated each other since the beginning. Even before I came into the picture. Why?"

He threw his head back and laughed. "You think I give a shit about him? He's not worth the time to even breathe over."

"If he's such a waste of your time, why do you even care?" she asked.

"I don't care."

"You're the one constantly bringing him up and I'm sick of it. He has nothing to do with you. You don't bully him anymore."

He was growing tired of her demands. She was nothing but trash and it was time she learned her place. He quickly pulled the car up against the side of the road. He saw the uncertainty in her eyes and was pleased he could get under her skin.

"Now, Trash, what was it you wanted?" he asked. "You want me to leave your little friend alone." She was taking long, deep breaths, and he liked that he made her nervous. This was what they did. The constant push-and-pull, and he relished it. Not that he'd ever tell her that. The best parts of his day were the interactions he had with her.

"Sean doesn't do anything to you."

"He breathes."

"Is that it? Is that all he's ever done wrong with you? Live? Get real, Drake. People you don't like exist. You can't just vanish them away because you can't stand them. You're going to be surrounded by people you don't like. It's the way of the world. I've got to put up with you."

"There you go again, constantly telling me how you can't stand me when it couldn't be further from the truth."

"Wow, you're really not listening to me. I don't want to be in this car with you. I don't even want to see you, ever. I'm so sick of this. Summer is supposed to be my time where I can do whatever the hell I want and I don't have to listen or see your face. I don't want to see your face and I don't have to keep on doing this with you."

He watched her unbuckle her strap. "What are you doing?"

"Getting far away from you." She opened the door and slammed it closed.

He rolled his eyes, watching her pull her bag up her shoulder.

She shouldn't look cute walking away from him. For a few seconds, he watched her walking. Tapping his fingers against the steering wheel, he didn't have a clue what he was doing or why.

His friends would gladly hang out with him, and they'd be a lot more fun. There were so many chicks who'd be willing to bounce on his dick. Her friend Ree being one of them, and yet, he was here. Why the fuck was he here in the first place?

He and Prudence didn't mesh. This was a waste of time.

He didn't even know why he was even trying. The moment he thought of that kiss, though, he couldn't walk away.

Opening his car door, he climbed out, determined not to let this go. He'd kissed hundreds of chicks. None of them had left him like this.

Even for him, this was fucking crazy.

Chasing after her, he caught her around the waist.

"Let me go. Let me the fuck go. I don't want you to touch me."

He knew that was bullshit.

He'd been watching her all day and when she didn't think he was looking, he saw the way she stared at him. Prudence didn't want to want him, but that didn't mean her feelings weren't heading down that path.

She fought him like a wildcat, hitting him, trying to throw herself out of his arms. He was shocked by her sheer strength. She was a fighter all right.

He had to let her go for a few seconds and that didn't stop her from running as far away from him a she could get. Watching her go, he couldn't help but admire her spirit. All it made him want to do was cage her. To keep that spirit for himself.

After catching his breath, he chased after her again. Only this time, he shoved her down into the dirt. He made sure not to hurt her in any way.

She tried to shove him up, pressing her ass against his dick, but none of it worked.

Hc was by far stronger than her. "Give it up."

"No!" She screamed the word.

He gave her enough space to roll over but that was about it.

When she started hitting at him again, he had no choice but to grab her hands and pin them above her head, keeping her still. "It doesn't have to be this way," he said.

"Yes, it does. You just won't quit. Why won't you leave me alone?"

In the process of her wriggling beneath him, he was now pressed up against her pussy. Her body fit perfectly against him, and as much as he wanted to complain, he knew he couldn't. Why would he?

She felt amazing.

The moment she realized what she'd done, she froze. "Get off me, Drake."

"I don't want to, Prudence."

"And what you want matters the most?"

"Pretty much."

"Why did you become such a dick?"

"It's a born talent." He expected her to keep on wriggling or to do all the other useless stuff she'd been trying to do that clearly didn't work. She didn't do anything. Prudence stopped fighting altogether.

Drake stared down at her and waited, but clearly, she had learned her lesson. "Seeing as we're in this predicament, I think it's only fair I get to ask you a few questions."

"Seriously?"

"You got a problem with me questioning you?" he asked.

"I've got a problem with you thinking you can do whatever the hell you want with no consequences. Why do you keep pursuing me?"

"We're going around in circles and I'm getting bored."

"So, get with the program and stop boring both of us. I don't want any more of this bullshit," she said.

"There you go cussing again. You're making me horny."

He watched her take a breath but there was no

other visible response or sign of annoyance. He was going to have to work a lot harder to get under her skin. She wasn't making this easier for him.

"You have questions. Ask them so I can go home."

"You think I'm going to take you home?"

"Drake."

He chuckled. "What do you see in Sean?"

"Sean? I don't see anything in him. He's my best friend."

"You haven't fucked him?"

"No, of course not. It's none of your business, but Sean and I are just friends. We don't have that kind of feelings for each other."

He stared at her. Drake didn't know if she was being fucking dense or if she really didn't see it. Sean had a crush on Prudence. He was sure of it, and the only reason he hung around was to be with her.

"You haven't kissed?"

"No, of course not. This is ridiculous."

Her lips were so close, and the memory of them against his was too good to ignore. Slamming his mouth down on hers, he traced his tongue across her lips. She didn't pull away and at first, he knew he had her stunned by the movement. He wasn't entirely sure what he was doing, why he felt the need to kiss her.

They weren't friends. Would never be friends, but he couldn't stop. The need was too strong.

She didn't fight him. After being tense for only a couple of seconds, she responded to him. Her body went lax beneath him and when he heard her moan, he was fucking lost. Why was their kiss so much more? He didn't understand it.

It was just a kiss. Two lips together, meaning nothing.

This was the third time he'd kissed her and it was even better than the first.

Pulling away, both of them panting for breath, he found the coil of hate inside him a little bit smaller.

She licked her lips and it made him want to taste her again.

"I don't want you ever kissing or touching Sean."

"You're not the boss of me," she said.

"The way you respond to me, I'd say differently."

"Let me up, Drake. I'm dirty."

"Do you want me to let you up?" He pressed himself against her and she rolled her eyes.

"Yes, enough."

"If you haven't kissed and fucked, what have you done?" he asked, more interested in how Sean could stay around her and not do something. For him, it was way too foreign a concept to have Prudence near him every single day and not do something about it.

He'd only had Ree around him for a couple of hours and he took care of it.

"Not everything has to turn into something so disgusting. It's not all about sex."

"Oh, please. You're deluded if you don't think for a single second Sean doesn't want to fuck you. He's a pussy but he still wants one."

Her attack took him by surprise as she suddenly drew her knees up and shoved hard. He wasn't expecting it and so he ended up on his back. This time, Prudence straddled him.

He gripped her thighs, unable to help himself from touching her at least once. They were so thick and juicy. He'd never really admired them before, but he wanted them on him now, wrapped around him.

"Let's get something straight. Not all of us are like you. We don't need to hurt or control people to be around them, and we certainly don't expect something from them just for the pleasure of their company."

He tilted his head to the side. "You could have run."

"Huh?"

Drake thrust up so she wasn't in any doubt to his meaning.

She could have run as far away from him as she could. It wouldn't have done any good. He'd have still caught her. When it came to her, he would always catch her. He didn't know why he had this sudden need to keep her close.

There was no way a kiss could have that kind of control, and yet here he lay underneath her, willing to do a hell of a lot more with her. "You know, for someone who hates my guts, you sure like sitting on me."

Rather than run off, she stayed perfectly still, surprising him once again even as he rubbed his hard dick against her. Finally, after what felt like an eternity but was only a couple of minutes, she got off him and marched back to the car.

"This is over. Stop following me around. Whatever you think is going on, you're wrong. We hate each other, Drake. Can't you just stick with that?"

Her face was all red and it looked to him like she couldn't handle her feelings. Drake made no move to hide his arousal. He wasn't ashamed of being horny.

Prudence had a body that he wanted and he wasn't going to think too much of it. She was curvier and heavier than any of the other girls he'd been with, but he wasn't picky. Climbing behind the wheel, he tried not to think of why his hands were shaking or why that fiery pit of jealousy seemed to spiral in his gut.

Prudence was nothing.

She meant nothing to him.

He didn't have to think about her, or even look at her.

They were enemies, not friends.

She didn't speak a word as he pulled back onto the road, doing a quick U-turn so he was heading back home.

He didn't need to justify his actions. If she wanted to be silent, then he was more than happy to stay that way. When he got back on her street, he noticed Sean the pussy was waiting for her.

Drake kept his mouth shut as Prudence climbed out. One look at Sean and Drake knew he wasn't happy. That only served to make him incredibly so. Sean was fake. He hid behind his glasses and nerdy tendencies and Drake had never liked it.

He turned his gaze to Prudence and saw she looked nervous, maybe even a little guilty. She had no right to feel guilty about anything. They'd done nothing wrong and if little baby Sean couldn't handle that, then it was his problem.

"See you around, Prudence." He winked at her and pulled away from her house, heading toward his empty one. He'd stayed behind this summer. The thought of going on any of his parents' trips didn't appeal. It wasn't like they wanted him there and if they did, he had to be dressed up as some kind of doll for them to show off to all of their friends. The lies and fakery didn't appeal, and with the end of school quickly approaching, he wanted to be on his own.

Glancing back in his mirror, he saw Sean and Prudence hadn't moved, and from the look of things, they were fighting. That, he found interesting.

Sean felt threatened by him.

It wasn't like he and Prudence had ever gotten along. Most of the time, he found a great deal of fun in making her life hell. She responded differently to everyone else around him.

Pulling into his driveway, he saw his friends waiting for him. They didn't look happy and neither was Drake. He wanted some alone time to start planning.

What he was planning, he didn't have the first fucking clue.

The kiss played again in his head. Prudence's lips had been so soft beneath his.

Would it be so wrong to find out what the hell was going on there?

He stayed in his car, waiting for the rage and anger to subside. When it did, he climbed out, facing his friends. They all looked like fucking idiots, waiting for their master to tell them what to do. He just wanted to tear them all apart.

None of them were as interesting as Prudence, but there would be time for him to have his fun. He could wait.

Chapter Nine
Save her from the penis

Boredom was not something Prudence was used to, especially not in the summer. Between her job and Sean, she kept pretty busy. Only, Sean wasn't talking to her. She didn't see what the problem was. Drake had taken her home and because she refused to explain what was going on, Sean had been avoiding her. He wouldn't even spend the day with her and that was why she ended up walking to the new tourist park alone.

She stretched her arms up above her head, lifting them and moving, trying to think of something that could end the boredom. She'd read about ten books in the last week alone. Her eyes hurt and her head pounded from all the knowledge she was sucking up.

Whatever happened with Drake was none of Sean's business. It didn't matter to him what she did, and she couldn't believe he was taking it this personally.

It made no sense at all. She wanted to believe it was all nothing, but the tingling she got on her lips meant otherwise. She couldn't stop thinking about the meanest little prick in the world. Drake wasn't the kind of guy she wanted to have a crush on or have any feelings toward. He was her enemy. Someone she had to steer clear of.

At night, when she couldn't seem to tame her thoughts, he was there, all the time. There was no getting away from the feelings he evoked.

This was why she had decided to go for a walk. What was the point of constantly calling Sean to have her calls ignored, or even standing outside his front door waiting for him to see sense just for him to close the door on her? There was only so much rejection she was willing to take.

She walked down the dirt path. The large trees

offered a reasonable amount of much-needed shade. It was way too hot, even for her. She had opted for a thin-strapped top and denim shorts, complete with a pair of sneakers. When she could only hear the sounds of distant birds, she paused, leaning against a tree, hoping Drake didn't invade her mind.

"Penny for your thoughts," Drake said.

She opened her eyes and tried not to sob as the person she was very much trying to escape stood right there in front of her with a smug smile.

"What do you want, Drake?"

He moved toward her but she didn't run.

Her heart started to pound and that curl of excitement that had been dormant for so long seemed to ignite the closer he got. She tilted her head to the side, waiting.

He placed a hand beside her head, and with his other, he cupped her cheek.

"What are you doing there?"

"I imagine I'm doing the exact same thing as you."

She didn't think for a second he was trying to run from his thoughts.

"You're not trying to pull away," he said.

"What?"

"Nothing. Just thinking."

"What are you thinking about?" she asked.

"Do you really want to know?"

Did she? This guy was her enemy. "Why not? It's not like we're going anywhere. No matter where I go, you're always there."

He laughed. "Seeing as we're being so honest." He pressed his body against hers. Rather than be repulsed, she liked it. Curious, she waited for what he had to say next. His gaze moved to her lips before going back up again.

"I'm thinking about kissing you right now."

"You are?"

"Yes." His thumb ran across her bottom lip. "What is it about you that I can't get out of my fucking head?"

"You think this is easy for me?" she asked. "I don't like you."

"But you want me to kiss you."

She didn't say a word. What was the point? He was very much aware of what she wanted, regardless if she really wanted it. Licking her lips, she stared at his, waiting.

The smirk didn't even distract her. "There is something really wrong with me."

She moaned as he slammed his lips against hers. He wasn't gentle. The soft hand on her cheek moved to grip her hair, holding her in place.

Putting her hands on his chest, she had no intention of pushing him away. She slid them up to wrap her hands around his neck, moaning louder as his leg pushed between hers. Everything in her mind screamed at her to tell him to stop. To not let it happen, but she couldn't bring herself to. She wanted this.

His other hand gripped her hip and he pressed against her. The hard ridge of his cock was easy to feel through their clothing as he made her very aware of how much he wanted to be close to her.

This was insane and crazy, but she didn't want it to stop.

The hand in her hair moved down, cupping her breast. Pleasure spread throughout her entire body, taking her by surprise.

She jerked away from the kiss, but there was nowhere else for her to go. Staring up into Drake's eyes, she was shocked by how much bigger he was than her.

"What is it?" His hand was still against her breast.

"I've … I've never…" She couldn't think of what to say because the truth was she'd never been in this position before.

The fact Drake was the one touching her startled her. She always imagined the guy to kiss her and touch her would be someone she liked.

"You've never been touched." He suddenly pulled his hand back and she wanted him to touch her again. To not hold back.

"I need to go." She went to move away but he caught her wrist, pulling her back.

"Did you want me to stop?"

"I don't feel comfortable talking about this."

"That doesn't answer my question."

She gritted her teeth, looking around for a joke to suddenly appear. There was nothing.

"Pru!"

"Where are they?" she asked.

"Where are who?" He frowned at her.

"Your friends. Do they have a camera waiting to take the moment?"

"What is going on here, Pru?" he asked.

"I don't understand what's going on. Why are you suddenly being nice to me? Why are you everywhere? What is with all the kisses and the touches?" Tears filled her eyes as she felt heartbroken at the thought of him playing her.

She didn't want to be toyed with. This was her life. Her summer vacation. The last thing she wanted to be doing was arguing with Sean and pining for Drake. Nothing made sense anymore.

Drake groaned. He pressed his head against her

shoulder but that didn't give her any answers. It only served to irritate her. She pushed him away and tried to leave, but he wouldn't let her go. "Please, stop."

"I don't understand. Okay? I know you want me to have some kind of evil plan. There's no one else here. No friend. No nothing. I didn't bring anyone else here. I saw you walking and I followed you."

"You followed me?"

"Yes."

"Don't you have something better to do?"

"No." He snorted. "What else is there for me to do?"

"I don't know. Get a manicure?" She smiled at him.

"I stayed home this summer. I didn't go with my family and for what it is worth, I'm confused as well. I've been with a lot of girls."

"I know."

"I'm not bragging here. I'm stating a fact."

"I get it."

"I don't think you do."

"You've been with a lot of girls. You've done it all. Kissing, having sex, all of it. There's not a lot to get but I'm guessing you've done it all, and what is confusing you even more is you're enjoying your time with me." She took a deep breath. She stared at his chest but knew she couldn't carry on without looking into his eyes.

Tilting her head back, she regarded Drake.

"I guess you do know what I mean."

"I happen to have a brain. I'm confused. I've never been with a guy. You're the first person I've ever kissed. Believe me when I say I don't have a clue what's going on here."

"I figured you and Sean were an item."

She looked away. Thinking of Sean made her feel guilty.

"What is it? What did I say to piss you off?"

"It's not you." She groaned.

"Sean?"

"Yeah, how do you know?"

"The only person I know you hang out with besides Ree is Sean. What's wrong with him? What does that have to do with me?"

"You know he doesn't like you and he wants me to talk to him about what's going on here, and the truth is I don't have a clue what's going on. I'm so confused all the time. This isn't supposed to be anything. It's getting too complicated and I can't stand it." She shook her head, staring down at where he still held her. "Please, let me go."

He didn't.

She waited.

His gaze was on her wrist.

"Drake?"

"Why do you have to go?" he asked.

Glancing around them, she saw no one was waiting or watching. His friends weren't there to bully or ridicule. "Whatever is going on here, I don't think it's a good thing."

"We kissed. So what?" he asked.

She took a deep breath. "Exactly, so what?" She shrugged. "You and I, we're not besties. We're never going to be anything more. It was one kiss today and that's all it's ever going to be."

She tugged on her hand and he finally let her go.

Turning her back to him, she clenched her hands into fists and walked away.

You can do this, Pru. It's Drake. Your enemy since you moved here. Your best friend is the only one who deserves your attention.

Drake didn't make a move to stop her.

Part of her was thankful and another was a little disappointed. She would be lying to herself if she said she didn't enjoy this attention. Not that she wanted Drake at all. Nothing between them would ever change. The kiss, though, his attention, and his gaze, that was enough to set her on fire, and she hated it.

Without looking back, she made her way home, only to stop when she saw Sean waiting on her front doorstep.

"No one's home," he said.

"That's because they're at work." She pushed a curl out of her eyes and waited. She didn't have the first clue what to say and part of her was a little guilty for the fact she'd spoken with Drake and kissed him.

They shouldn't be kissing and she wouldn't allow herself to be put in that compromising position again. Nothing good could ever happen to her if she was around Drake and she needed to remember that.

"I stopped by your work place as well. They said it was your day off," Sean said.

"I did try to call you. A lot."

"I know."

"I don't know why you're so angry at me. I've done nothing wrong." She hated this stalemate between them more than anything.

"I hate Drake."

"So? It's not like I'm sleeping with the guy."

"But you didn't see the way you and him looked at each other, Pru."

"We didn't look at each other in any way." She wasn't going to get into her confused feelings with Sean. He wouldn't understand. He was the only person she could talk to. Ree hadn't even bothered to stop by or to speak to either of them since the party. She figured sleeping with Drake had been her only goal, and now that she accomplished that, she and Sean weren't worth her time.

"I don't like him being near you."

"He brought me home. Nothing more." She wasn't about to tell him about Drake destroying her phone. She'd been using her dad's old phone, claiming hers had been stolen.

Sean sighed. "I'm sorry. I shouldn't be a dick to you. I can't believe I've been acting like this. It's not me and I shouldn't take my issues out on you."

"It's fine."

"No, it's not fine." He moved up toward her and wrapped his arms around her. She closed her eyes, breathing him in. This was her best friend in the entire world. The one person she could share everything with and yet, she couldn't tell him her thoughts or her confused feelings about one particular guy. He wasn't ready to know about that.

Wrapping her arms around him, she pushed her worries and concerns down. Whatever was going on between her and Drake, Sean didn't need to know.

Pulling away, Sean kissed her head. "Come on, I'll go and make us some coffee."

She followed him into her house and for now, she was able to relax. Everything else could wait.

Chapter Ten
The prick needs a punch

Drake wasn't the least bit surprised to see Prudence and Sean hand-in-hand as they walked through town. He sipped at his shop-bought coffee and chewed on his doughnut as he watched them. They looked so happy.

All friendshippy and all the bullshit he knew he couldn't stand.

Whatever was going on between them, Sean wasn't getting any. He didn't believe for a second that little shit knew what to do with his dick.

He stayed in his place, leaning against his car as they approached. Prudence had just laughed at something Sean had said, and for whatever it was, Drake wanted to hurt him. The laughter died the instant she caught sight of him. She looked nervous and he liked it.

"Look what we have here," Drake said, drawing their attention.

"Drake," Sean said.

"Asshole."

"Come on," Pru said.

"Yeah, take your little dog. He needs to be put on a leash."

Pru glared at him and he smiled right back. She had the cutest angry look.

Sean shook his head but put his arm around her shoulders. Drake clenched his teeth, growling at the sight. He watched the two friends pass and it made him lose his appetite. After throwing away the last of his coffee and doughnut, he climbed into his car and headed home.

The house was quiet and it would be all summer. He moved out toward the pool, pulling off his clothes and diving into the water buck-naked. Trying to unwind from the anger simmering inside, he swam laps. But all he could think about was snapping Sean in two.

As he broke the surface, he saw his friends waiting.

"Hey, man," Marco said.

"You haven't called," this from Nick.

"Yeah, we've been worrying about it," Carl said.

They all looked bored and the last thing he wanted to do was to hang out with them. "I've been busy. What the fuck do you guys want?"

"Figured you needed some company," Nick said. "You haven't got arrested or shot in the past couple of days. What's up?"

Drake snorted. "What do you guys know about Sean?"

"Sean as in pussy Sean?"

"The kid that hangs out with Trash," he said. He thought about her lips and how good they felt against his own. It didn't matter about the kiss. She was still trash.

"Not a lot to know. He grew up in this town. Judgy little prick. You probably beat some sense into him," Marco said.

"The only one," Nick said, in agreement.

"I want him out of the picture."

"What do you mean?"

He thought about Pru. As long as Sean was in the picture, there was no way he'd be able to explore this thing he had with her.

"Yeah, Drake, why the fuck do you want to mess with those losers, anyway? They're so beneath you," Marco said.

"I want to mess with whoever the fuck I want to. Last time I checked, I didn't answer to you."

Marco shrugged. "Whatever."

He didn't know why the fuck he was putting up with these assholes. Leaning back in the pool, he thought about Prudence. She was clearly guilty when it came to him. He didn't even know why he was wasting his time with this.

After climbing out of the water, he walked past the guys and went straight to his room. He pulled on a pair of sweats and a shirt and made his way back downstairs. His friends were already playing on one of the games. He didn't bother to interrupt them as he left his home. He got into his car and drove toward Prudence's house. There was no sign of Sean or his car.

He moved toward the small park where there was a lot. Once he'd parked his car, he walked over to Pru's house.

No one was around. He checked in the windows and walked around the back. He had no idea what the fuck he was doing. Taking a seat on the back porch, he waited. Several times, he got up and was about to leave, only to take a seat again.

He needed shit to go back to normal between him and Pru, where he hated her guts or just liked to watch her suffer. She was always so open with her emotions and it was one of the reasons he liked to attack her.

He was playing on a game on his cell phone, waiting for Prudence and Sean to arrive. It didn't take long for Sean to drive up to her house. He moved toward a large bush where he could watch without being caught. Drake pocketed his cell phone and watched as she climbed out of the car but leaned down to look through the passenger window.

Whatever Sean said made her laugh and he saw the blush on her face.

Clenching his hands into fists, he wanted to go over there and pound that smug bastard's fucking face in.

There was something about Sean that really rubbed him the wrong way and he wanted nothing more than to take him out, to fuck him up.

Finally, the feeling ebbed away when Prudence stood. She gave Sean a little wave, making her way up to her house. Sean didn't drive away until she was in her house.

The moment Sean was out of sight, Drake moved toward the back door and knocked but he didn't have a clue what he was doing or why he was even here.

Prudence walked into the kitchen, looking toward the door. He saw the surprise flash across her face when she caught sight of him. She hesitated but finally opened the door. "What are you doing here?"

"Is that any way to greet your friend?"

"We're not friends, Drake."

"Are you just going to leave me at the back door?"

"I'm tempted."

He gripped the edge of the doorway and pushed hard. She stumbled back, and he let himself into her house.

Prudence was back in his face within a second. "Get out or I call the cops."

"You won't call the cops."

"Really? You think I won't?"

"No, you won't. Not if you want to answer questions as to why I came over in the first place."

"I didn't invite you here."

"We've been seen together, Pru. You think anyone is going to believe that you don't want me here? I'm the richest kid in town. I've got power, money, and what do you have? Nothing. Money talks, baby, and no one will believe a word you say. Not when I'm such a catch. Any girl will throw themselves at me."

"Ugh, I don't like how smug you are. I don't want you here. Get out."

"I'm not leaving."

"And I don't want you here. How's that going to work?"

Drake laughed. "I've always been curious about how the other half lives."

"Other half?"

"Your house is really small." He smiled as he heard her growl. She was so freaking cute when she was angry. Seeing her lose control made him hot as well.

"Damn it, Drake. I mean it. My parents could be home any minute."

"And you'd only introduce me as your friend. Let's not think anything else that would happen. They'd probably be happy that you've finally gotten a good friend."

"They adore Sean. They wouldn't care about you. They're not greedy and won't be bought off just because of who you are."

"For a clever girl, you sure do act stupid." He saw all the pictures on the wall. None of them were from famous artists. They were all family photos of Pru at different ages, and also of her parents.

In all of them, they looked happy. They weren't even professionally done. For the only photos he'd taken with his parents there had been a minimum of three photographers, along with makeup designers, and everything that a set would need to make them all look like the perfect family.

He'd hated it. The fakeness of his family. The lies each photo sold. There was no truth in a single image. The pictures here, they were all natural. There were no expectations.

"It must be nice," he said.

"What must be nice?"

He turned to find Pru with her arms folded. He had a slight smile on his face. "Nothing."

"Do you and your family have pictures taken? I don't see the draw."

"Do you like your parents?" he asked, avoiding her question.

"Of course. I love them. They're my parents and they'll do anything for me. I don't understand what all of this is. Why are you even here?"

"I figured we could hang out."

"Hang out?"

"Do you have a repeat button on or something?"

"I don't understand what you want from me, Drake. Why do you want to hang out when you've got all of your other friends?"

He stared at her, wondering the exact same thing. There were his friends back home. The ones who were playing his games, probably drinking his father's expensive scotch. There was any number of girls he could call to keep him company, and yet, here he was. Waiting for something.

Hanging out with Pru seemed like the best idea of them all.

"You know, I can't have a picture taken unless it's a selfie and then my mom likes to photoshop it so it's perfect. I'm not allowed to upload anything that makes me look bad." He didn't know why he was talking. "We don't have stuff like this. We're always standing there stiffly as if we've got a giant stick up our asses."

"Drake?"

"I don't want pity."

"I'm not giving it to you. I just ... you're confusing me. I don't know what you want from me."

"I don't want anything from you. Believe it or

not. My friends came by and I just, I wanted something real."

She gave him that confused look again and he didn't like it. "Real? You think you can be real with me but not anyone else?" she asked.

"I don't know what I'm saying." He shoved his hands into his pockets, looking at anywhere but her.

"Drake, you don't have to lie to me."

"I'm not lying to you. Okay? I don't know what the fuck I'm doing here. You can't tell me you don't feel it whenever I'm around."

She didn't say anything and he had to look at her.

Pru was staring right back at him. "The kiss again?" she asked.

"Tell me you don't think about it."

"Drake, we're enemies."

"We don't have to be."

"But we are. You need to see that. We're not good for each other."

He took a step toward her, then another, not caring about anything else but to see her, to feel her against him. When he stood right in front of her, he reached out, cupping her chin. This, to him, felt like the most natural thing in the world. He didn't get it or understand it, but it was there.

"Drake?"

"Shut up, Pru. Haven't you ever noticed that things get complicated when we talk?"

She snorted. "What are you wanting from me?"

He looked at her lips. They were so ripe and full. He wanted to taste her again. He ran his thumb across her lip, watching her.

Why hadn't he ever realized she was pretty?

Leaning forward, he found that her lips were just too much temptation to deny. He should stop, he knew that. His parents would hate for him to be with someone like Pru. She wasn't in the same league as him. They probably already had a wife picked out for him. A girl with way more money than sense and who knew how to prance around in their world with the right image. Pru was so far removed from what his parents considered a good match. They wouldn't see anything other than her lack of wealth and prospects.

Slamming his lips down on hers, he threw caution to the wind and just took what he wanted. As he slid his tongue across her lips, Pru surprised him, opening her mouth. He plundered inside, moaning at her exquisite taste. He didn't even know why the kiss felt so fucking good, but he couldn't stop. He didn't want to.

She let out a moan and it was almost as if she was relenting. Her arms went around his neck, and he slid his hand down her back to cup her ass, holding her as close as he physically could. Moving back, he dropped her onto the sofa, following her down. He pressed between her spread thighs, wishing there was nothing between them.

He didn't want anything to hold him back from touching her. From taking her, and from making her his. Drake pulled back from the kiss, staring down at her, a little startled by his sudden change of … feelings.

"What is it?" Pru asked.

He saw how tense she got the longer he just watched her.

Obsessing about a kiss was one thing. Craving Pru was an entirely different experience.

"I've got to go."

"Drake?"

He got to his feet, very much aware of his raging erection, ignoring it and Pru's voice. He needed to get the fuck out of here, and not just out of her house but out of town. The longer he stayed here, the harder it was to ignore these messed-up feelings.

Chapter Eleven
It only lasts so long

One week went by where Drake was nowhere to be seen. Not that Pru was complaining. Having a break from him was what she needed. He'd been confusing her with his kisses and attention. Even down to him ruining her phone. She needed to demand a new one from him when she saw him.

She didn't have a clue when that would actually be because he'd decided to completely disappear. It wasn't a problem for her, though. The break was nice, even if she did check across the shopping mall to see if he was camped out eating or following her around. But she didn't miss him. That would be freaking crazy on her part to miss him, wouldn't it?

Sean helped to make the time go faster. He stopped by to have lunch with her whenever he could, and they hung out when her parents weren't around. She did notice he rarely stopped by if her parents were home.

If they were, he'd take her out somewhere. They'd go driving or watch a movie. Neither of them brought up Drake. The last thing Pru wanted to talk about was Drake. Sean was her best friend, her only friend, especially as Ree wasn't talking to her. She hadn't heard from Ree since the party, not that it was any surprise. She'd see Ree around town but the blonde completely ignored her. Pru wasn't losing sleep over her friend's sudden dislike of her. Clearly, screwing Drake had helped her climb the social ladder of high school.

Into the second week, Pru said goodbye to her boss and left the store. The mall was closing, and she quickly slipped out one of the side doors, rushing through a cloud of cigarette smoke as she did so.

Sean wasn't picking her up tonight and her

parents were out, so no car.

After pulling her jacket around herself to ward off the cold as the temperature had plummeted considerably and it was raining, she folded her arms across her chest and began to walk. By the time she got home, she'd be soaked to the bone, and the idea of being at home alone didn't appeal to her.

A car passed her, throwing water across her legs and covering her shirt. The person who was driving the car didn't stop to offer a single apology, which she found rather rude. She carried on walking, dodging the water splashing up against her and hating that driver all so much for it. When a car pulled up beside her, she tensed up, only to freeze when she noticed the window slid down and there, waiting for her, was none other than Drake.

"What are you doing here?"

"From the looks of it, I'm about to offer you a ride."

"I don't need a ride."

"Really? You clearly need it. Or do you like getting splashed with water?"

She glanced up and down the street, knowing there was no choice but for her to take the offered ride from Drake. Why should she put up a fight? He wasn't asking for anything in return and the idea of walking home soaked really didn't appeal to her.

"Fine."

"You know, a *thank you*, and *yes, please*, would be more than nice."

Glancing over at him, she slammed the door closed. "Thank you, Drake, I really do appreciate you stopping by. Was it out of your way?"

"You know it was."

"Then why did you come and pick me up?"

"I knew you'd need a ride and well, I don't see a reason why I can't give you one. We're friends, aren't we?" he asked.

"You know we're not friends." They weren't anything.

He shrugged. "If you don't want the ride, get the fuck out of my car."

She stayed perfectly still, staring straight ahead of her.

"Just what I thought." He pressed his foot to the gas.

Pru couldn't bring herself to look at him. To do that, she'd be admitting she liked that he'd come to pick her up.

"Where's Sean when you need him?" he asked.

"He's busy."

"Of course he is. The wimp is probably playing on his computer or something."

"He's probably studying. Next year is important. He wants to get into..." She couldn't remember the college he'd picked. She was a really bad friend. Gritting her teeth, she growled. "It doesn't matter. I know he's busy and he only wants the best."

"Have you ever noticed, Pru, you've surrounded yourself with an asshole and a whore who are both self-centered pricks?"

She glared at him. "I didn't hear you had much of a problem with Ree."

He laughed. "Are you jealous?"

"I'm not even going to give that one an answer." She wasn't jealous. Whatever he wanted to do with his body was more than fine with her. It was his, anyway.

Resting her elbow on the door, she stared out of the window, watching the world go by. It was still pouring down rain and she felt a chill to her bones.

"She didn't mean anything," Drake said. "I was angry at you. She was just a distraction."

Pru looked at him, not understanding him again. "Pull over."

"What?"

"You heard me. Pull over."

"I'm not going to let you get out in this weather. You're stubborn, but that doesn't mean I want you to get hurt."

"Ironic coming from a guy who has hurt me every single step of the way. It doesn't matter. I'm not stupid and I'm not going to get out to walk. Just pull over." She rubbed at her head, feeling the stirring of a headache. This wasn't how she wanted to spend her evening but there was nothing she could do about it.

Drake flashed hot and cold and it was starting to give her whiplash. One moment he seemed like the asshole bully, and the next, a reasonable gentleman, calm and collected. She was starting to wonder if he had multiple personalities with the way he was behaving. He pulled over to the side of the road. A car blared his horn at him, but Pru didn't care.

"Well, what was it you wanted to say to me that couldn't wait until we got somewhere private or at least safer?"

"What the hell is wrong with you?" she asked, turning toward him.

"There's nothing wrong with me."

"What is this? What do you want from me?"

Drake sat back. "You want me to make a list?"

"I want to know what the hell is going on here, Drake. One moment you're hating me. We've hurt each other for as long as we've known each other. We fight all the time. I avoid you as much as possible and I don't for a second think you like me." Even as she was speaking, she remembered their kisses.

Locking of lips did not make for such a dramatic change.

"Then you leave like I've done something to you. I don't get you. You've gone from being the bane of my existence to demanding I be at your party. You've slept with Ree and bragged about it. We kissed and things got weird, and then you were suddenly everywhere I turned. You disappeared again, and now you're back. You seeing this here?"

"Yes."

"What is going on? Why are you doing this to me?"

"I don't know!" he yelled at her.

She pulled back, the anger taking her by surprise.

"You think I've got a clue what's happening here?" he asked.

Pru shrugged.

He shook his head. "You're beneath me. You're so far fucking beneath me it's not even funny."

She rolled her eyes. "Back to money again. Why am I not surprised?"

"It's easy for you. Your parents don't expect you to do the right thing by their books."

"What the hell does that even mean? Of course they want me to do right. It's not always about the money, Drake. It's about being a good person. Is that all your parents want? You to make money? To only associate with people who will better you in some way?"

"Yes."

His answer surprised her.

"We're the wealthiest family in town. They want to keep that title. Why is it so hard for you to see that?"

"Why are you hanging around with me then? I can't give you anything. I'm just me, Drake. No matter how many times you kiss me or how much you want me to be different. It's never going to happen. I'm only me and you're only you. Just tell me what it is you want." This wasn't doing any of them any good.

"You."

"What?"

"I … I want you. I don't want this to mean anything but when I'm with you, I forget all of the other shit and I can think. You're all I can think about, and I don't get it."

She turned toward her door. "You're confusing me. This can't be happening between us. We're going over the same old ground. We sound like a broken record."

He gripped her arm and she turned toward him. "I know. I really do."

She couldn't help but look at him. He sounded so lost.

"All of my life I've been told to look at people like you as if you're nothing. You're nothing to me because you could never be in the same league as me. My parents would make your and your family's life a misery, and that's being nice about it, if they even knew I was driving you home. This can't be anything."

Pru sat back. "Then what do you want?" She kept asking the same question in the hope that he would just tell her what he wanted. This back-and-forth was grating on her nerves. She didn't know what to expect and, quite frankly, it just wasn't worth the pain or the confusion.

"I want you," Drake said, completely shocking her to the core with his honesty.

"What?"

"You heard me and I'm not going to repeat myself." He turned to face the road once again.

Pru opened her mouth, then closed it, and opened

it again. "You can't be serious."

"I am serious, Pru. I know you feel it too. I get that we're different people. That this is completely fucking stupid and you know what, you're right. It's crazy and stupid but I still don't care because it's what I want."

She licked her lips. Drake made no move to pull away from the curb. The windshield wipers moved back and forth. She looked around at the passing cars. None of them stopped or belted out their horn, they simply moved around Drake's car. Did they know who he was? What he was capable of? She didn't have a clue.

"Let's go back to my place," she said. The words fell out of her mouth before she could stop them. Once she had spoken, there was no taking them back. She didn't want to. This was her choice to make, and she chose finding out more about where this would lead with Drake. It wasn't going to end well. She knew that, deep down into her soul. This was going to end badly for both of them.

Drake drove and they stayed silent.

There was no need for words. What was the point of talking? She nibbled her lip, recalling her parents weren't home. They were busy working as they usually were during the summer season. This was their time to put in as much overtime as possible so they could pay off all their debts.

It was the only time in her home there wasn't a single argument about money. For a split second, she worried Sean would see Drake's car but then pushed it to the back of her mind. Sean was busy doing whatever it was he was doing.

Climbing out of the car, she was all too aware of Drake's presence at her back. He stood right there, waiting. Sliding the key into the lock with a surprisingly steady hand, she twisted the key and entered her home.

The silence was deafening, if that was even possible. Her heart pounded as she closed the door behind Drake, who had slid in behind her. With the door locked, she turned toward him. He simply watched her.

As she clasped her hands together, the metal of the key dug into her palm, but she made no move to stop it. Maybe the bite of pain from the key would help her to get her head on straight.

Drake took a step toward her, then another. She didn't move back, simply tilted her head to look at him. Like this, he seemed so much taller than her. He reached out and she didn't even flinch as he cupped her cheek. His touch felt right, natural, and at that moment, she knew she had to be losing her mind. How could his touch feel like this?

"Do you feel that?" he asked.

"Yes." There was no point in arguing.

They'd been arguing for too long now and it hadn't gotten them anywhere. She didn't want to argue or fight with him anymore. She placed her hands on his shoulders, feeling the strength within him.

One look into his eyes, and Pru stopped fighting. She let her body take control and she closed the distance between them, which wasn't much. She couldn't believe Drake was in her living room, or that she was about to do what she was. Pressing her lips against his, she kissed him. This wasn't their first or second kiss, but this did feel like it was going to change her life.

Drake sank his fingers into her hair, and he held the back of her head, kissing her harder. He bit down on her lips and she moaned, holding him tightly to her. He moved them both back until she hit the wall, and in some way, they clawed at each other's clothing. Their jackets were on the floor, their shoes were kicked off, and before

Pru knew what was happening, they were in her bedroom. She couldn't even remember walking up the stairs.

All she wanted was Drake's lips.

His touch, his everything.

They collapsed to the bed, and even then, Pru didn't put a stop to it. Even as her body shook, she wanted him and didn't wish for him to stop. The pleasure rushed through her body, and she couldn't imagine being anywhere but with him.

She climbed over him, straddling his waist and pulling him up. She kissed him back as he ran his hands over her panty-covered ass.

She was in her bedroom, in her underwear, with her bully. What the fuck was she doing?

Chapter Twelve
Can't get her out of my head

Drake had tried avoiding her. He'd done everything he could think of to put some perspective on his life away from Pru. She wasn't good for him, not when it came to his parents. There was no future here, and at the same time, he didn't understand why the fuck he was even thinking about a future.

What was the point? They were never going to be together.

It didn't matter how much he wanted her kiss, or how good it felt having her wrapped around him right now. The truth was this wasn't going to work out.

This, whatever *this* was, couldn't work. His parents would ruin her, and he'd bullied her. For as long as he'd known her, he'd bullied her. He'd enjoyed it as well. There were no excuses for his behavior. He liked to hurt her, plain and simple. There was no logic into why he did it.

Pru fed a part of him that no one else seemed to be able to touch, and now, he couldn't make it stop, didn't want it to. There were a million girls out there just like Pru, so why was he fixated on her, just her? None of it made any sense. He'd tried to stay away, to clear his mind of whatever this was, but nothing worked.

He wanted her.

Staying away was hard work. He was tired of yearning for her and not getting what he wanted. This time, he was going to take her.

Running his hands down her back, he cupped her ass. Her underwear didn't do a good enough job of hiding her from his gaze. Her tits were nice and large. He'd noticed them long before now. When they were in class and she'd been leaning forward, looking over her book, he'd seen right down her shirt. Chemistry class where he'd been at the perfect angle to see everything so clearly.

Drake remembered being so angry at her for making him realize she was a girl, he'd spilled some of the iodine over her pristine-white shirt, soaking it a nice dark amber. Then he'd ruined her books by setting them on fire in the sink.

He'd been an asshole, but everyone had laughed and he'd felt a lot better. The memory of how much he'd wanted to touch her faded as she'd merely looked at him with no reaction whatsoever.

This past year, she'd learned not to give him the time of day. He'd waited for her to explode, to retaliate, and nothing. Hurting her had become a bore, and now, as he grabbed her full ass, he didn't want to think about all the other shit he'd done to her.

She moaned. Her head tilted back and he couldn't resist sucking on her neck. Flicking his tongue across her pulse, he bit down, relishing the feel of her squirming in his arms.

"Drake?" she asked, moaning.

"What?"

"I don't … not yet."

"You don't want to fuck?"

"No."

"Why not? We're going to end up doing it anyway." There was no point in denying the inevitable.

They were almost naked, in her room, on her bed. Sex was going to happen.

"You don't know sex is going to happen straightaway and I'm not ready." She tucked some hair behind her ear and seemed nervous. He found it cute. Stroking the tips of his fingers down her arm, he had to remind himself she was still a virgin. She didn't party like him or the other girls he'd been with. None of them had cared about where they had sex or even when. They threw themselves at him in the hope of snagging the wealthiest guy in town. Always looking toward their future, never once considering what he wanted. It was why he always made them jump through his hoops, giving them tasks so ridiculous, they shouldn't ever agree to do them, and yet, they did.

Pru wasn't like any of them. She didn't come to him when he called.

"I can wait," he said. The words slipped out of his mouth before he could stop them. He didn't even know why he said them. This wasn't going to be a relationship.

All he wanted from her was her cherry. That was it.

She offered him a smile and all the vile insults he could throw at her left his mind. He didn't want to hurt her. Not right now. It didn't seem right.

"I don't know what's going on inside that head and I've got a feeling I don't ever want to know." She cupped his face, her touch shocking him even more. There was something in her gaze. He didn't know what it was, but he couldn't look away. He held on to her arms, hoping to ground himself, to hold on to this moment and never let it go. Was it possible to love a single second so much you didn't want it to pass?

She leaned in close and her lips crashed against his.

Sinking his fingers into her hair, he pushed his thoughts and fears aside and simply basked in all that was Pru.

She wrapped her legs around his waist, and he kissed her harder. She opened her lips and he slid his tongue across her mouth before plunging inside. Pru released a moan, and he loved the sound, especially as she ground herself against him. His cock was so close to her.

Pru didn't want to have sex but that was more than fine with him. There were other enjoyable ways to have some fun.

Running his fingers across her back, he touched her panties, giving them a little tug.

She pulled away from his lips, and without giving her chance to stop him, he moved her so she was beneath him and he had all the control.

"What are you doing?"

"Don't worry. I know your limits. I'm not going to push you yet, but I'm not going to be a good boy for long."

They were chalk and cheese, and yet, he didn't want to be anywhere else. How the fuck did that work? There was no way this would ever last, but it didn't mean they couldn't have some fun.

Kissing down her body, he pressed his face against her tits, relishing the feel of them. He pulled back one of the bra cups and out popped her tit. She had large, pointed nipples.

"Someone is very happy to see me," he said, sucking on her nipple.

No one had done this to her. He was the first and only one to be with her, and that did something to him. Virgins weren't a conquest for him. The prospect of being with a virgin didn't fill him with excitement. When it came to Pru, though, he liked that she didn't know anyone else.

Pushing all of his confusing thoughts and feelings aside, he focused on her. Touching her body, kissing her, wanting her. Every single part of him was excited at just being with her.

Moving between her thighs, he pulled down her

panties and spread her legs apart.

"Drake?"

"It's okay."

She nibbled her lip, and he saw how scared she was.

He kissed back up her body until he was at her mouth, taking her lips, and he knew he didn't want to rush this with her. How crazy was it that he didn't want to rush? He was more than happy to take it at Pru's pace. It didn't mean he couldn't get her used to his touches.

When he cupped her pussy once again, she gasped, holding his hand. "Drake?"

"I'm not going to hurt you. I've promised you I won't do anything that you don't like."

"You don't know that."

"I know what I can do to you, and believe me, you're going to like this."

She stared at him with that cute little frown.

"You're still doubting me."

"It's hard not to. You've got all these other girls screaming how good you are, but what if you're not? What if the only reason they say those things is so you'll buy them nice things?"

"Do you want me to buy you nice things?"

"No. I don't want anything from you, Drake."

"Money is a huge incentive."

"For what? To do something illegal and wrong?"

He groaned. "I don't want to argue with you. I'm just saying a lot of people will pay a lot of money for bullshit."

"I'm not like a lot of people, Drake."

"I know that." He kissed her again. "I don't want to argue."

She still held his wrist. "I … I'm not ready."

He pulled his hand away. "Then I'll stop."

"Just like that?"

"I'm not a rapist, Pru."

"I know that."

"You didn't think I'd stop."

"I honestly don't know what to expect from you. I'm sorry."

He sat back. "I'm not going to hurt you. I'm many things, but forcing myself on you, I'm not going to do that." He sat back and groaned. "I've got other shit to do."

He got off the bed and began to put his clothes on.

Out of the corner of his eye, he saw Pru pull her panties on and then she wrapped her arms around him. "I'm sorry."

"You don't need to apologize."

"I do. This isn't what I intended. I mean that. I like it when you kiss me. I'm not ready for something more. It scares me."

"Do you think this is easy for me? I don't have a fucking clue what I'm doing. This isn't me, Pru. This isn't the kind of bullshit I'm used to." He pulled out of her arms, tugging on his shirt.

"You're just going to run away again? Like that? Just because I won't spread my legs for you?"

He turned toward her. "I need to clear my head." He left her bedroom and made his way out to his car. There was no reason to drive it so he crossed the road and started to walk. No one stopped him, which he liked. No one would be willing to get in his way, and they often moved to avoid him.

He wasn't the kind of guy to search for conflict. It just always had a way of finding him when he least expected it.

Apart from Pru.

She didn't move out of his way or give him a break. She would stand and fight. To get around her, he would have to walk or knock her down to keep on moving. This made him stop and glance back. He'd been walking in a straight line but he could barely make out her house. With hands on his hips, he looked back, wondering what the hell he was going to do.

****

The only guy Pru had ever chased down was Sean. Since he was her best friend, it had never meant anything to her to go looking for a guy.

Leaving her house, she saw Drake had left his car. She didn't even care what that would mean to people passing by her house. She had to see Drake again.

Pulling her hair up into a tight knot, she walked across the street. She saw a couple of kids playing and she went around them. She'd watched Drake come this way, and now she was chasing after him.

It was Drake Connor. Why the hell was she chasing after him? It made no sense, and yet, here she was, doing all the chasing. When she saw him, standing there, staring at her, hands on his hips, she stopped running, slowing down to a walk. "Drake."

"Do you have a reason to follow me?" he asked.

"No." She stepped up to him, putting her hands on her hips and looking right at him. "Look, I get there's something going on here. I don't understand it. I don't even know if I want to. You're used to girls falling all over you. I'm not going to be one of those girls. I'm not going to fall for you and let you do whatever the hell you want. I'm not ready for sex. If that's what you want, then you've got to find some way to get it. It's not going to be with me."

"And if I don't want it with anyone else?" he asked.

"I don't know, Drake. We're not friends."

"I'm not offering you friendship. Can't we just be this?"

"What is this?"

"I don't know. I don't fucking know!" He grabbed the back of his head, pacing. "We can't do this in public. No one can know about us."

Pru laughed. "We really should get inside. We're probably scaring the neighbors or something." She didn't want to have to deal with a whole host of questions. "We can take time to figure this thing out."

"Yeah, that does sound like a solid plan. Do you want me to follow you?" he asked.

"Come on, it doesn't matter now. We've been seen together." She reached out, taking his arm, ignoring the sting as she walked with him back to her house. There was no one on the street. The kids playing just a few moments ago had vanished.

Arriving back home, she didn't go to her bedroom but to her kitchen. "What do you want to drink?"

"Coffee, unless you've got a beer."

"No beer. Dad hasn't been shopping and whenever my mom goes, she always forgets it."

"By mistake or on purpose?"

"She's always saying it's by mistake but I doubt it. If it was just by mistake, she'd only miss it once, huh? I'm not sure. Oh, well." She flicked the coffee maker on, so very aware of him in her kitchen.

He didn't speak and she chanced a glance over at him to see him watching her. "What?" she asked.

"Nothing. Your kitchen is really small."

"Of course it is. It has to be." She rolled her eyes. "We don't all have millions to waste on big homes." She shrugged.

With the cups waiting to be filled, she turned toward him.

"Rules then."

"Rules are good," she said. "No one can know anything about us."

"It has to be top secret," he said.

She chuckled. "It feels a little over-dramatic. We're just two high school kids and yet we're acting as if we're doing something wrong."

"We are," Drake said. "We're planning on hooking up and it's against my parents' rules. What about yours?"

"They adore Sean. I think if I was to have any kind of boyfriend-like material, it would be him."

"Don't talk to me about him. Seriously, he's off-limits for anything." Drake slashed his hand across in front of him and she nodded.

"No Sean, got it. I don't want to hear about all your conquests either."

"No previous girls, got it."

"I'm not going to be with anyone else. We're secret but we're also exclusive."

"I hate to break this to you, Pru, but we're not fucking."

"I don't care. You've already made it abundantly clear it's where we're going. I'm not going to risk getting any kind of diseases."

"I do know how to take care of myself, you know."

She was going to retaliate but instead held her hands up, counted to ten, and forced a smile. "We can't argue. Unless you're doing something to keep up appearances."

"This sounds like a good one." Drake crossed his arms across his chest and smirked. "Are you going to give me more details?"

"When we're alone and together, we can't argue like this. We either agree to disagree or we move on. If we're in the company of other people, I don't want you to treat me any differently."

"Are you giving me permission to bully you?"

It sounded stupid even to her. "Yes." She wasn't looking forward to being on the receiving end of his brand of bullying but she also had to keep up appearances. If Drake suddenly started to treat her fairly, others would want to know why. "Why not?"

Drake smirked. "I can't believe you're giving me permission to hurt you."

"It hasn't bothered you before. Why would you care now? This is only going to be until we head to college next year."

"You're going to college?"

"I want to. I don't know where yet. I'm keeping my options open." He wouldn't want to know the truth. Sean wanted her to go to the same college as him, but that meant being miles away from home, which sounded awesome, and it truly did, but for her, she wanted to be a little closer to her parents.

"Isn't that something you'd have figured out?" Drake asked.

"You'd think so, wouldn't you? But no. I haven't made any plans." This summer was about her making a final decision. Her parents only wanted the best for her, even though they were on a limited budget. Anything she wanted would have to come through a scholarship.

"Moving on. What other conditions you got?" Drake asked.

"You can't push me either. I'm not ready for sex."

"I can't even believe I'm discussing this with

you."

"I don't have anything else to add."

"Let me get this straight, we can't be with anyone else but each other. I can't push you into fucking, but I can't be with another girl. No one else can know about us. Behind closed doors, we're good and friends, but to the outside world, I hate your guts and can bully you."

"Yes, that sounds about right. What do you think?" she asked, biting her lip.

"Whatever. Can I kiss you now?"

Just as she was about to tell him to go right ahead, the door to her home opened.

"Raincheck?"

Chapter Thirteen
Just for the summer

"So, I was thinking we could go and see a movie tonight. What do you think?" Sean asked.

Pru glanced at her friend. She stood at his bedroom window overlooking his yard. He had a nice place and his parents were able to afford a gardener.

"Pru, is there anyone in there?"

She pulled out of her thoughts as Sean came over to her, waving a hand in front of her face. "Sorry, I was kind of off in my own world. What?"

"What's with you lately?"

"Nothing is with me." It had been three days since she and Drake had made that agreement. Three entire days of her thinking the absolute worst about her own decisions. There was no one for her to talk to other than Drake and he'd been shockingly silent.

"Are you sure? You've been … quiet."

She chuckled. "Are you trying to tell me I'm a bit of a loudmouth?" she asked.

"Trying to?" Sean asked, laughing.

"Hey, don't be mean." She tapped his arm playfully.

"In all seriousness, you'd tell me."

"Of course. You're my best friend. I'd tell you anything." The lies rolled off her tongue and she felt sick to her stomach. "You know, I think I'm going to head out, actually. It's nothing bad, but I'm not feeling so good."

"Do you want me to drop you off at home?"

"No, I prefer the walk. It might help make me feel better." She grabbed her jacket. "I'll talk to you soon, right?"

"Yeah, of course. Let me know you got home

safely. You know I don't like you walking out all alone."

"I'll be fine. Believe me." She gave Sean a quick hug before leaving his home. What she really needed to do was clear her head. She didn't go straight home but instead walked to the private land that was once a park. It was nearly thirty minutes away from her home, but it was torn down years ago since addicts would leave used needles in the sand pits.

After much-heated debate, the park was torn up, moved, and the ground was closed off, ready to be used for a building site that never actually happened. The company that bought the land ended up going bankrupt and the last Pru heard, the possession of the land was still being argued in court. So until a resolution was found, nothing could be done to it, which was a shame.

It was a huge piece of land. Homes would be a waste but a nature reserve or something else would've been far more fitting to the space. Still, it helped her to sit and think. No one would be stopping by, and as she lay down on her back, staring up at the sky, she had to wonder about what she was doing with her life.

In a matter of months, she'd be entering the last year of high school, preparing for the day she'd go to college. She had to make so many decisions and on top of everything, she had Drake to deal with.

"You know you shouldn't be out here alone," Drake said, taking the spot next to her.

She didn't gasp or scare. When she glanced at him, he smiled at her. "I shouldn't be surprised you knew where I was."

"True," he said. "I seem to know where you are all the time."

"You followed me from Sean's. It's not hard to guess."

"Yeah, and you're still seeing that asshole."

"Don't, Drake."

"Don't?"

She sighed. "Why do you have to keep bringing him up? I told you you've got nothing to worry about. We're friends. We're only friends. Nothing else is going to change that. I promise you."

"And what if I say differently?" he asked.

Pru chuckled. "You can say whatever you want to say. It's not going to suddenly change anything, is it?" She shrugged. "I don't want to argue or fight with you over this."

"We're going to anyway until you do as you're told."

Pru flopped back to the ground and stared up at the sky. The colors were so clear and bright. Soon they would be full of fall clouds, of the threat of lightning, thunder, rain, and storms. She loved summer clouds. The heat offered a calmness that was also silently deadly. With the heat, it brought its own bunch of problems. What would she be doing come fall? When they were both back in high school? Already, they were complicating their relationship and Drake was making this far more difficult than it actually needed to be. She didn't understand.

Sean had been her friend for so long. He'd been the one constant in all of her life during Drake's bullying. Was that why he wanted him gone? Did he feel threatened by her best friend? It made some sense, but she had told him, repeatedly, nothing was going on. She hadn't told Sean about her time with Drake. What was the point when their relationship was supposed to be secret?

They weren't dating. They had shared a few kisses and had seen each other nearly naked. That didn't mean anything. Not in this day and age. She knew her peers were doing all kinds of crazy stuff. For so long, she'd been living a rather boring life. Hanging out with Sean, watching movies, or just driving around, not really doing anything.

This, with Drake, was the most adventurous she'd ever been. Glancing at him, she found Drake staring right back at her. "Stop telling me what to do."

"Or what?"

Before she had could come up with a witty comeback, he moved on top of her. He ended up between her spread thighs. His hands were beside her head, trapping her against the ground.

"What are you going to do to me, princess?"

She smiled. "Princess? I thought I was trash to you?"

"You are to everyone else, but not today. Not when no one else is looking."

Should she like their secret relationship?

It's so brand new, it doesn't matter if I like it or not. It's what is going to happen.

She reached out, touching a strand of his hair. "You need a cut."

"Not yet."

She stroked a finger down his cheek, crossing over his pulse and resting it across his chest. His heart raced beneath her hand and she was utterly fascinated by it. "Kiss me," she said, hungry for his lips.

Drake slammed his lips down on hers. One of his hands went to her head, gripping the back of it as he ravished her mouth. The other locked their fingers together, holding her hand directly above her head. His tongue traced across her lips and she let out a moan, giving him access. This time, Drake groaned and he nipped at her bottom lip.

"I have no idea what it is you do to me."

"Shut up and kiss me," she said.

He tugged on her hair, making her tilt her head back and giving him as much access to her as possible.

She didn't fight him. There was no reason to. More than anything, this was what she wanted. "Yes," she said as he broke the kiss to trail his lips down to her neck. She sank her teeth into her lips, waiting for more. Closing her eyes, with her head tilted back, she didn't have to think about what she was doing. She could only bask in the feelings he inspired.

"I want more, Pru."

"Not yet."

He groaned and his hands moved up to cup her breasts. She didn't push him away. He didn't scare her. His touch only ignited the pleasure within her.

Wrapping her arms around his neck, she forgot about all the expectations from her and took what she wanted. At this moment, who cared that he was her bully? Who cared that he didn't want anyone to know about them? Neither did she and when it came to Drake, she was no longer going to think about what she could or couldn't have. These stolen moments were everything to her.

Sinking her fingers into his hair, she tugged on the strands, hearing him hiss. Pulling away from his lips which she'd been ravishing, she asked, "Did I hurt you?"

"You know how to bite."

"Are you complaining?"

"Fuck no. Kiss me, Trash."

She couldn't help it. The smile on his lips had her giggling. Kissing him back, she felt his hands wrap around her, gasping as he ground his hips between her thighs.

"I don't mind us not fucking. I can wait. It seems with you, Pru, I can wait."

"Good. I won't be an easy ride."

"Oh, believe me, when I do finally pop this cherry, it's going to be easy. I'll make sure of it." He kissed her hard, stopping her from arguing with him.

Wrapping her legs around him, she pressed her pussy against him, needing the friction that only Drake could give her.

"Fuck, you're going to make me break every single rule."

"Then we better stop." She broke from the kiss, dropping to the ground and staring up at him with a smile.

"What's that smile all about?" he asked.

"I don't know. I'm happy."

"That's not a bad thing though, right?"

"No, it's not bad at all. In fact, I'd say it's very, very good." She giggled. If he wasn't holding her hands in place, she would have covered her mouth. "I can't believe I'm giggling."

"It's a cute sound. You should make it more often."

"Please, you're probably used to girls making that noise all the time."

"I'm not going to lie to you. I am used to it, but from you, I'd say it's pretty fucking cute."

She nibbled her lip. "You're a charmer."

"You better get used to it. I'm going to charm the pants right off you."

"There you go, talking about my underwear."

"Unless you're not wearing any?" he asked.

"I'm wearing a pair, thank you very much. They're white, as well."

He let out a groan. "You shouldn't tell a guy what panties you're wearing unless you're willing to take them off."

"Nope, not taking them off. There are some things you're going to have to wait for."

"Moving on. Why are you here, anyway?"

"Why are you following me?"

"You own my dick for the foreseeable future. It's a given I'm going to follow you every single chance I get."

"If you do that, people will find out about us. What then?"

"We live in a small town. Come on, people bump into each other all the time. I don't see why us being seen together is going to be a problem."

She ran fingers through her hair and shook her head. "You know what, let's not think about what could happen and what might happen. I'm tired of being worried about something that's not even going to be reality."

"Thank you. Now, will you shut up and let me kiss you before I die of old age or something else?"

Pru giggled. Wrapping her arms around his neck, she pressed her lips against his. "Like this?" She wasn't kissing him and he sighed.

Gripping the back of her head, Drake showed her exactly what he wanted and as he did, all of her worries faded away.

Why should she worry about anything when he kissed her like she was his entire world?

****

"Dude, where have you been?" Carl asked.

Drake looked up from washing his car to see his three friends entering the yard.

"I've been here." He'd been washing his car so it would look just right for his and Pru's date that very night.

They'd been in a relationship now for a week,

and he wanted to do something nice. It wouldn't be long before they headed back to school for the final year; he didn't want to think about all of that shit though.

Not yet.

"Washing your car? Don't you have a bazillion servants to do that for you?" Marco asked.

"Yeah, I totally do because I'd trust anyone to wash my car."

"When did you start washing your car? I thought you liked to go through the drive-thru. Manual labor has never been your forte," Nick said.

His friends had been with him less than ten minutes and they were already pissing him off. There was a time he didn't mind hanging out with them—before he knew how fucking fake they were, of course. They were only here because of the money, and what he could provide them. He gave them an easy fucking life, and now all he wanted to do was to see how Pru was doing.

They had been hanging out at her home last night, watching a movie, eating popcorn, and just spending time together. Of course, they'd also made out, and he'd even gotten her shirt off and had some tit action, but nothing too far that made her uncomfortable.

Most chicks would have pissed him off by now, but he had yet to get annoyed with their slow pace. Besides, he happened to like hugging and holding her. He'd never taken the time to simply enjoy a girl's company, and Pru, she didn't want anything from him.

When they weren't arguing about something, she was amazing for just listening to him talk or speaking about their futures. She never pushed him for information, always allowing him to go at his own speed. It wasn't lost on him that the most comfortable he'd been in years was with the girl he'd spent a lifetime bullying.

"Dude, what the fuck?" Carl asked, snapping his fingers in front of his face.

He shoved Carl hard. "Get out of my face."

"Okay, now you really do need to spill. What's your problem?" Nick said.

"Nothing is my problem. I'm cleaning my car and now you're pissing me off."

"You got a girl?" Marco asked.

"Seriously? I clean my car and you think I've got a girl."

"You're cleaning your car. The only reason for you to do that is because there's a chick somewhere." Marco shrugged. "And you're blowing me off."

"Yeah, I'm blowing you all off, so get the fuck off my porch." He picked up the hose, pointed it at his friends, and aimed the blast of water right at them. It was the only way he could figure out to get them off his lawn and away from him.

"Fuck off," he said.

He was tired of their bullshit and with their constant, never-ending questions. He wanted a break.

This thing with Pru, it was crazy but it was also true to him. He didn't have to put on any kind of show with her, and she didn't expect anything from him, which was refreshing. Of course, it meant he still had to deal with her hanging around with that piece-of-shit coward Sean.

He'd just have to live with it.

When his friends were gone, he finished washing the car and headed back into his home. Pulling out his cell phone, he found her name.

Drake: **What r u doing?**

Pocketing his cell, he grabbed a bottle of water out of the fridge and downed half of it before the text came in.

153

Pru: **Working. You should try it.**

Drake: **Nah, sounds kind of boring. I've got more important things to do.**

Pru: **Like what? Play video games? Do you have a high score?**

Drake: **Do u even know what a high score is?**

Pru: **Nah, got more important things to do like study, work. You know mature adult stuff. I don't have time to play being a kid.**

Drake: **I'm not a kid.**

Pru: **If you say so.**

Drake: **I can have u screaming in a way no kid could.**

Pru: **Gross. You took it to the gutter. Why are you texting me?**

Drake: **It's not against the rules.**

Pru: **But what if someone steals your phone?**

Texting bored him. After closing the message, he dialed her number, holding his cell phone to his ear, waiting for her to pick up.

"You know this isn't any better," she said.

"I don't care. What are you doing?" he asked.

"I'm working." She released a sigh.

"What's wrong?"

"Nothing. Just … it's nothing."

"Tell me." He could imagine her biting her lip, wanting to tell him anything but. "You know, you could learn to trust me and open up to me."

"It'll go against everything I know," she said.

"I'm not going to hurt you. What do you have to lose?"

"My sanity."

"I don't want your sanity."

She chuckled. "Yeah, I know what you want." She let out a breath. "I'm just tired of the way people talk to me, you know? As if I don't matter. I can't stand it. I hate being treated like shit. It's not something I enjoy."

"Who has done this to you?"

"Besides you?"

"Yes. I'm allowed now, remember? Tell me."

Pru did. She told him about the women who'd been in the shop, throwing clothes at her, screaming at her because they didn't fit.

"It's not like it's my fault. They yelled at me that I'm thick and stupid. A lot more not-so-nice words. I don't think I can take this."

"Then don't."

"I need this job."

"I could pay you."

"To do what?"

Drake smiled. "Well, I hate to say it."

"Stop it, Drake. I'm not interested."

"I'm just saying. It could be interesting. You know, me paying you for certain services."

"I'm not a whore. I appreciate you think I'm worth paying for. I must be a damn good kisser."

"I can't wait to get your hands on my dick."

"You had to go straight to the gutter. I need to get off now."

Drake chuckled.

"Seriously, how old are you?"

"Old enough to know I want to take you out tonight after work."

"Tonight?"

"If you've got plans with fuckface, cancel them."

"That's really rude."

"It's the truth and he's not more important than me. Are you rolling your eyes at me?"

"No, of course not."

"You lied to me."

"I've got to go now. I've got customers waiting."

"You're lying to me again."

She burst out laughing. "I'm not lying to you. Not even a little bit, but it would serve you right. I've got customers. Bye, Drake."

He hung up the phone and smiled, actually, a full-mouth smile.

Chapter Fourteen
Dinner date

Blowing Sean off was way easier than Pru expected it to be. He already had plans and was going to cancel on her, which she did feel sucked a lot, but at the same time, it meant she was free to spend time with Drake.

She couldn't believe *spending time* and *Drake* were in the same sentence.

Fluffing out her hair, she made her way downstairs just as the bell rang. Drake stood on the other side, in jeans and a crisp, white shirt. He looked, sexy, in control, and even though he was dressed in casual clothes, he looked wealthy.

"Well, well, well, you clean up nice."

She'd gone for a plain white summer dress. Her mother had picked it out of a second-hand store and washed all the stains out of it. It was a rather nice-fitting dress. She gave a little twirl, and Drake whistled again.

"Will it do?" she asked. Nerves hit her hard and she hated feeling anything but confident around Drake. She didn't want him to think she wasn't capable, which was crazy.

"I don't know, you have to give me another little twirl," he said.

Holding her hands out, she turned around so he could look at her. "Well?" She dropped her hands down.

"Your ass looks so hot and full."

"You always go to the gutter. Always."

She let out a squeal as he suddenly held her. "You love it, admit it."

"I don't know what I do and don't love yet." She nibbled her lip. "Where are we going, anyway?"

"Out."

"You're not going to give anything away?"

"Not yet. It's all going to be a surprise."

"I'm not sure if I like surprises."

"You'll love mine. Don't worry about everything so much. You need to learn to relax. Take a breath and trust me."

"Are you ready to go?"

"Yes, but first, I want you to have this." He stepped out and bent down. When he stood, he held a single red rose in his hands. "This is for you."

"Thank you. I should go and put it in a vase."

"No, you're going to hold it for tonight. We've got to keep to our conditions, and you can't let anyone else see it. This is all for you." He stroked some hair behind her ear.

"It's beautiful." She put her hand on his chest and kissed him. He'd even taken off all the thorns so she wouldn't cut herself. Who would do that? Only someone who gave a shit, that was who.

"Look, if you want to remain a virgin past tonight, we're going to have to go."

She rolled her eyes. "Not everything leads to sex."

"It does for me, and I'm practicing being the perfect gentleman for you."

"You're so sweet."

"I know, I plan to knock your socks off with just how fucking amazing I can be." He moved aside, giving her room to pass him.

She closed and locked the door, following him to his car. He placed a hand on her back as they walked. She wondered who was watching them. If there were people twitching their curtains, nosey to see what was going on between her and Drake.

Drake opened the door and she climbed inside.

The rose caught her attention. It was a really sweet gesture. She took another sniff and the subtle floral scent was so nice. The leather of the interior of the car smelled a little overwhelming, on the other hand.

He climbed into the passenger side and started the car.

"Where are we going?" she asked.

"You'll see."

"You do seem to like being a mystery."

"Do you mind me being that way?" he asked.

"Not at all. I rather like it."

"This is going to be weird, you know?"

"What is?"

"When we head back to school. My friends are already riding my ass, wondering what's wrong with me."

"Why would anything be wrong with you?" She stroked one of the flower's petals as she watched him.

Every now and then, Drake would glance in her direction but not for too long. "I've rarely hung out with them the past couple of weeks. I keep blowing them off and normally, I party and fuck around."

"Do you want to party? Mess around?"

"No, I don't. That's it. Don't you think that's fucked up? It's what I'm used to."

She chuckled.

"What are you laughing at?"

"Nothing. I just wonder if you always enjoyed partying and fucking around, or if it was just easier for you."

"Easier how?"

"No one else expected anything from you, and you just dealt with whatever they threw at you, you know?"

"I … I honestly don't know how to answer that."

She smiled. "It's not supposed to be a hard question. You don't even have to answer."

"But the truth is I have no idea. I mean, I love to party. I can make people do whatever the hell I want, and that's fucking fun." He laughed.

"Cool." Now she didn't know what to say. This was awkward.

"I shouldn't have said that."

"Drake, you don't have to pretend with me, or try to say things that you think will make me feel better. Be honest with yourself, not with me."

"I haven't enjoyed hanging out with the guys for a long time. How's that for honesty?" he asked.

"Why not?"

"I don't know. I guess I don't trust their bullshit anymore. They're only around because I'm rich."

"I doubt that."

"You don't know them. They laugh at whatever I do. They don't call me on my shit. I could be beating the crap out of someone and because they're afraid of me, they won't say anything."

"Do you really want them to say anything to you at all?" she asked.

"Of course."

"They're your friends and you're not the easiest guy to get to know or get along with. From day one, you've had a hatred for me. I've seen your anger. I've been on the receiving end of it so many times. I don't think you should expect them to want to get in the way of that. I don't know what you're like around them. Only what you've been like around me, and trust me, there were times you did scare me."

"I did?"

"Yeah. I didn't know how far you'd go. The hatred you had, it was scary."

He took her hand. "Don't be afraid. I'm sorry. Not tonight. I don't know why I even asked about this. I want tonight to just go well."

"You sound nervous, Drake."

"I am. This is the first date I've ever been on."

"I still find that hard to believe."

"Well, believe it. Also, I'm the one that has done all the organizing here. Remember that."

"I won't forget it. I love the rose and you said I looked beautiful. Of course you also referred to sex but I'm not going to hold that against you. I promise." She gave his hand a squeeze before letting him go.

"Let me get this out of the way. How's the pussy?"

"Sean is doing really well but I would appreciate it if you didn't think of him as the *pussy*. He's got a name and he's really nice when you get to know him."

"You see, that's where you and I will always have differing opinions. I see Sean for what he really is."

"Really? You think you know my best friend more than I do?" she asked.

"Sweetheart, you know the Sean he gives you. The fake little show he puts on for you. Believe me, I'm a guy and I've seen the real dude hiding underneath, and he's not pretty."

She turned to look at him to see if he was lying.

There didn't seem to be any lies or any indication he was trying to tell her fake truths. "You really think so?"

"I know so. It's why I make sure to keep Sean in my line of sight. There's nothing worse than having an enemy who can strike out and you don't see them coming."

"Is that how you see the world? People are only out for what they can get? No one is genuine anymore?"

"You don't know guys. You're a freaking virgin, for crying out loud. Sean is like every single other guy."

"He's not."

"Yes, he is. I bet he goes to bed at night with his dick in his hand. He probably thinks about you as well. Comes all over himself thinking about you riding his precious dick."

"You're disgusting." She didn't want to hear this.

"Look, you don't like the truth, and that's fine. I really couldn't give a shit. You want to believe he's above everyone else in the scheme of things. He's a teenage boy. I'd be surprised if he hasn't already gone and seen a whore to take care of his problem."

She closed her eyes. "I want you to take me home."

"No."

"Yes."

"No. We're going to have this date." He flicked the locks on in the car.

"Seriously? You're going to lock me in your car?"

"It's what you deserve. You don't want to hear the truth about Sean, that's on you. I'm telling you to be careful. That's all I'm doing. I will do everything in my power to keep you safe."

Pru turned toward him. "Keep me safe?"

"Yes. I know you only want to see Sean as if he's some kind of angel. Well, I know this angel has a darkness within him and I'm not going to let you get hurt by him."

"Drake, you know it's not your responsibility to take care of me." She was oddly touched that he actually cared about her. Was she crazy? Insane? All she could think was *yes* to both of those answers. There was no way she couldn't not be. She was alone in the car of a guy who loved to bully her. "Drake?"

"I know it's not my responsibility, and I'm not behaving like it is. Fuck! I didn't want this, okay? Just promise me you'll be careful when it comes to that asshole," he said.

She stared at him and saw he was indeed worried about all of this. "Drake?"

"I know you don't believe me and think I'm over-reacting and fine, maybe I am. I'm concerned."

There was so much she wanted to say but instead, she nodded her head. "I promise I'll be careful. You have nothing to worry about. Believe me, Sean won't hurt me." She truly believed that.

"We'll agree to disagree or whatever. So, you like the rose. The trip sucked but I'm blaming Sean for his little part in all of this. Now, let's get back to our date." He didn't unlock the doors.

"You're going to keep the doors locked?"

"Until I know you won't throw yourself out of the moving car."

She chuckled. "I'm not going to do anything stupid. You can trust me." She reached out and took his hand. "I rather like you being really protective."

"You do? From where I'm sitting, you've got a real issue with it."

"Nah, it's fine. I know deep down you worry because you care."

"And I shouldn't. We both know the way this is going to end."

Unfortunately, she did. There was no point arguing with him. They weren't going to get a happily-ever-after. His life had already been decided for him, and well, she could live hers however she wanted.

"Let's forget about all of it. Just you and me tonight. How about that?" she asked.

"I really do love the sound of that."

She smiled and rested her head against his arm, staring out of the window. After a few seconds, she did pull away since she didn't want to risk him hurting himself or anyone else while driving.

Drake drove for what felt like hours before he finally pulled into a lone parking lot. The restaurant looked very humble and she saw it was an Italian place. Her first-ever date was about to start. So far, her nerves were getting the better of her.

****

Drake gripped the steering wheel tightly. They'd argued about Sean again. He had to get to a grip on his anger when it came to the little prick. Sean wasn't as good as people liked to think. Drake seemed to be the only one to see past his fake bullshit to the lying turd he really was.

One day, someone else would see what a manipulative peeping tom he really was. He knew all about Sean's hidden cameras and sneaking into the girls' locker rooms to film them. It was why he knew Sean wasn't to be trusted, and whenever he went into Pru's room, he always checked.

It was one of the many reasons why he opted for her to hang out at his place. His parents would be returning soon and he'd have to find a whole new excuse to hang out with her. He had no doubt in his mind he'd find something to do.

"This place looks nice," she said.

"It is. I don't know for sure. I've only seen the reviews. All of them are good. Good food and all the stuff." His palms were sweaty. Why was he suddenly so nervous?

This was Pru. She'd been on the receiving end of his bullshit for a long time now. He'd just used her, hurt her, and not cared about what he'd done before. Why did this matter?

Because you're trying to impress her, asshole!

"This is your first time coming to this place?"

"Yeah, pretty much. We get to try the food together."

"Cool." They climbed out of the car and his nerves didn't disappear, not one bit. This was the most he'd ever done to impress a girl and he wasn't even getting sex at the end of it. He really had to take a good long hard look in the mirror at himself.

Neither of them spoke as they entered the restaurant. He'd called ahead to make a reservation and they were shown to their table. He made sure to help Pru into her chair, thanking the maître'd for his help.

"This place seems really fancy."

"It's not up there on a scale of what I'm used to. I figured you'd like this one better. I'm not trying to sound spoiled."

"I know you're not trying to sound like it." She laughed. "You can't help it. Do your parents take you out to dinner often?"

"No. Only when a certain look is required."

"I hate how it all sounds with your folks."

"They do their best, I guess."

"Does it bother you?" she asked. "Being used in their game?"

"It used to. My parents would try to compete with who looked better with me. My mom, for instance, loved having me in a tux, and she'd like to show off to her friends. My dad, he was the same, only he liked me to learn a script. Never had a clue what was being said."

"You were like a toy to them?"

"As I got older and I could tell them to go and eat shit, the whole social thing changed. I'm now the rebellious hot son. Someone to mock, ridicule, or to look like they're doing the right thing."

He watched her smile. "I love how you added the hot son. You think a lot of yourself, don't you?"

"It's what I am. You have no idea how many women hit on me."

She chuckled. "Doesn't it ever bore you? The same old lies and the bullshit?"

"Yeah, it does. It's why I'm here with you. You don't bullshit me, Pru. It's really rather refreshing and also interesting. No matter what I do, you always call me out on my shit."

"This isn't exactly how I imagined our conversation going, you know," she said. "If someone was to have told me I'd be sitting having dinner with you, I would've laughed."

"Me too." He held up his glass. "How about a toast?"

"All right."

"To changes and different ideas."

"I like it."

She pressed her glass to his, sitting back. They were silent for several moments. He watched as she glanced around the restaurant. These were the kind of treats she deserved and should have on a regular basis. Her mother would have scoffed and scorned anyone who dared to bring her to such a place. For his parents, it always had to be expensive, the new biggest thing.

They were never happy with something low-key like this.

"What are you thinking right now?" Pru asked.

"How beautiful you are," he said.

"If my supposed beauty makes you look like that, I'm scared."

He frowned at her.

"You look like you were thinking about wanting to kill something, not a woman's beauty."

"Oh, well, you caught me in a lie. I was thinking about my parents. They'd hate this place."

Pru grabbed his hand. "I love it. I think it's perfect. I'm hoping the food is going to be just as good."

"You mean it?"

"I won't lie to you, Drake."

He stared at her, not really sure if he could trust her. All his life, he'd been lied to in some form or another. She smiled, but it wasn't a happy one. He saw the sadness in her eyes.

"What is it?"

"Nothing."

"It's not nothing."

"You're right. It's not. I can see you don't believe me and I find it sad." She shrugged. "I haven't given you a single reason to not trust me."

"Pru—"

"It's okay, Drake. Things like this take time. We're both young. You know a whole lot more than me. I get it. I really do."

She tried to pull her hand away but he wouldn't let her go.

"Drake, you don't have to do this."

"I do. I want to. This isn't about … look, I wish I could say I'm different and you're only going to see the good, or whatnot, but I'm not used to being this guy."

"I'm not looking for a guy. I told you I won't lie to you and already, you don't believe me."

"It's not you."

She burst out laughing. "Seriously, you're going to play *that* card?"

He sighed.

So did she. "This isn't working out," she said. "I

think we're making a mistake."

"No," he said. He wouldn't let this be the end of it. He was trying. Really fucking trying and there was no way he was going to let her go, just like that.

"Look at us, Drake, we can't even have a simple conversation without one of us ending up arguing or feeling aggrieved by the other. This isn't the way life is supposed to be."

"Don't … please, just stop. I didn't think it would be so hard to be like this," he said. "I know what I'm used to. With you, you've always been different and I'm not trying to make this harder or easier, I'm just saying what it is." He held on to her hand, not wanting to let her go. "I know I'm not a good guy. There are a billion other guys you could be with right now, and none of them would have treated you the way I have in the past."

"You don't have to do this, Drake," she said.

"I know I don't have to, but if I don't, you'll walk right out that door and out of my life. I don't want to lose what we've been able to find."

"We haven't really done anything."

"The last couple of weeks have been the best of my life. A guy who has everything and he can count in weeks how good it has been." He stared down at their hands. "I'm not trying to get sympathy."

"Don't worry, I won't show you any."

He chuckled. "Just don't walk away from this. Please, I know I'll fuck up. I'll make mistakes."

"Drake, you're not superhuman. You need to stop apologizing for everything. I overreacted. You've got to learn to trust me, I get it. You're not used to trusting people or them telling you the truth. I can promise you I will tell you the truth, always." She gave his hands a squeeze. "Don't give me a reason to really walk out that door."

"You mean I can piss you off a couple of times?"

She laughed. "I doubt we're going to agree on much, but I can see us being really good friends if we try. I know when I'm around you, I love being with you, and I do think about you when you're not there."

"You do?"

"Yes. Do you think about me?"

She looked nervous and he couldn't think of a single reason for her to be so.

"Yeah, I do."

"Really?"

"That surprise you?"

"I guess it does. I never think of you and me and you know, all the other stuff in between."

"I'm sure I'm not the first guy to think about you and want a hell of a lot more than what I'm getting."

"Nah, I don't believe it."

"You've got a low opinion of yourself."

She snorted. "For years, you've told me I'm not pretty enough. I've seen the kind of girls you go for."

"I'm sorry," he said. The words fell out of his mouth with ease. He didn't like apologizing to anyone about anything. Most of the time, he truly didn't believe he was in the wrong.

"What for?"

"For all the shitty things I've said to you. I didn't mean them, and if you believed them, please stop."

"You don't mean all of those things weren't true."

"I do."

She shook her head.

"Pru, I mean it."

"So you don't think I'm a smartass? Or a know-it-all? You don't think I should give someone else a chance to get it right?"

He couldn't help but smile.

"Or how about calling me a nerd, or a bookworm? Those have no meaning?"

"You're being a smartass right about now."

"Yeah, well, sometimes I've got to accept that you mean what you say. Other stuff can be said in the heat of the moment. Not all of it. I don't believe everything we say to each other is true."

"Is there anything you've said to me you regret?" he asked.

She sat back, pulling her hands away with her as she did. He wanted her touch more than anything, and he didn't like feeling her withdraw.

"You don't have to think too hard about it."

"I do though. I can't think of anything I regret saying to you. Every single time I've lashed out, it has always been in the heat of the moment. I don't know." She frowned. "Is there anything I've said that you've hated?"

"You've called me rich boy."

"Drake, you are a rich boy."

"Can't help who I am."

"I hate it when you call me trash."

"It does?"

"Yeah, it makes me feel quite sick. It's hard to explain."

"Try, please, for me."

"I know when we head back to school, if we're still doing what we're doing, then it's going to start up. I guess deep down, I believe you when you call me trash."

He wanted to hold her. To kiss those pretty lips and tell her she had nothing to be upset about because she was the furthest thing from trash.

"I'm not wealthy. My family, we've struggled all my life and when you say it, I feel like I'm exactly that. I try not to let it bother me but, it does, and I can't help it."

He saw tears in her eyes.

She sniffled, looking away. "I'm sorry. I didn't want to cause a scene."

"You haven't. You've been completely honest with me, and I appreciate that." He wanted to hold her, but he'd have to get up, and he didn't want anyone turning to look at them. This was his and Pru's time. No one else had a right to barge in on them. This was going to be one of those rare times he got her to himself. "You're not trash, Pru. I'm an asshole, but you will never be trash. I'm an idiot for calling you that."

"How about we forget all the bad shit we've said to each other and move on?"

"You want to do that?"

"I know we're going to have to change the rules come high school, and we'll deal with them then. We've got a couple of weeks left until school starts. When are your folks back?"

"Tomorrow unless they find something far more entertaining than being back here."

"So, we can hang out tomorrow as well? My parents are working again, and I'm off. You could come to my place. We could watch a couple of movies, eat popcorn. Order some pizza."

"What about when your parents return?" he asked.

"We can tell them I'm tutoring you or something like that. Believe me, they won't mind."

"They'll know who I am."

"Just be nice or be yourself and they'll ignore it."

He'd never actually met Pru's parents. Being in a small town, he'd seen them from time to time, but he'd never been interested in anyone or anything but himself.

"How do you make everything sound so easy?"

he asked.

"Practice. I was also thinking about it for a couple of days. I figured there was a chance. I'm not worried. I don't think you should be either."

He wasn't worried. No one would believe there was anything between them. He didn't know if it made him happy or sad.

Chapter Fifteen
School came around too soon

How had two weeks gone by so fast?

Before Drake's parents arrived back in town, he'd spent every moment with her, and now, Pru looked at the main doors of the high school.

Senior year.

After this, high school would be finished. No chance to change her path. She had to work her ass off to get a scholarship no matter where she went. The question was, did she stay close to home or go with Sean? He'd been her rock for so long, but she loved her parents, even if she didn't agree with them about a lot of things.

She was fighting a losing battle.

Taking a deep breath, she walked up to the main school gates. Everyone was all excited about it being their first day back, and she had to agree, it was a lot of fun. Running fingers through her hair, she headed toward her locker. The first day of the final school year, and she had a secret.

She and Drake were still dating.

No one knew.

It was kind of exhilarating to have a little secret no one else knew. Probably stupid of her to even go along with it, but being around Drake, the one who was sweet and kind, she liked him. Really liked him.

She worked the combination of her locker, opening it up. Bare, just the way she liked it. As the day progressed, they'd have books, notes, and all manner of things to store inside.

Once she had emptied out her gym kit and removed most of her books, she closed the door.

There was no sign of Sean, and she'd told him she'd rather walk, to give herself a chance to get her bearings before being driven to school. Also, she didn't know how the first meeting with Drake was going to go down. Last night, they had texted until the early hours, and she was still tired, but she was ready to go for the day.

She felt this hum of excitement inside her at what they were going to have to do to keep their relationship a secret. She didn't want to think of him with other girls. That was a big no on her list, but if he had to keep up appearances, she'd have to deal with it. There was so much she didn't know how to handle.

Walking down the corridor, she went toward homeroom and hoped to stay out of the way of seeing Drake at all costs.

No such luck as he suddenly appeared around the corner.

The moment he saw her, the glare on his face turned into a smile.

"Well, well, well, if it isn't who I was looking for."

No one was around and he suddenly had hold of her arm and began pushing her into the janitor's closet.

"What the hell are you doing? Drake, we agreed not to do this."

He pressed her up against the door. "The place is empty. No one saw me and it means I can do this."

Before she could protest, his lips were on hers, and she didn't have time to think or process, just to feel. He sank his fingers into her hair, cupping the back of her head. She couldn't help but moan as his tongue traced across the seam of her lips and she opened up on a gasp. Drake plundered inside and she couldn't help but hold on to his shirt, pulling him close against her, never wanting to let him go.

"Fuck, I don't know how I'm going to be able to

cope knowing what's waiting for me when school is over," he said, breaking from the kiss.

"We can't do this. We could get caught."

"I'm always going to be careful when it comes to you. I'll do whatever it takes to protect you." He stroked his fingers down her cheek. "Whatever happens after this, don't believe it. Okay?"

"I was thinking of avoiding you. Staying as far away as possible."

"If you can do that, please do. I don't want to hurt you if I don't have to."

She rolled her eyes. "You do realize how fucked up this is, right?"

"I know. I wish we didn't have to put on this charade, but we have no other choice. Unless you've got some bright ideas."

She groaned. "I wish I did. Kill your parents? Run away together?"

"Now that could be an idea."

"Killing your parents?" she asked, jokingly.

"No, running away together. We could do that." He looked at her, seeming serious.

"I was joking."

"I'm not."

"Drake, you've said so yourself, you can't just run away and leave. It's not the way it works." She cupped his cheek and quickly withdrew. There was no way either of them could get used to touching the other.

"I can already see the change inside you. I don't want what I know is going to happen." He pulled her close and kissed her again.

She let out a moan as he claimed her lips. It was addictive. They couldn't stay locked in the janitor's closet all day. At some point, the janitor would return, and people were waiting for him.

Sean would also be waiting for her, but she wasn't going to remind Drake of that.

"After school," he said. "I'll come by your place."

"I don't know if that's going to be possible."

"Tell fuckface to piss off."

"Drake, come on, don't be like that."

"I told you, I can't stand Sean. You think what we're going to be doing is fake, you should see him."

"I really don't want to argue with you."

"Then don't. It's pretty fucking easy, really. All you've got to do is see me after school. You know you want to. I'm so pretty to look at. I'll make it worth your while."

"Now I'm curious. How?"

"I can make up for whatever shit is about to go down."

"Tempting."

"And true."

"Ugh, this is … fine, I will blow off Sean if that's what you need me to do."

Drake grabbed her face and kissed her hard and passionately. "You won't regret it, baby."

"I hope not. What about your parents?"

"They don't care. They're only back in town because commitments say they have to be. I better go out first. I'll slap the door if it's clear. If not, stay inside." Drake kissed her again and left the closet.

She couldn't believe he dragged her in here. With hands on her hips, she waited, and then he slapped the door.

She opened the door and stepped out. Just as they were about to go in separate directions, his three friends arrived. Her stomach twisted and pulled. Marco was the first one to whistle.

"What's going on, Drake? You ran into Fatty already. Wow, you don't know how to leave well enough alone."

She looked down at the floor and quickly rushed off.

Drake grabbed her. It wasn't tight, but to anyone looking, it wouldn't seem all that nice either.

"What? You think I'm stuck to her? Please, you're lucky I made it out alive by passing her."

Okay, that one hurt.

"Get off me," she said.

Drake let her go and she chanced a look at him. He suddenly grabbed her and pulled her close. "Hit me or something. Call me an asshole and leave." He whispered the words against her ear but she refused to use violence.

Pulling away from him, she glared. "You're an asshole." She shoved him, and not hard either. Hurting him was the last thing she wanted to do. This was going to be a lot harder than she anticipated.

Rushing away from him, she walked toward her class just as Sean was coming around the corner. "Hey, Pru, I was wondering where you were. I waited near your locker but you never turned up," he said, grabbing her arms.

She glanced behind her and saw Drake with his friends. The smirk she associated with her bully was back in full force. He glanced her way and it was just a subtle change, but it was there nonetheless. He didn't like her being with Sean.

"What's his problem?" Sean asked.

"It's nothing." Turning back to her friend, she tried to get the niggling doubt out of her mind. It was next to impossible to do because Sean had been with her since day one in this town. He'd stood by her side.

Should she trust Drake, her bully, when this guy

177

in front of her didn't give a shit about her social standing or anything? He liked her. They did movie marathons together, studied, listened to music. He was her best friend in the entire world. There was no one else she wanted to be around more than him.

"That doesn't look like nothing. Drake's glaring at me. What did I do to piss him off?" Sean asked.

She saw the tension mounting in Sean and she didn't like it. Grabbing his arm, she laughed. "What's gotten into you? Why are you all macho all of a sudden?"

"I made a pact with myself, Pru. It's our final year and I'm not going to stand by while he does all of his bullshit with you. If he starts, he's going to have to deal with me. Punk-ass bastard."

"Whoa. What have you done to my best friend?" She placed a hand on his forehead, smiling at him. "I don't know what is going on with you."

"Nothing is going on with me. There is nothing to go on with." He winked at her. "I just don't want you to be miserable for our last year. I think we've let Drake and his goons have at us long enough. I'm not going to allow it to happen again."

She didn't know if she liked this newfound confidence within him.

Sean had always been a bookworm, a nerd. Someone she could identify with on a very basic level, and yet here he was, talking about hurting Drake. Was it possible for him to even go through with it? She had no idea what to think or do.

"Let's just go." The last thing she wanted was for Drake to approach them. She didn't like confrontations and after their kiss and the horrible words he threw her way, she just wanted to have some peace and quiet, for once. That was all she wanted. Was it really impossible to ask for that much?

Sean wasn't budging.

"Sean, seriously, what is your problem?" she asked.

"First day of school. I'm not going to allow him to bully us. It's time for us to take a stand."

"You've been watching way too many movies. We're not making a stand against anything. All we need to do is leave. That's it. Plain and simple. We can go to class and forget about everything else. It's what I want to do, and I bet it's what you want to do as well," she said.

At the end of this day, she was going to need a hard drink of alcohol. There wouldn't be anything better for it. Not that she drank. Ever. Right now, she felt it would be a real good thing to take up.

"I'm not moving."

"Sean, please, not right now."

"No. I told you, Pru. Not this year. I'm not taking it anymore."

"You really don't need to do this for me."

Sean wasn't moving.

She wanted to walk away, but she'd never been the kind of person to do that. Regardless of Drake's warnings, Sean was her best friend.

"Well, well, well, if it's not the fucking nerd," Drake said.

"Piss off, Drake," Sean said.

The hatred was easily detected in Sean's voice.

Pru didn't recognize him. Most of the time, Sean was the voice of reason and yet, here he was being the complete opposite.

Marco whistled, which in turn attracted attention from others in the corridor.

Great.

Just great.

This was what she wanted to avoid on her very

first day back. The encounter with Drake in the closet was nice but not worth this.

"Look at you, Sean. You finally decided to grow a pair?" Carl asked.

Drake snorted. "He probably got some cheap whore to rub him dry. I bet he didn't last two minutes with her. Probably got her lips right near his junk and he blew all over her face."

Pru felt sick. "Come on."

"I bet he was fucking Prudie right here," Nick said. "Let's face it, the only way either of these two are getting any is if they're fucking each other."

She didn't need to listen to this. "Come on," she said.

There was no way she could look at Drake. He'd be able to easily see how hurt she was, and she couldn't stand to show weakness.

"Pru's more woman than any of you guys could manage," Sean said, wrapping his arm around her.

Her face heated up. This wasn't what she wanted and the fact Sean was doing this made her really uncomfortable. "Sean, stop it."

Sean suddenly turned her, grabbed her face, and kissed her hard. She was so shocked that for a few seconds, she didn't do anything. Her best friend was kissing her and she didn't know how to make him stop.

What the hell?

Quickly, she became aware of Drake grabbing Sean and yanking him away. Before she knew what to do, he was slamming his fist repeatedly against Sean's body. Not his face, though.

Without thinking, she jumped on his back like she had done when he would bully Sean in the past. Wrapping an arm around his neck, she tried to pull him away, to get him to stop.

"Stop it!" She yelled the words as she tried to pull him away.

When that didn't work, she had no choice but to slide down his body and rush between him and Sean.

He raised his fist, and it took every ounce of willpower not to panic, not to scream, and not to beg for him to stop.

Holding her hand up, she waited and waited until he finally, slowly, lowered his hand. They had an audience.

Could he walk away without hurting her?

Every single time, he'd done something to hurt her. What would he do now?

She waited for him. The tension in the hallway grew. She felt sick to her stomach.

The decision was taken out of his hands as three teachers rushed toward them. Like all the other times, it was right after the problems had been done. The damage was already there for everyone to see.

Sean was a bloody mess. Drake stepped back, his fist lowering. She turned toward Sean and tried to help him up. He pushed her away and she stumbled back.

"What is going on? Our first day back, and already a fight."

"It was nothing," Drake said. "Or was it, Sean?"

Pru looked at Drake then back at Sean, who glared at Drake. Her heart pounded and she had never felt so afraid in her life. This was the worst kind of feeling in the world.

"It was nothing," Sean finally said after a couple of minutes passed.

"If it was nothing, then why are you bleeding?" Mr. Wheeze said. He taught English and she knew from experience that he wasn't the best kind of teacher. He liked to pretend to be everyone's best friend. She didn't find him the best person to be around and there were far better teachers at the school.

"I fell into the locker. Honestly, it's nothing."

"Sean!" Mr. Wheeze didn't look happy.

"I'll get him to the nurse," she said, putting a hand on his chest and hoping that would do the trick.

"I don't like lies and I know something was going on here," Mr. Wheeze said.

With no one willing to stand up and say what was going on, there was nothing anyone could do.

"What about you, Prudence?" Mr. Wheeze finally looked toward her.

"Me?"

"Yeah, what did you see?"

The sickness had come in full force now. Licking her dry lips, she glanced at Drake before looking at Sean. Every other time, she wouldn't think twice about speaking out against Drake. This was different. Sean went after Drake. He'd wanted to start a fight.

She didn't know why and didn't know where this new best friend had made an appearance. They hadn't spent all that much time together in the summer. Had she missed so much?

"I didn't see anything."

****

The first day of school could have gone a million times better as far as Drake was concerned. He never wanted to hurt Sean, especially not after getting his goodbye kiss from Pru. He'd promised himself he wouldn't do anything to hurt her and all he'd ended up doing was just that. He couldn't win.

He didn't know what the fuck to do anymore.

School, this relationship, it wasn't supposed to be this hard, and yet, it felt so far from what he'd ever wanted to do. By the end of the day, he was pleased to see the back of school, and he wanted no part in it, no part at all.

Ignoring his friends, he climbed into his car and took off, driving out of town. He knew he had to see his girl, but before he did, he really needed to get control of himself.

This thing with Pru was turning into a nightmare, not one he wanted any part of, either. When had his life gotten so fucking complicated? He drove out to the middle of nowhere just so he could think. With his parents back in town, he wasn't going to get much time away from them. They were going to want him to play the doting role of a loving son, of course, and he'd try to fake through it.

Climbing out of his car, he looked out at the view. Nothing really caught his attention. There was a light breeze, which was nice for the time of year. He could get used to the weather like this.

You've got to get back in the car and go and talk to Pru.

He didn't move.

Maybe ignoring her was for the best? He hated second-guessing himself. There was nothing worse. There was no way he could stay and wait this out. He had to go back and talk to her, at least clear the air between them. Their first day of school and already he'd fucked up. Seeing Sean touch her had pissed him off more than he realized. Sure, Pru thought she was friends with Sean, but Drake wasn't an idiot. He saw what the guy was all about, and he despised him for it.

Giving up on his little tantrum, he rushed to his car and climbed inside. After starting up the engine, he took off, going toward Pru's house. With any luck, Sean wouldn't be around, trying to make her feel sorry for him.

Damn it.

Why did he have to let the little prick win? Why couldn't he have just walked away? It wasn't exactly hard to do.

Parking his car twenty minutes from her place, he clicked the button, locking it, and made his way toward her house. This secrecy shit was getting old, really fast, and he didn't know how much more he could take. The moment he got to Pru's house, he was happy to see there was no one home. That was what he wanted.

Breathing out a sigh of relief, he made his way up to her front door. Knocking on it, he waited. He counted to ten then to twenty before the door finally opened and there she stood. At first, she glared at him.

"I didn't mean for that to happen today."

"Then what did you mean to happen?"

"I don't want to argue with you, Pru."

"I don't want to argue with you either but I didn't agree to you starting a fight with Sean."

"He fucking started it."

"Seriously? You want to do this? You want to start throwing blame?"

"I don't want to argue with you."

"I don't want to argue with you either, but you're making it really hard for me to want to take your side," she said.

This wasn't what he wanted.

"You do know I didn't want any of this to happen, right?"

"Yes, I know that." She wouldn't look at him.

"Dammit, Pru, look at me."

She waited a couple of minutes before finally giving him her full attention. "What?"

"What's going on here with us?" he asked.

"Nothing."

"Nothing?"

"Yes, there's nothing going on. You're here trying to tell me what went on back at high school."

"You're withdrawing from me."

"I'm not."

"Yes, you are."

"I honestly don't know what you want from me anymore, Drake."

"It has been one day and we can't even remain friends because of it." He couldn't lose her. There was no way he could allow her to go. They weren't done. "I'm sorry."

"Please, stop saying that."

"I mean it, though."

"I know. You keep saying it but I really don't need to hear it." She released a breath and looked incredibly nervous.

"What's going on?" he asked.

"I'm just thinking this is a lot harder than it was supposed to be."

"Dammit, Pru. Don't do what I know you think you should do."

"He's my best friend and you pummeled him today."

"He deserved it."

"No one deserves that, Drake. No one. Why can't you see that?" she asked. She ran her fingers through her hair, and all he wanted to do was hold her, not fight. Fighting was the last thing he wanted to do.

"Can't I do something to make it up to you? Surely there has to be something?" he asked.

"There's nothing. We were wrong to think we could even try this." She pulled away and he couldn't let that happen.

"No, don't do this. I fucked up today, but we

knew it would be hard for us to get this right. Don't give up on me or on this." He reached out to her. She didn't fight him as he caught her close to him.

Drake honestly didn't know what to do next. Here she was in his arms, exactly where he wanted her to be, but there was a divide between them. He shouldn't have fucked with her best friend but he'd seen the crazy look in Sean's eyes. That dude wasn't right in the head or in any part of his body.

He didn't like him and no matter what he said to warn Pru, she wasn't listening to him. Not that he could blame her. Why would she listen to him? He'd spent most of his life making her miserable. There was no way he was ever going to be able to pay back for all those sins.

Kissing the top of her head, he felt her sink against him.

"I don't want to fight with you, Drake. I feel like we're always fighting over something and I hate it."

"Me too."

"I need you to leave Sean alone. You messed him up today."

"It didn't stop him from going to class." Drake had seen him walking the halls. There was something that really bothered him and he couldn't for the life of him think of what it was. Sean wasn't the same.

"Don't," she said, sounding really tired. "I just want you to hold me."

Drake's heart started to race. She just wanted to be held. What did that mean?

He wasn't going to question her, not when he had her in his arms. "All I could think about all day was that kiss."

"I wish we could have spent all day in the closet and not come out. I would've loved that."

"Me too," he said, being completely honest with her. There was nowhere else he'd wanted to be than with her. When his friends had arrived, he'd hated it. All he wanted to do was tell them to fuck off. Then the shit with Sean. It seemed that no matter what he did, he was always screwing up in one form or another.

Running his fingers through her hair, he closed his eyes and breathed her in. For now, he didn't have to worry about anyone or anything. He could just enjoy being around her, and it was all he wanted, all he craved, all he wished for.

"Will Sean be coming here?" he asked. He didn't want to leave her but for tonight, he would give her this chance to be with her best friend if she needed it.

"No. He wants to take some time at home. I did offer to cook him something but he said he wanted to be alone." She pulled away with a sigh. "I don't know when everything got so complicated."

"It's not complicated, not even a little bit."

"Really? You don't think this is weird?"

He laughed. "Come on, let me make you something to eat."

"I don't think food is going to help what is going on, Drake."

Still, he wasn't going to take no for an answer. He took her hand and led her through to the kitchen where he let her go to check out the fridge. There were a lot of cheeses and cold cuts of meat.

"Do you even know your way around a kitchen?" she asked. "I seem to recall in all the time we've spent with each other, I'm the one that has been doing all the work."

He blew her a raspberry and then stopped himself. He'd just blew her a fucking raspberry. When did that happen? Why was he joking around like this? He wasn't the kind of guy to be doing these things and yet, here he was, in her home, making her some food.

"You okay?" Pru asked.

"You're changing me." He turned to look at her. "I don't get it."

"You don't get that you're turning into a caring person?"

"No, I'm not. This isn't me."

"Well, maybe I bring out the best in you."

Drake stared at her.

"You're kind of freaking me out here, Drake. I don't know what you want from me." She put her hands on her hips and stared at him. He liked looking at her like this. She always looked so in control and it never failed to turn him on.

They hadn't even had sex yet. The highlight of his day was kissing her. That was all he needed from her, one single kiss and he was happy.

"I'm sorry," he said. "I guess this whole thing has affected me more than I thought it would." He gripped the edge of the counter and took several deep breaths. "I didn't mean to freak you out."

"Drake, it's fine. Really. I don't mind."

He stepped up close to her so she had no choice but to look at him. He liked being near her and often found any chance he could to get as close to her as possible.

"What are you doing?" she asked.

"I know today was crazy and I'm sorry about what I did with your friend. I shouldn't have hurt him." They were all lies. The truth was, he shouldn't have hurt Sean, and he got it, but it didn't mean he didn't get at least a little bit of pleasure knowing he'd taken a swipe at that fucker. "From now on, I will find any number of reasons to walk away."

She tilted her head to the side. "I think this is going to be the closest I ever get to an apology, isn't it?"

"Pretty much. I've got nothing more to give."

"Huh," she said. "You don't have to have my forgiveness. You didn't do anything wrong with me."

"What I said to you after the closet."

"Drake, stop. We both know why you did that and I can't fault you. I don't want to talk about it. We don't need to talk about it." She placed a hand on his chest. "We both agreed this was going to be secret. The only way we can make it play out this way is if we do this where nothing has changed. If all of a sudden you jumped to my defense, people would get suspicious. Neither of us wants that, do we?"

Did he?

He looked into her eyes. She was so fucking beautiful. Why hadn't he ever realized just how beautiful she was? All of this time he'd wasted bullying her.

Get a grip and answer the question.

"We don't." As much as he hated to admit it, he couldn't fall for her. He already had, but this was as far as it would ever go. This wasn't for the long term, not for them. The moment high school finished, they were going their separate ways, and he was going to have to deal with that.

"Now, how about I get you something to eat?" he said.

Chapter Sixteen
Lies are easy

Against all the odds, the first month of the final year of high school was in fact easy. Drake kept his word and she never saw him go near Sean again. Whenever he entered a room and he caught sight of them, he would often turn the other way or show someone else more interest.

If anyone even pointed in their direction, Drake would always look as if they were beneath him. Pru didn't mind. She found the peace and quiet somewhat refreshing. Sean, though, didn't like it. In fact, her very best friend seemed to believe that he had in some way scared Drake.

"I tell you, if he comes near me again, I'm going to fucking have him."

Pru held her pencil over her paper and glanced over at him. "What?"

"You heard me. I bet he's afraid of me."

"No, I doubt that's it."

She hadn't spent all that much time with Sean in the past couple of weeks. With Drake sneaking around her place every single chance he got, she had been making every single excuse she could think of to be with him. When they were together, she forgot about everything.

There were no cares in the world.

Just each other.

It was refreshing for her to just feel rather than have to think about every little detail of her life. For Drake, she didn't know what he felt. He smiled a lot more and on the whole, he did seem happier.

The days in high school were always the longest, and Sean made her nervous. There was no way she could expect Drake not to retaliate if Sean decided to start a fight. She wished she knew what had gotten into Sean for him to change.

"You don't think I could take him?" Sean asked.

It took every single ounce of composure not to respond to his claim. None of this made any sense. Why was he suddenly so intent on taking Drake on?

"You really don't, do you?"

"Sean, please, I have no idea what's going on," she said. She licked her suddenly dry lips and wished she knew what to say to calm him down. "Why do you feel the need to fight him? If Drake's leaving you alone, then I don't see a reason to get into any conflict at all."

"You don't?"

"No. It seems kind of pointless." She tried not to wince.

Sean kept on staring at her. She quickly glanced down at her book and hoped against hope he wasn't reading too much into this.

"Pointless?" Sean slapped his hand on the table, making her jump.

Looking around, she saw a couple of other people staring at him.

"Sean, really."

"You know, I don't get it. I spent most of our school years together watching the two of you fight it out. I've had no choice but to put up with it and now that I'm doing something about it, you're not happy."

"It's not that I'm not happy about it, I just don't see why you should have to risk hurting yourself for no good reason." She reached out, taking his hand.

"What has happened to you?" he asked.

"Me?"

"Yeah. You're never around anymore. I don't get it."

"I don't know what you're talking about."

"I think you do."

Her heart started to race.

"There was a time we'd do everything together. The old Pru would have loved this new fighting spirit I've got."

He was right. There was a time she'd have begged him to find that fire inside him so no one could hurt him. Only now, the person he was intent on hurting was the guy she'd fallen for, and it wasn't fair to him for her to force him to stop being this guy.

"I've got to use the bathroom." Without waiting for a response from Sean, she got to her feet and rushed out of the library. No one followed her, least of all Sean. He never did. She was thankful since she didn't want any company today, she just needed a minute.

Bursting through the doors, she was pleased to see the bathroom was empty.

Gripping the edge of the sink, she stared down into the plain white porcelain sink.

"It's fine. You're fine." She took several deep breaths and realized her hands were shaking. She didn't know why, and her gut was twisting as well.

This wasn't good.

Whenever she was with Drake, she felt like the world could just disappear and she wouldn't have to worry about a thing. The moment they were apart, everything seemed to turn to shit and she couldn't focus, not even for a short while.

"I can do this," she said.

"What can you do?" Drake asked.

She spun to see he'd entered the bathroom.

"You do know this is the girls' bathroom?"

"Yeah, I know. It doesn't mean that I can't be worried about you. No one's here."

"Why are you here?" she asked. They had avoided all contact at school, leaving their make-up sessions for when they were together.

"I wanted to make sure you were okay. Don't worry, I didn't beat the shit out of Sean even if I wanted to."

"He wants to hurt you. I don't get it." She burst out laughing. "I mean, all this time he doesn't want to do anything with you and now when we're doing whatever it is the hell we're doing, he now wants to start a fight with you." She pressed her hands to her face to try to contain the hysteria that was building. "Do you see how messed up that is?"

"That's why you're upset?"

"I'm upset because I can't tell my best friend about us. I'm upset because he even wants to hurt you in the first place. This is all fucked up." She turned back to the sink and gripped the edge. She had to get control of herself.

"What do you want me to do?" Drake asked.

The question took her completely by surprise. She closed her eyes but felt him get closer.

"Don't," she said as he put a hand on her shoulder.

"I don't like seeing you like this. You think this is easy for me as well? I don't know what the hell I'm doing anymore."

She lifted up and put her hands on his chest, hoping to find some kind of comfort just by holding him. After opening her mouth to speak, she closed it.

"Don't say anything," he said. "Neither of us can make a decision right now. I'm not going to hurt your best friend."

She snorted.

"For the past month, I've kept my word. You

think this is easy for me?"

"I know it's not," she said.

The stolen moments were starting to wear on the both of them.

"I just wish for once I could be selfish," she said.

"Selfish how?" he asked.

It was on the tip of her tongue to say but she smiled. "Don't worry about it."

"Pru, we've spent a lot of time going over this." He pulled her close and she just wanted to sink into the warmth of his embrace. "I'm going to worry about you."

He ran his fingers through her hair and she breathed a sigh of relief at his touch. It meant a great deal to her just to have him here with her. Wrapping her arms around him, she closed her eyes, breathing him in.

"Now, tell me what you want me to do," he said.

"I don't want you to do anything but hold me."

"That's the easy part."

She laughed. Pulling away, she stared up into his eyes. For so long, she was used to anger and rage staring back at her. Right now, she only saw concern and it meant the world to her. Placing her palm against his cheek again, she stroked her thumb back and forth.

"Come away with me this weekend," he said, surprising her.

"You want me to come away with you?"

"Yes. I wouldn't have asked if I didn't want it."

"Wow," she said.

"You didn't see that one coming, did you?"

She chuckled. "We're sneaking around and no, I didn't imagine for even a second that we'd be doing something like this. It's crazy." She whispered the last bit.

"Yeah, well, I'm tired of all the sneaking around. There's only so much a guy can take and well, I want to be with you without looking over my shoulder. You think we can do that?" he asked.

She nibbled her lip. "Going away together is a huge step."

"It is. One I think we can take. Remember, we only live once and well, our time is running out. You know we're on a countdown."

There it was.

Their time was running out fast.

They weren't going to remain together once school was finished and that upset her more than she cared to admit.

"Come on, come away with me. You know you want to," Drake said. "You and me."

"No one else."

"No one."

"Okay, then we'll do it." She wasn't about to tell him this weekend was her birthday. Her parents had already apologized for not being able to get off work. The thought of not being alone all day was far too tempting, and well, any time with Drake where they didn't have to pretend to fight was also a relief. "Wow, I can't believe we're going to do this."

"Yes, we are."

She was about to kiss him when she saw the door about to be pushed open.

Without thinking, she quickly shoved him into a stall, flicking the lock into place. Drake sat on the toilet and lifted his feet up.

He laughed and she pressed a hand against his mouth in the hope of trying to contain his noise.

He didn't make a sound.

"Ugh, I hate math so much. It's, like, so boring. Why do we even need it? It's what accountants are for anyway."

Pru couldn't make out the voice.

"Since when do you know a thing about accountants?" another said.

"Since my daddy has been telling me that they are pissing away his money again. I mean, I get it, they deal with taxes and shit, but I'm so bored."

There was silence after a couple of giggles.

Pru had managed to sit on his lap and keep her feet from being seen.

"So, are you going to tell us about your night with Drake?"

She tensed up and even Drake frowned.

"Oh, please, a girl never tells. You know that."

Again, she had no idea who these girls are.

"Shut up, you've been trying to get with Drake for over a year and he finally paid you some attention."

"I know. He shut my locker as he walked past. It had to be love."

Now, she couldn't help but smile. Drake stroked her back and rolled his eyes.

"We could make out," he said, mouthing the words.

"Well, I went around to his house last night and you know he lives in that big mansion of his, it is so amazing. So huge as well. He has a pool…"

This conversation was starting to annoy her.

"Nothing happened," Drake mouthed. "She's fucking lying. I don't even recognize who it is."

Pru believed him.

Whoever the girl was, she was only trying to score some kind of points with her friends and she was using Drake to do it.

For the first time, Pru saw Drake as a victim. There were people out there, women, who would use him to get ahead. She wasn't using him for anything and didn't expect anything from him in return. Sure, he'd been an asshole, but that didn't mean he deserved to be hurt.

She couldn't help but wonder if a time would ever come when he'd be wanted for himself rather than the money and wealth people often sought him out for?

****

Friday night, Drake checked the clock for what felt like the hundredth time. So they wouldn't get caught, Pru had offered to meet him up by the lake, and now he was waiting. He didn't like the thought of her walking through town on her own, but this was the only way they would get any privacy.

Rubbing at his temples, he tried not to think about what he hoped would happen this coming weekend.

Not that he'd force her.

Of course not.

He was more than happy to wait until she was ready, another big shock for him because he didn't wait around for anyone. Pru had surprised him at every single turn, and he loved it. He loved to be taken by surprise.

Running fingers through his hair, he looked around and didn't see a thing.

"You look nervous," Pru said, rounding the corner.

"You took your time."

"Well, I had to make sure I wasn't being followed."

"We're not spies."

"True, but I like the mystery."

He pulled her in close. "Are you ready for your birthday tomorrow?"

"No. Is anyone ever ready for their birthday?"

"I don't know." He pressed a kiss to her lips but it wasn't enough. He wanted more. He gave her another kiss. "You taste amazing."

"Yeah, that's coffee for you."

"You had anything to eat?"

"Nope. I'm starving."

"Lucky for you, I know what to get us both." He took her hand, grabbing her overnight bag and tossing it into the back of the car. He helped her inside and couldn't resist leaning in close and pulling her seatbelt on.

"You're such a gentleman."

"You have no idea just how gentlemanly I can be." He winked at her and then felt like a crazy person for doing exactly that." Walking around the car, he felt nervous.

He was. His hands were shaking a little bit, and his stomach, well, he felt incredible about what was going to happen.

"Where are you taking me?" she asked.

"It is a surprise. Your parents aren't going to think I kidnapped you, are they?"

"Nope. They don't know I'm going away. I said I'll be in and out all weekend so if they don't see me not to worry."

"And they fell for that?" he asked.

"Yes. What? You look shocked. Are you telling me your parents are at home right now, worried about you?" she asked.

"No, they don't even give a shit that I'm gone."

"Exactly, and neither do my parents, so why don't we just worry about the two of us, and leave the rest of the world to fend for itself? How does that sound?" she asked.

"It sounds exactly like what I want to do."

"Good. Me too." She leaned over and kissed him. "Take me away, honey."

"Honey. I like it, baby."

"Ugh, that sounds so bad," she said, giggling.

He loved the sound of her giggle. Pulling away from her, he turned over the engine and moved away from the curb. He wanted to get this show on the road, but first, they needed to have some food.

"So, did your little friend want to spend some time with you?" Drake glanced over at her and she was looking right back at him. "What?"

"You want to talk about Sean?"

"Why not? He's your friend, so why not? You like him. I guess I will tolerate him."

"You don't have to. He's fine with it. He had some thing with his parents."

This time Drake paused. "He did?"

"Yeah, why?"

"I just … it's weird that on the weekend of your eighteenth birthday, he'd leave you all alone. It doesn't exactly sound like the Sean thing to do." It was the oddest thing.

"They're going up to some kind of museum. He and his folks and he's been talking about it."

"A museum."

"Yeah, it's … damn, I can't think of what it is called. It has lots of old English artifacts. Anyway, they'd been waiting to go for a long time, and now that they can, I don't want him to miss it."

"I'm not going to complain. I've got you all to myself." He grabbed her hand, locking their fingers together and kissing her knuckles.

"You can be sweet when you want to be," she said.

"You got it, and yes, I even got you a present as well."

"Is it you wrapped up in a big bow?"

"Not even close, but we'll see. You never know, I might let you unwrap me. It'll be a good gift." He glanced over at her and winked.

"Look at you, showing off like that. You never know, I may want to unwrap you."

Drake gripped the steering wheel tighter. "I don't want you to feel pressured."

"I know. I'm not feeling any pressure. I'm getting hungry. What about you?"

"Yeah, I'm starved. Another twenty minutes and I'll feed you."

He focused on the road and tried not to think about the girl sitting beside him. Every now and then, he chanced a look at her, but she kept looking out the window.

None of his friends had even asked him what he had planned for this coming weekend. He'd been ditching them as often as he could. The time he wanted to spend with Pru was far more important to him than any time spent elsewhere.

"So, er, is there anything specific you'd like to do for your birthday?" he asked.

"Not really. Is it corny if I say I just want to spend it with you?"

"No, not corny at all."

She leaned over and rested her head against his shoulder. "I find it strange that I really do enjoy being with you, Drake."

"I'm going to take that as a compliment."

"You really should because that's how I meant it." She glanced up at him. She opened her mouth to speak but all of a sudden, her stomach growled and he laughed. "Damn, that's embarrassing."

"It's cute. Don't worry. I know what to do. I need to feed the beast."

She chuckled. "I can't believe this."

"I'm starving as well."

He saw the diner he was looking for and pulled in. There weren't a lot of cars around, and so he found a parking space easily.

He climbed out of the car and Pru did the same.

They came together inside, holding hands as they made their way into the diner. He loved being able to hold her hand, to be close to her. It was moments like this that Drake realized how much he actually hated being in school. He couldn't hang out with her. He had to sit in each class watching Sean sit with her, or she was on her own. Rarely did anyone else sit with her, and he hated it.

Lunchtimes, she would either sit in the cafeteria or outside, and he found himself finding her, watching her. Sean was always with her, and it only served to remind him of what he didn't have, what he could never have. They both knew this was going to end at the end of the high school year, but it didn't make it any easier.

Entering the diner, they found a small booth, and he let her go to sit on one side.

"What do you think is good here?" she asked.

"Anything. I'm paying."

"You don't have to pay for everything," she said. "I can pay."

"This is my treat. Consider it a treat for your birthday."

"When did you get so sweet?" she asked.

"It comes naturally to me. You know you find me adorable because of it."

She giggled. "This is nice. I like this—"

"I don't like seeing you hanging out with Sean," he said.

"Drake, don't do this. I thought we were past

this."

"I did as well, but clearly not. This bothers me. Can't you see that?"

"What do I have to do? We can't change what our lives are about." She grabbed his hand. "There is nothing going on between Sean and me."

"I know there's not." When it came to Pru, he didn't doubt her. It was her best friend he doubted, but they were going over the same ground they'd been covering for a while now. He wasn't going to spoil her weekend because of his own anger issues when it came to her best friend.

Chapter Seventeen
I want this

Drake's family owned a lot of houses and because of this, he could go anywhere he wanted in the world. Pru didn't care about his money. Never had. What she cared about was the time spent with people she loved and cherished.

As Drake let them into his old country beach house, she was a little nervous.

This was her first time away with a guy. She hadn't told her family anything. No one knew she was away with Drake, not even Sean. Her best friend had been willing to stay behind, but she'd told him not to. Instead, she'd told him to go and take his time and that she was just going to relax for her birthday, and not really do a whole lot.

Drake flicked on the light and the beach house came into view.

"I had no idea you had a beach house."

"This one is rarely used because it's quite small and when my parents want to go away, they like to do so in style, if you know what I mean."

"I know."

Drake dropped the bags on the floor.

"How long has it been since you last came here?" she asked.

"A couple of years. We're going to have to eat out. The kitchen is really for show. My parents are not domesticated at all. They either hire a cook, order in, or go out."

"It's fine." She took a step into the room. Considering the beach house was *small*, it was bigger than her own home.

"Do you like it?" he asked.

"Do you really need to ask me that?"

"I don't know. I brought you here to be impressed and you're not giving anything away."

She rushed toward him, wrapping her arms around his waist. "Drake, I like your family's beach house but I don't need it. It's just a house."

"Now you're just hurting me."

She chuckled. "You're crazy, but that's okay because I like your brand of crazy." She pulled him down, pressing her lips against his. "I like this so much."

"What?"

"Not having to hide. I like kissing you and not having to sneak around."

He pulled her close and sank his fingers into her hair. She gasped. "If you like that, I can keep on doing it." He slid his tongue across her lips, plunging inside, and she moaned, wanting more. He pressed her up against the nearest wall. "Now I don't have to pretend with anything. I can kiss and touch." He slid his hands down her body, cupping her hips before going to her ass.

She cried out as he held her close and she felt the hard ridge of his cock pressed against her stomach. Rather than be nervous by his blatant display of need, she relished it.

"Please," she said.

"What are you asking for?"

"I don't know. I don't want you to stop."

"You don't have a chance of me stopping, not ever." He lifted his head and yelled, "Hello, anyone home?" Then to her, he said, "We're all alone. I've got no reason to pull away. No parent is going to come barging into this place. You're completely at my mercy, Pru. Are you afraid?"

"Not even a little bit. I'm ready for whatever it is you've got to throw my way." She ran her hands down his chest, feeling a little brave. She stopped at the edge of his jeans, jerking her hand away.

She didn't exactly last long with feeling brave.

"We're not in any kind of rush," Drake said. "You. Me. This weekend. It's for all of us. Let me give you the tour."

He held her hand and they walked into each room. He showed her the living room, kitchen, dining room, library, and study. Upstairs, there were two bedrooms, one she figured were for his parents, the other, for him.

"It looks amazing."

"It is."

"You love it here?"

"I do. I don't come here as often as I'd like, but for the most part, this is home."

"I can see that," she said. Drake put their bags on his bed. Considering this room was smaller than his parents', the space was still large, huge even. "Your parents won't know you're here?"

"No. Like I said, they don't come here. It's not exposed enough."

"It still seems kind of strange they'd want a place they consider exposed."

"My parents like to be the center of attention. I've told you that before."

"You have. And you don't like the attention?" she asked.

"I used to. Not anymore. Not when I'm used as some kind of toy in their never-ending power play. You want to take a walk down to the beach?"

"I'd love to."

"We've got a private access to the beach at the back. You don't have to wear any shoes. You can feel the sand between your toes."

She slipped off her sneakers, putting her socks inside each shoe. Drake did the same and it was rather odd again to see him without any shoes. He looked a little normal to her now, but she didn't have a problem with that.

Hand-in-hand, they walked down toward the beach. The access was a private gate that he had to press in a code for.

"This isn't accessible to just anyone?" she asked.

"No. My parents, for all of their need to be exposed, don't like to have just anyone walking on their land."

"So they like to be exposed to the right kind of people?"

"You got it."

Each time he talked about his parents, she noticed he always sounded bitter, resentful.

As he led her out to the beach, she saw the tide was in. There were several lights casting down across the beach, and she heard people up ahead, laughing, joking. They were normal people with normal lives. They didn't have to sneak around with anyone, like she was doing with Drake.

"What are you thinking?" he asked.

"About us. About the people up there."

"You don't have to think about them up there," he said.

"I know. I'm just wondering how this would have been if it was different."

He held her hand a little tighter. "In what way?"

"In a way that we could have come to the beach without sneaking. Don't you ever think about just saying fuck it, and the two of us trying to make this work without worrying what others would think?" she asked.

"Yes, all the time. When we pass in the hallway, I

want to grab you, push you up against the locker, and kiss you. You know that. You know I want to hurt your best friend every single time I see him with you because he can do what I cannot."

"What's that?"

"Touch you. Make you smile."

"You can make me smile, Drake."

"Not in front of everyone. No, I get to cause you the most pain." He made them stop, and he pressed his head against hers. "You have no idea how much I wish things were different for us."

"We could make them different," she said.

"How?"

"Do you really need to be here with the money? Why don't we make a new life, away from all of this? Away from all the expectations from other people. I'm willing to take this chance with you. Won't you take it with me?" She didn't know why she was even suggesting this.

"Pru, if I do this, I will be completely cut off."

"I know. Is it so bad?"

"I will have nothing."

She felt tears fill her eyes.

"You have your parents who will be more than happy to keep you with them. I won't have a home or anything."

"You told me once that your parents would even try to ruin my parents."

"They would."

"So I wouldn't have anywhere else either."

"Okay, say we do this. We say screw it to my parents who have all the power back in town. I lose everything, your parents lose their jobs, and move. You're gone then, and we can't even have this."

"What if we run?"

"Run?"

"You know, away together. We can graduate and then while people think we're partying, we can run?" She couldn't believe she was even suggesting this. It was completely crazy and stupid.

Running away wasn't the answer. She knew that, and yet, she couldn't help but think it would be the right decision to make.

"Pru, are you serious?"

"We can run and no one would need to know what we're doing. Your parents can think you're partying around the world, and in truth, we're making a life for ourselves. We just have to get to graduation," she said.

"You'd run away with me. Start over, even without the money."

She rolled her eyes, which seemed to be a never-ending habit with her when he asked certain questions. "Drake, I'm not here because of the money. I don't know how many times I'm going to have to tell you that. I'm here because I want to be with you. I know it's shocking and scary, but you're not going to get rid of me that easily." She placed a hand to his chest. "You're going to keep me around for some time."

Pru knew they were taking a risk being together but what kind of life could they have otherwise? Would she have to walk away knowing what they could have?

"I know a way where I could keep my money and we could stay together."

"Killing your parents?"

"Nope. Nothing as drastic as that."

"Then I'm all ears," she said. She was willing to listen to his reasoning no matter what.

"So, I'm thinking, you and me, we keep doing what we're doing, keeping up appearances and stuff like that, then I pay for your college tuition. We move away from town, and I keep you as my little secret in the city."

"And then when your parents want you to marry someone they decide?"

"You'll always be with me."

"You're thinking of turning me into your mistress? You do see that, right?" she asked.

"Yes. But not as bad nor as seedy as you're making it sound."

She laughed. "Okay, then, tell me how you being married to someone else, having sex with them, and me being kept in the background isn't anything like a mistress? How is that light and fluffy?"

"Saying it like that doesn't make it sound great. I agree."

"You agree?" she asked. She folded her arms across her chest.

"No, I don't agree. I'm looking for solutions for us to be together."

She started to laugh. "Okay, then if you're being so stubborn and refuse to see it from my side of things, think of this. What if I was the one with the money? How about my parents pick me out a handsome, sexy guy for me to marry, and you're the one that gets to have the cushy life but knowing when I'm not with you, there's a chance I'm with my husband and we're having sex."

"No!" He yelled the word.

Pru knew in that second she had won. "See, if you can't stand the same thought, then you and I both know this is a really bad idea."

"Fuck."

"Is it really so bad to live without money?" she asked. She'd never been rich or even well off. Money had always been a sore and uncomfortable topic at home. Nothing would ever change that. Her parents were always wanting to make more. It was one of the many reasons she was home alone. Not that it was a problem. She knew her parents were trying to make a good life for her. They didn't want her to go without, even though she didn't care about money. She never needed a brand-new phone or a new car.

Sean often drove her to school or she walked. It wasn't a big deal.

"It's okay for you. You know what it's like to live without it. I don't know that feeling. I've never experienced it."

"Oh," she said.

"Fuck, I don't mean it as a bad thing." He ran a hand down his face, looking increasingly frustrated. "I … you…"

"I get it, Drake. I do." She couldn't even be mad at him. He didn't understand. He'd never been without money. "I can promise you, it's not a scary thing. At least, not how you're treating it. I survived."

"That's the thing, Pru, I don't want us to survive."

"So, we continue on with the path we've chosen." She didn't have anything else to say. "I don't want to fight and no matter what, when we talk about the future or the past, we always do."

"Pru?"

"We've only got a couple of days here. Let's make the most of them. Can't we at least do that right together?" she asked.

She saw he wanted to argue. In the time they had spent together, she had started to read his many tells. It saddened her how things were turning out between them. There was no future between them and of course, like always, she was trying to make it work. She had to learn to accept there was no way they could be together. They both wanted different things and even as they wanted each other, there were too many differences between them to make this work the way she wanted to.

It was time to just enjoy and to stop trying to change the outcome of their inevitable future.

****

Once again, the walk across the beach didn't go to plan for Drake. He wanted to make this romantic but when their future was set to change in a matter of months, which neither of them wanted, it caused a few difficulties.

Arriving back at the house, Pru went into the kitchen and made them some food while he paced the sitting room.

He'd never been without luxury of some kind. It was second nature to him. Running his fingers through his hair, he tried to think of how to fix this mess. Why couldn't he not fuck this up? No matter what he did or where he turned, he seemed to be constantly making a mess.

This is why it's never going to work long-term.
Why not?
We don't have to fuck this up.

Needing to see her, he moved toward the kitchen. He stood in the doorway and her back was to him, so he only got to watch her. She stood at the counter, chopping away at something, he didn't know what. When he'd checked out the fridge, he saw it had an abundance of vegetables so he imagined they were having lots of them.

Not that it mattered.

He heard her sniffle and he couldn't help but tense up.

She turned away from the counter and sure enough, she washed her hands, grabbed some tissues and clearly not realizing he was watching her, she sobbed into the tissue.

His heart fucking broke. "Please don't cry."

She gasped as she pulled down the tissue. "You're not supposed to see this."

"It's kind of hard not to see it even with you trying to hide your face."

"I'm fine. You don't have to worry."

"Stop trying to hide everything from me. I know I caused this."

"Yeah, well, I don't want to talk to you right now."

"I know I've upset you."

"It's fine."

"It's not fine. Stop pretending everything is fine."

"What do you want me to say? Look what you did to me? This isn't supposed to be complicated, Drake. We keep saying the same old thing and we're not getting over it." She sighed. "I don't want to argue with you. Not anymore. I think you should take me back home. It will be for the best."

"No, I won't." He stepped right up to her, pulling her in his arms. "We're not going to let this go. We're going to resolve it."

"How can we possibly resolve anything? We keep coming back to the same thing. Can't you see we're constantly going around in circles?"

"We don't have to be. We've got to learn to compromise."

She sighed then laughed. "You think I don't know how to compromise? Look around you, Drake. This is me compromising. I'm not at home alone, or with Sean. I know you hate me talking about him, but tough. Live with it. I have to live with your hatred of him. You think he's such a bad person, but I can promise you he is far from anything bad. He's one of the best guys I know."

Drake stepped away from her and closed his eyes. He counted to ten inside his head before staring at her. Again, they were back to that fucking pussy. He wasn't going to let Sean get between them. No matter how often she threw that shit in his face. He didn't need to keep on telling her the same thing. One day soon, Sean would show his true colors and when he did, Drake would accept Pru with open arms.

"Are you done?" he asked.

"Yeah, I'm done. I really think you should take me home."

"Not going to happen. Not on my watch." He folded his arms and stared at her. "My parents will destroy us. They have the power to and can do it easily. You think I don't want to run away with you? All I can think about every second of every day is how I can spend time with you. This isn't easy for me either."

"It's not easy for either of us."

"Here's the thing, Pru. I'm in love with you," he said.

She gasped and put a hand to her face in shock.

"Yeah, I know. It surprised me as well."

"We promised each other not to develop those feelings, Drake. You shouldn't have said anything."

"I can't help the way I feel. I love you and I want to spend the rest of my life with you. It's hard for me when you constantly talk about what a good guy Sean is. You think there are times I don't feel ashamed? Jealous?"

"Why would you be jealous of him? There is nothing to fear with him."

He laughed. "He gets to hold you in front of everyone. He gets to be the guy by your side. He knows you, and what do I get?"

"You get all of me, Drake," she said.

"Do I? We're always fighting about the same thing. No, I can't walk away. I've seen my parents in action. I know what they're capable of and I know what they will do to you, your parents, and even me. They have all the power here. We won't ever be able to run from them. They have all the power and we have nothing. I don't want to lose you but unless you can come to me with some compromise, come May, we're done." He didn't like how much it broke his heart to say it. He didn't want either of them to be done. They had so much to give.

"I ... Drake?"

"I don't want you to tell me an answer now. I know it's a hard decision to make. Yes, one day I could be married to someone else, but there is also a chance that I could become stronger than them. I could make sure they don't hurt either of us and then we can live happily ever after." He stepped back up to her and cupped her face, tilting her head back. "I know it's what I want. For you and me to have a chance. Don't you ever wonder what it could be like?"

"All the time," she said. "Then I feel like I'm living in a fairytale land."

"No. I think we've got a chance. You've just got to learn to trust me. Can you do that?"

"I don't doubt you or your ability, Drake."

Her lips were just too tempting to let go. Leaning down, he took possession of her mouth and she let out a little moan as he sank his fingers into her hair, holding her in place as he kissed her, deepening it. Sliding his tongue across her lips, he moved her back until she was sandwiched between the counter and his body.

Banding her arms around his neck, she cried out as he lifted her, pulling her against his body. He made sure she felt the hard ridge of his cock.

"Drake?"

"I know. I'm not going to do anything. I promise."

Not until her birthday.

"Please," she said.

"Don't beg me, Pru. I can't handle it when you beg so nicely."

"I want you."

He growled. Breaking from the kiss, he trailed his lips down to her neck but he kept his hands at her waist. "I promised myself I was going to be a good boy with you."

She giggled. "I'm giving you permission and you want to be a good boy?" she asked.

"Always. I've hurt you enough and I promised myself no matter what, I would wait. This is me waiting for you." He stroked her hair back. "You're so beautiful."

"You're just saying that."

"No, I'm really not. You may not believe this, Pru, but you've changed me in ways no one else ever could." He was speaking the truth. There was no one else in the world who could make him feel this way.

They had fought so much and he wasn't even talking about the bullying all those years ago. No, he was talking about their constant bickering. How neither of them would ever back down. He knew if this had been with anyone else, he'd have quit long ago, but no one he'd ever known was quite like Pru.

He was starting to think of her as more, as his Pru. Not Trash or any other word he used to call her. She was his just as he was hers. It was cliché as fuck, but he couldn't bring himself to part from her. He didn't want to part from her, ever.

"How about I finish us some food?" she asked.

"We watch a movie or something? Maybe go for a walk."

"Food sounds good. So long as I'm with you. I'll do anything."

"Just how long do I have this more amenable guy around?"

"Consider this a special gift as it's your birthday."

"Oh, I'm lucky?"

"That you are, baby. Really lucky. I will be on my best behavior from now until, well, we head back home Sunday."

She wrinkled her nose. "Let's not think about Sunday. Let's just think about this weekend. Taking each moment as it comes and not freaking out about it. What do you think?"

"I like that sound of that." He kissed her lips and when she moaned, the sound went straight to his cock. All he wanted to do was take her to his bed and have her.

You've got to take your time with her.

She's a virgin.

You love her.

You want to care for her.

You don't want to leave her.

Against all the odds, he had fallen for her, and now, he had to find some way to keep her. He wasn't under any illusions about his parents. He knew they both cheated and there were men and women waiting for them back at any location where they put them.

You could just kiss your wealth goodbye and run.

It wasn't the running away that scared him when it came to spending his time with Pru. Far from it. He'd gladly run anywhere she wanted to go so long as he got to spend every second with her.

No, it was what his parents would do to them.

They could run and he could live without his

wealth but if they set out to destroy them, could he protect her? He honestly didn't think he could, and that scared him. All he wanted to do was protect her. Love her. Take care of her.

The real truth was he wanted to spend the rest of his life with her without anyone interfering or thinking they could run their life. That wasn't ever going to happen with his parents already making plans for him.

They always wanted what they did and he couldn't figure out a single way to stop it, unless he became more powerful than them. The fortune becoming his, and he forcing their hand by being bigger, meaner, and turning the cards on them. It would take time.

He'd have to do it slowly so they didn't suspect anything. He had his own ideas. Regardless of what others thought, he wasn't stupid. There was a chance of him taking it all from them, and he would.

He watched Pru as she walked back to their food to finish it off. He would have her all to himself, and no one would ever harm her.

He'd make sure of it.

Chapter Eighteen
Birthday

Pru couldn't believe she was eighteen today. It seemed almost too surreal to think of herself as an adult. Not that her age mattered. She'd been taking care of herself for a long time. At least since they moved to the new town all those years ago when she was just five years old.

Up until that point, she'd been a happy, oblivious child in the city, playing in the small garden. She had no idea her life would change so much, or that a small town could be so … different.

Then, of course, there was Drake, who she had left back at the beach house. Not to punish him or anything. She just needed a little time and space and the only way to get that was to leave him behind.

Running fingers through her hair, she tilted her face up to the sky and closed her eyes. She was alone with Drake. They had argued last night, but that seemed to always be in the cards for them. She hated arguing the most. There were times she wished she could rewrite their summer together. They shouldn't have ever been alone in a room, let alone kissing or doing anything else.

The moment she started to think about not being around him, though, guilt flooded every inch of her. Could she really be so cruel to him? He'd done nothing wrong to her.

"It's fine," she said to no one.

"Are we talking to ourselves now?" Drake asked, startling her as he wrapped his arms around her waist.

"I guess we are."

"It's kind of sexy," he said.

She giggled. "You're a strange man, Drake. What do you really think is sexy?"

"You. The birthday girl." He kissed her neck. "Do you feel any different?"

"Did you on your birthday?"

"Nope. I was just older. I already did a lot of stuff eighteen-year-olds are allowed to do."

"It doesn't feel any different," she said. "The view is breathtaking though."

"The view always is." He kissed her again. "I missed waking up beside you."

"I didn't want to disturb you and I wanted to see the sun rise."

"I could have joined you."

"You looked so peaceful, all asleep with nothing in the world to trouble you." She turned in his arms. "I wasn't excluding you. I just needed a short time to think."

He stroked a curl out of the way. "I wish I could stop you from worrying."

She chuckled. "What makes you think I was worrying?"

"I know you. I know you worry about everything and anything. I wish I could make it all stop for you."

"You're sweet."

"I'm the best kind of guy." He smiled. "I have a present for you back at the house."

Her heart sped up at his words. She didn't know what it was, just that it made her feel … alive when he talked like that.

She knew why he didn't want to run away. The power his parents had. They scared him, not that he'd ever admit it.

"Can we just stay here a few more minutes?" she asked.

"It's your birthday. We can stay here as long as you want."

He didn't let go of her, and she didn't want him to. She wanted his arms wrapped around her so when they were apart, if they ever were because she still held hope, she would have these precious moments to remember.

Leaning back, she closed her eyes and just relaxed against his touch. Nothing could take this away from her. Not now.

"It's your birthday and I have to wonder what you'd like to do on this magical day."

She laughed. "Magical? How do you spend your birthdays?"

"I tend to get drunk. That's how I do it."

"Ah, drunk. Maybe we should do that?" she asked. "I've never been drunk before."

"You haven't?"

"Nope. Come on, my rebellious lover, show me how a real rebel parties." She spun in his arms, wrapping hers around his neck.

"You want me to show you how to party?"

"Why not? It could be fun."

"No, today you're not getting drunk. You're going to remember every single moment of your eighteenth." He grabbed her ass and kissed her hard, taking her breath away.

He slid his tongue into her mouth and she moaned against him, feeling an answering heat within her body. She knew what she wanted. Their time together was destined to end. They had put a time limit on it themselves, and she didn't want to waste a single moment of it.

"First, I'm going to take you for breakfast," Drake said, breaking the kiss. She didn't want him to ever stop kissing her or wanting her.

"Breakfast?"

"Yes. I'm not going to cook for you and you're not going to be cooking today either." He took hold of her hand and they started to walk along the sea front.

"Breakfast is our first stop?" she asked.

"Yes. Then I think we can go for a walk before heading back home for the evening. I'll be ordering takeout."

"Did you buy me any presents?"

"Yes. I have one I want you to have." He gave her hand a comforting squeeze. "What did you get from Sean?"

"Do you really want me to tell you? I know you hate talking about him."

"It's your day and I can handle hearing his name or what it is he thought was appropriate to get you."

"He didn't get me anything," she said. "I got a text this morning. That was pretty much all I got." She shrugged. "I imagine there will be something when I get back."

"Or he's being an asshole and you're finally seeing it. That's the only comment I'm going to make. Don't you worry about him or your parents. I've got this covered. You're going to have the best time with me. I promise." He pulled her close and kissed her again.

She didn't care about Sean forgetting a present.

Even though she had asked Drake if he'd gotten her anything, she didn't actually expect anything from him. She didn't need gifts to have a good day. Having him for her birthday was all she needed.

Last night, they had slept together in bed, and it had been ... surreal. At first, she'd been a little uncomfortable as they had been together all night without any fears of their parents walking in. She didn't realize how much of a strain it was trying to keep everything a secret. It was exhausting in more ways than she had ever realized.

Anyone who looked at them or watched them would see there was no hatred or animosity. She didn't want to go back to what they were. More than anything, she loved who they had become.

Pushing those thoughts aside, she instead focused on the day. Looking to the future was too painful. They both wanted the same thing but had to go about it differently.

The scents of fried foods filled the air as they neared the pier at the edge of the beach. A small café with a broken neon sign filled the spot. She saw only a couple of people were inside.

Drake opened the door and she smiled at him. They found a small booth near the window.

"This is nice," she said.

It wasn't overly fancy, which part of her was afraid of. Drake's need for money kind of made her nervous most of the time.

"You can order whatever you want."

"Are you after my heart?" she asked, jokingly.

He didn't respond and she looked up to see him staring at her.

"You've got to stop taking things so … personally. It was just a joke."

"I know. Can't a guy just like looking at you?" He winked at her.

"You do?"

"Of course. You've got beautiful eyes and a nice pair of tits. What's not to like?"

She rolled her eyes. "Of course, you're a guy. You'd go toward the guy things."

"Hey, I'm keeping it real."

She laughed, loving this banter between them. It was moments like these that made their arguing so …

frustrating. Neither of them should be arguing about anything and yet, they always found themselves back to that.

No! She wasn't going to allow herself to do that.

Today was her birthday. She would enjoy it with Drake. Not thinking about their problems or what they had to face. That would all come very soon.

"What are you looking at?" he asked, nodding toward the menu.

"I'm thinking waffles. I haven't had them in a long time. At least ones I didn't make myself."

"Get them. Lots of waffles and coffee sounds good to me."

The waitress came over and Drake ordered them a lot of waffles with syrup.

"You think I can eat all that?" she asked, smiling.

"They're not all for you. A man is starving here." He patted his stomach.

"You see, I didn't think you ate."

"Please, you've seen me eat lots."

She smiled. She had. They just rarely got to eat together like this. "This is fun."

"It is." He took her hands once again and ran his thumb across the back of her knuckles. "I want today to be really special for you."

"Drake, it is. I'm with you." She held his hands a little tighter.

Neither of them spoke for several moments. Neither of them wanted to ruin the peace they had found together. She licked her suddenly dry lips and wished they were alone. At least she could kiss him. While they were kissing, she couldn't think about all the things they couldn't have together.

"So, how are you doing at school?" she asked, breaking the silence. Even though they spent as much time as possible together, she never really got to ask how he was doing in classes. They shared a couple and the teachers rarely asked him to answer any questions as most of the time they would get a joke or a witty comeback. It was his thing, and she didn't mind. At the end of the day, it was his life and he could do with it what he wanted.

She let go of his hands to push some of her hair off her shoulder.

"You want to talk about school?"

"It's a safe topic. Besides, I don't recall you doing any homework. You watch me do mine and I'm a little worried I'm turning into some kind of bad thing for you."

He stroked her cheek. "One, you'd never be bad for me. Two, I do my homework. Don't worry."

She tilted her head to the side, trying to think about it. "When?"

"When I get home. I'm not much of a sleeper. Never have been. So when you're asleep and I've got to sneak out, or just head home, I do all my homework then, and I don't carry it around with me. I simply email it to the teacher. Easy."

"So all this time, you've been a good guy?"

"I wouldn't call it being a good guy."

"Then what would you call it?"

"Doing what I had to do."

She giggled. "Look at you, being the good guy."

"I'm not."

"Come on, you email the teacher homework, but you're too afraid it'll damage your rep. Oh my, I can't even … this is really good."

"Really good?"

"Hell yeah."

"Who are you going to tell about it?" he asked,

brow raised. "I don't see anyone paying much attention to you."

"Damn, you're right. I'm going to have to catch you in the act. I didn't ever think of you conforming to anything, and now look at you. Conforming. Being the good guy."

"How do you think I kept up in grades?" he asked. "I never flunked a class."

She winced. "Can I be honest with you?"

"I don't see why not. I know this is going to hurt my feelings, though. Isn't it?"

"Little bit. I thought your parents paid for your grades."

Drake put a hand over his heart. "Now you really do hurt me. You're not wrong, though."

"I'm confused. Your parents do pay for you?"

"No. They don't pay. What I mean is, if I was flunking and giving them a bad name, they'd pay to move me up and have someone do all my homework."

"You were never tempted to make them do that so you could have fun partying or whatnot?"

"Yeah, I was tempted but why make it easy for them, you know?"

"I wish there was something I could do to make your life easier."

He laughed. "My life is easy."

"Is it? You try hard at school to spite your parents. I…"

"Neither of us have great parents, Pru."

She winced. "You're wrong about that."

"I am?"

"My parents. They're not the best, but I know they love me and want what is best for me." She felt a little guilty because she knew deep down her parents loved her more than anything. Yes, they were working, but that was because they needed the money for rent and to live. They didn't have it easy like Drake's family.

Drake once again took her hand. "Look, I'm not denying that your parents care. I bet they do. Think about the last thirteen years."

"Why?"

"Think about them. They've been called to the school because of what I've done to you, and not once did they stand up for you. Not once did they fight me or my parents."

"We know why."

"Yeah, well, some people would still fight. My parents have a lot to protect and their reputation is one of them. Believe me, if your parents had any kind of backbone, they would have seen that."

She didn't pull away from him.

There were times over the years she had been so angry with the way they treated her. How afraid they seemed to go against his family. She, to a point, understood it, but they should have loved her, trusted her. They hadn't fought for her. They had simply wanted her to forget and to pretend it didn't happen.

The waitress brought their breakfast. The mood was broken.

"Thank you," she said, speaking to the waitress.

"I'm sorry."

"It's fine."

"No, it's not. I should have kept my stupid mouth shut. I wanted today to be perfect for you."

She picked up her knife and fork and took a bite of delicious, syrup-soaked waffle. Closing her eyes, she let out a moan. "It is perfect," she said after finishing.

"I'm sorry," he said.

"Don't be. You're right. I don't have to like it, do I?"

"I don't want you to be upset."

She chuckled. "Drake, we're both free and clear to be upset about something." She shrugged. "There's nothing we can do about the past or the future. Let's enjoy today. Take it one day at a time. It's all we can do." She took another bite of her food. "Now, please, just take a bite and enjoy. Share this day with me. All horrible and shitty truths aside."

He stared at her and she smiled.

There wasn't going to be anything to spoil their day. Too much time had already been taken from them. No more.

At least not today.

****

After nearly fucking up breakfast, Drake vowed not to bring up their rocky past or what little hope they had of a future. It wasn't going to help either of them anyway, so he wasn't going to do anything to hurt her.

He knew he was right, though. Her parents could have forced his parents' hands. They were too afraid.

When he had kids, no one was going to hurt them. If he had a little girl and there was a punk-ass kid like him hurting her, he would destroy him.

Taking Pru's hand, they walked through the town, looking through the market stalls. He offered to buy her anything, but in true Pru style, there was nothing she wanted. She simply liked to look and move on.

He wanted to give her a day to remember but it would seem he couldn't even do that. They walked around the town together and had another meal, one she didn't have to cook, before returning to the beach house.

Pru pulled away from him and went to have a shower while he found her gift. He sat on the edge of the bed, waiting for her to return.

Twirling the box between his fingers, he couldn't

help but smile. This was the first time he'd ever given some real thought to a gift for a girl. He hadn't cared about anyone else in his life to ever put in this much effort.

Most of the time, gifts were items they got PAs or secretaries, or even nannies to buy. With this, he wanted to give Pru something with meaning, something he'd taken the time to think about.

It wasn't long before she finished in the shower and entered the bedroom, wrapped in a towel, looking sexy and innocent all at the same time.

"Drake," she said. "You look … serious."

"I didn't mean to mess up your day."

She laughed. "There's no way you could do something like that. I had a lot of fun today."

"You did?"

"Yes. Couldn't you tell?"

"I don't know. You've wanted to leave and you looked like you wanted to kill me."

"We're still new at this."

"We've been dating for months and we spend a great deal of time either making out or fighting."

She stepped up to him. "I don't want to fight tonight."

"I don't want to fight either." He never did but they were always pushed into the tight corner and he was getting ever increasingly tired of it.

"Drake, I know we don't make the best of our situation sometimes, but our relationship is different than others."

"How is it different?"

"For one, how many people do you think enter a relationship knowing it wasn't going to last? We've done that."

He stared at her hands, knowing deep down he

didn't want to lose her. Not even for a second. They were not, nor would they ever be coming to an end.

"It's why I can't walk away. Even when we both say mean things to each other. I don't mean half of them. We've spent so much of our time hating each other, I truly believe we don't know how else to be."

He stood up and pulled her into his arms, kissing the top of her head. "You're amazing. You know that, right?"

"Not really." She tilted her head up to smile at him. "I just know we're doing the best with what we know, and what we know isn't a whole lot."

He chuckled, stroking her cheek. "I got you a present." He'd put it on the bed so he could hold her.

"You really didn't need to buy me anything. I've had so much today already. You, the beach house. Falling asleep with you. I don't need anything more."

"And I get to spoil you this one day of the year. You can say a relative bought it for you." He held out the box. "Please, take it."

"It's expensive, isn't it?" She looked nervous.

"I took my time and the moment I saw it, I thought of you."

She opened the wrapping and he saw her hands shake a little. "When it's your birthday, I won't be able to get you something like this, Drake."

"I didn't buy this for you to buy me something. Let me have some credit."

"It's not that, I want to be able to get you nice things as well." She'd stopped unwrapping to kiss him. He loved her kisses, but he wanted to put his present on her.

"You give me more than enough nice things. You don't have to ever worry about that. Besides, you may hate what I got you." He kissed her again.

Taking her hand, he made her sit beside him. He was a little nervous, but he wanted her to like it. This was one of the many reasons he never picked out gifts. Not that it mattered to anyone else. Their feelings meant nothing to him. Pru, she wasn't just anyone, at least, not anymore. She was someone.

She glanced at him. The velvet box wasn't a wedding ring size or anything. He'd seen a couple of engagement rings and they'd taunted him. He wasn't going to marry Pru, not yet, at least.

Opening the box, she let out a little gasp. "Drake, it's beautiful. It looks like a teardrop."

"I know. It's what I thought when I saw it. I … I didn't want you to cry any more tears. It's a symbol. This is my way of telling you I'll never be the cause of any more of them. I stopped hurting you and I started loving you."

She looked up at him and much to his surprise, she had tears in her eyes.

"You shouldn't be crying. This isn't what it's about. I don't want you to be sad. Shit." He got to his feet, rushing to the bathroom to grab some tissues. Why couldn't he have gotten this right?

Returning to the room, he quickly pressed the tissue to her eyes, trying to capture them.

"They are not bad or sad tears, Drake."

"They're not?"

"No. I'm happy."

"You're crying but happy?"

She nodded.

"That makes no fucking sense." He had bought her the necklace because it felt to him like it had so much more meaning.

"I don't care. I'm telling you the truth. You've made me so happy." She pulled him close and he felt her soft body against his.

Since the summer, he hadn't been with anyone else. There had been so many offers and he'd turned them all down. The only person he wanted was right here, next to him. The girl he really shouldn't have but one he couldn't walk away from.

Pushing some of her hair off her shoulder, he stroked her cheek. She smiled up at him. The tears had faded and she had this amazing smile.

"Let me put this on you." He took the necklace from the box and put it around her neck. His fingers were shaking a little as he fixed the clasp.

"It really is beautiful," she said.

With it in place, he stepped in front of her and she took his hands, going to her tiptoes to kiss him. Something changed in the air. He didn't know what it was, only there was something happening between them. She pressed her head against his. Neither of them spoke for several seconds, or maybe even minutes. He didn't care about the ticking of time. All he cared about was Pru.

"Drake," she said.

"Yes."

"Make love to me."

Her words took him completely by surprise. "Pru, are you ... ready?"

"Yes. I know I want you to be my first."

Her first.

For Drake, he'd be her fucking only. He couldn't even stand to have Sean touching her, let alone another man. It wasn't possible. He didn't share and never would.

"I didn't bring you here expecting this to happen." He'd hoped something would, but it wasn't that he faced being her first. Something else had overcome him. Fear.

Sex for Pru on her first time could be painful. He'd never been with a virgin before but at the very thought of hurting her, he didn't want to do that. He'd spent too much time causing her pain to experience it.

If you don't do it, someone else will. Think about it. Another guy seeing her naked, spreading her thighs, making her come, giving her pleasure that only belongs to you.

He didn't want to think about it.

"Do you want to? I assumed you'd enjoy it. It's sex. Don't all guys like sex?" she asked. Her nerves were clearly showing through.

"I don't want to hurt you."

"You won't. Not in the way you think." She touched his chest and began to work the buttons of his shirt open.

He didn't stop her. He wanted this and letting her take the lead, at least for this part, he could do. If she got naked and was ready for him, he could do the rest.

She pushed the shirt from his body and it fell to the floor in a heap. He made no move to help her as she worked on his pants. This was all on her.

She was the one in control.

Not him.

She had to do what she wanted to him.

Pru tugged on his belt and he waited. "You're really not going to help me?"

"I will when you need help. For now, let me enjoy this. You want me, Pru. This is a first for me."

She smiled at him. "But you do want this?" she asked.

"Yes. More than you know."

"I've never gotten a man naked before."

"I had figured that little detail out." He winked at

her.

She worked at his belt and finally got it free. The sound of his zipper seemed to echo in the room. She put her hands on his hips but didn't move or push his jeans down. They stayed up and he cupped her under the chin, tilting her head back.

"I want this," she said. "With you. I don't know what I'm doing, Drake. I'm so nervous."

He had to take the lead. This wasn't something Pru could do alone.

He stroked her cheek, pushing some of her hair out of the way, watching as it fell down her back in beautiful waves.

"I know what to do," he said. "Relax. I'm going to make this amazing for you."

Was that his first lie?

He let her go and began to work his jeans down, followed by his boxer briefs. He was already hard, not that it would have taken a lot. He wanted this woman more than anything. Pru had gotten under his skin and now he couldn't be denied what he wanted.

She was perfect for him, and he couldn't believe he hadn't seen it before, or had he? Was that why he wanted to hurt her? He finally realized what a precious person she was and he couldn't stand that he didn't get her.

He pushed those thoughts aside as they were irrelevant now. Nothing mattered, apart from showing Pru an amazing time and how he felt about her.

With him completely naked, he captured her chin and made her look at him. "Don't be afraid."

She smiled. "I'm not. How could I be afraid? I trust you, Drake."

He pressed a kiss to her lips and slowly worked her towel off. He was shaking a little bit as he was nervous. The women he'd been with before, they knew what they were doing. They weren't virgins. This was all so different.

He dropped her towel to the floor in a heap and picked her up in his arms.

"I'm heavy," she said. "You'll break something."

"Shut up."

He lowered her to the bed and joined her. He moved between her thighs and she spread her legs for him. There was no reason to rush. He was more than happy to take his time, letting her get accustomed to him.

Kissing her lips, he stroked his tongue across her mouth before plunging inside. He didn't linger too long, trailing his lips down her body, going to her neck and sucking on her pulse. She let out a gasp, tilting her head to the side to give him better access.

Take your time, Drake. It's not a race.

He didn't want to come all over her since he hadn't been with anyone for some time. Continuing his kisses down her body, he went for her tits. They were so perfect he wanted to suck on them. Pushing them together, he stared at her body. So full, so ripe. Not fat like he'd always called her, but perfect. Pru was sheer perfection and he'd been too stupid to fucking see it before.

Now, she was all his for the taking and he was going to do exactly that. After he flicked his tongue across one hard nipple, he heard her gasp and moan. Glancing up her body, he found she was staring down at him, watching.

He bit down and she let out a whimper. Smiling, he circled the bud with his tongue before sucking it back into his mouth. He licked across each stunned peak, lavishing the other nipple with the same kind of attention, wanting to drive her wild just as she did him.

He loved her tits and wanted to spend a lot more time there, but he also knew he was stalling.

Before he got to the good stuff, he wanted to make her feel amazing. To experience a real, powerful kind of pleasure. The stuff he always wanted to give her but never could. After running his hands down her body to her thighs, he gripped them tightly then slowly spread them open.

"Drake?"

"Shh, it's okay. Trust me. I know what I'm doing." None of the girls he'd been with before had ever come close to meaning this much to him. She was everything and he wanted her so badly.

Take care of her.

Moving away from her glorious tits, he began to work down her body, kissing her stomach before going between her spread thighs.

No one had ever touched her.

Not Sean.

No one.

He found that highly addictive and couldn't get enough of her sweet cunt. Opening the lips of her sex, he stared at her clit, and his mouth watered for a taste of her. Untouched, virginal, all his.

Stroking a finger between her slit, he felt how wet she was for him. She was perfection as far as he was concerned. Replacing his finger with his tongue, he finally got to taste her and he wasn't disappointed. Flicking his tongue back and forth across her clit, he glanced up to see her eyes were closed. Her hands were clenched into fists and he teased her even more, wanting her to be wild with the pleasure only he could give her.

"Drake?"

"Shh, it's okay. I know." He stopped licking her pussy long enough to speak before going back and sucking her clit into his mouth. He'd never been one to go down on a girl. For the most part, he didn't know where they'd been before and he didn't want to taste another man's dick, but with Pru, she was all new at this.

His untouched woman.

Running his hands up to her hips, he held on to her tightly before caressing her skin all the way up to her tits. He worked her nub while he pinching her nipples, drawing her closer to her peak, wanting her to come before he took her virginity.

He had wanted this to happen on her birthday but he'd also been prepared for them to share a bed with nothing else happening.

"Drake … I'm … coming."

She let out a scream. The sound filled the air, echoing off the walls with the force of it. He felt and watched her as she came beneath him. His touch drove her ever higher, and he was desperate for her.

Using his fingers to tease her, he moved between her thighs and gripped his cock, knowing in the back of his mind he should wear a condom. It was insane for him not to, but he didn't want anything to be between them. He wanted to feel her wrapped around his dick. To have every inch of him bare as he sank inside her.

Staring down at her, he stopped playing with her pussy and lined his cock up to her entrance. In one swift thrust, he tore through her virginity. The pleasure she'd been experiencing seconds ago came to a close and she whimpered, but he didn't stop. He took her hands, holding her down as he allowed her to get accustomed to his cock. The pain in her eyes tore him apart. He wanted to stop it, but this was what he had to do.

Seconds passed.

Minutes.

Tears trailed down Pru's cheeks and he hated

them.

"Ouch," she said. "That hurt more than I thought it would."

"I'm so sorry." He really didn't want to hurt her.

"It's not your fault," she said.

"It really kind of is."

She chuckled, which again, didn't exactly do well for him.

"I'm sorry, I'm not laughing at you. I'm laughing at this. How nervous we are and the fact I'm not a virgin anymore."

"And we're talking like this. My dick's inside you, and we're here now, talking." He wasn't going soft any time soon. She felt amazing.

"I know. I read that if you give it a little time, it might not be so bad."

He stroked her cheek. "I cannot believe I'm here right now with you."

"Me neither. I don't want to go back."

"Then let's stay here for as long as we can. You and me." He pressed a kiss to her lips before she could allow their reality to set in.

There was nothing either of them could do. As he traced the seam of her lips, she let out a little moan and he cupped her hip, holding her in place, not wanting her to move, otherwise, she'd make him come. He didn't want to orgasm without feeling her come at least once more. She moaned and began to rock against his cock.

"Pru, don't."

"But I want to. I know it's going to be sore, but I want to feel you, Drake." She cupped his cheek as she slowly thrust against him. Her movements weren't practiced. She really didn't have a clue what she was doing and he found it even more charming.

This girl, this woman, she was … more than he

had ever hoped for. All this time she'd been right in front of him, but he'd been too blind to see just how precious she was. And for a short time at least, she belonged to him.

Chapter Nineteen
The day after

Opening her eyes, Pru blinked against the sunlight and quickly turned her head away, letting out a groan. Her body was sore and a little stiff. It wasn't her birthday anymore and the memories of last night rushed back to her.

"Morning," Drake said.

She tilted her head back and sure enough, he was awake and smiling at her. "Morning."

He stroked her cheek and she couldn't believe she'd had sex with Drake last night.

"You're not regretting what we did, are you?"

"What? No, of course not. Don't be crazy. I'm not regretting anything. Are you?"

"No, not a thing." He stroked her cheek again and leaned in close.

"I've got morning breath," she said.

"So do I, but I don't care." He took possession of her mouth and she closed her eyes, letting out a little moan. Drake was the first one to break the kiss. He pulled back and offered her a smile. "How are you feeling?"

"Okay, I think. How are you feeling?"

"I'm fine, Pru. Please, tell me if you're hurting."

"I'm not hurting. I'm not really feeling anything, to be honest. I'm all good. I promise." She licked her swollen lips. They were tingling from his kiss. "So, er, what are we doing today?"

"We've got to head back home today. School tomorrow."

She wrinkled her nose. "Or we could forget about it all and stay here for a couple more days? What would it hurt? I can call my parents and you said yours don't really check up on you. What harm could it do?"

"I'm starting to think I've made a bad impression on you."

"You're tempted?" she asked.

"Baby, I'm more than tempted. It means I don't have to worry about driving. We can stay in bed until it's really late." Drake grabbed her and pulled her down to the bed. She let out a scream, a little taken aback by his sudden mood change.

"What are you doing?" she asked, laughing. He stared down at her and she touched his face, cradling his cheek. "You look so serious."

Before she had a chance to know what was going on, his lips were on hers. She let out a little moan, to which he growled. Her entire body woke up. She was a little sore, but she wasn't going to allow her body to stop her.

"When it comes to you, I can't get enough." Drake broke the kiss, trailing his lips down her neck, toward her tits. He pressed them together and she gasped as his tongue stroked over the hard buds. She watched him, mesmerized as he continued to touch her. "I love these. You have no idea how many times I've thought about touching you, tasting you, wanting you."

"Please, Drake."

"I hope you can handle me. I want to get my fill of you while I can."

She pushed aside the quick pulse of pain that flashed through her at the reminder they weren't going to be together. She had to get her head together when it came to Drake.

This wasn't going to last.

He bit down on her tit, and she moaned his name, wanting him again.

"Please," she said.

The hand on her waist slowly stroked down, moving across her stomach to settle between her thighs. He didn't touch her right away, just put his hand directly over her pussy. She stared at him as he looked down at her.

He didn't avert his gaze as he slid a finger between her slit, touching her clit. She let out a gasp. His gaze remained on her as he moved down to plunder inside her pussy. She spread her legs wide.

"Are you sore?"

"A little, but I don't want you to stop."

"I don't think I can stop." He teased her, drawing his finger back up to stroke her clit before moving down again to work her body.

She had no control over it. Her body burned with need and as he stroked her, she melted against him, wanting him even more than last night.

He suddenly pulled his fingers from her body, and she groaned, not wanting him to stop. Only, Drake had no intention of stopping. He started to kiss down her body, going toward her pussy.

She watched him as he hovered over her, crying out his name when he sucked on her nub. He held her pussy open and ravished her, his tongue repeatedly stroking over her clit. Next, he began to work her entrance, teasing her before coming back up and sucking at her nub once again. She couldn't keep looking at him, not when the pleasure was so intense. She fell back to the bed, grabbing the sheets beneath her as he toyed with her, playing her pussy to the point she couldn't even think straight. All she wanted was her orgasm and he was the only person to give it to her.

"Drake, I'm going to come," she said.

He didn't stop and as she came, he held her in place, keeping her down on the bed. She wasn't silent.

Her body complete, sated, and ready for more of what he could give her.

Drake wasn't finished with her yet. He wanted more. He kissed his way up her body, and as she cupped his cheek, he reached between them, grasping his cock. She didn't need to see him do it to know what he was doing. She spread her legs and he slid the tip of his cock between her slit, bumping against her clit before moving down to her entrance.

She was still sore but there was no way she wanted to stop this. Not now, not ever.

Drake stared into her eyes as he began to sink within her.

One inch.

Two inches.

By the third, he held her hips and slammed in deep. They both cried out. It was a little uncomfortable for her but not painful. Wrapping her legs around his waist, she held on to him, staring up at him and marveling at just how perfect he was.

"I can't get enough of you," he said, pulling out of her only to slam back inside.

She gasped.

"I'm never going to forget this, or you." He kissed her hard as he took her and she moaned his name, not wanting him to leave her alone. Drake held her in place as he fucked her and when he broke the kiss, he did so to trail his lips down. With his cock still working inside her, he cupped her tits and began to tease over her nipples.

With each flick of his tongue, she felt an answering release in her core. She knew he wasn't long from his own release as he took her hands, pressing them above her head while he fucked her. He held her down and she watched as he came, thrusting in deep as he did so.

It was quick, intense, and as he collapsed on top of her, she knew this was how it was going to be between them. There was no way it could be any other way.

"I had hoped to last a little longer," he said. His voice muffled as his face pressed between her breasts.

She let out a chuckle. "I don't mind."

"I don't know what it is you do to me, Pru. I can't seem to get a hold of myself."

"I'm not going to complain." She cupped his cheek. "I really like doing this with you."

He lifted up. "You do?"

"I don't even know why we're having these kinds of conversations. They're weird."

"When I'm with you, I feel like I can be myself."

"You can. There's no reason to hide."

Drake's stomach began to rumble and she laughed. "We're going to need to get up and deal with your growing problem."

"I've got two growing problems. Give me a couple of minutes and I'll be ready for round two."

"You're always ready," she said.

"Only for you." He kissed her again.

"I'm going to have to feed you. I don't want you passing out on me and then I'll have to scream. It'll be a scary thing."

He laughed. "I could eat."

She lifted up but he was still inside her. "Drake, you have to move."

"I'm not ready to move just yet." He took her hands and placed them back above her head. "I rather like having you here, at my mercy."

"You do?" She tried to lift her hands away but as she knew, he had her trapped in one place. "You're right, Drake. I'm here. I'm all yours. What will you do with me?"

"There is a lot I want to do to you." He pressed both of her hands together so he was only holding them down with one. "Are you going to beg me?"

"Do you want me to?"

"I don't know if I should get you to beg me to let you go, or to ask for more."

"What is it you want to do to me?" she asked.

Before he got a chance to respond, they heard the front door of the beach house open up.

Drake tensed and quickly climbed off her.

"Who is that?" she asked.

She lifted the bedsheet just as the doors to the bedroom opened.

"I've found them."

Pru recognized the man as Drake's father. She couldn't recall his name but the look he gave her would stay with her forever.

Seconds later, they were joined by Drake's mother.

"How … disappointing," his mother said.

"What the hell are you two doing here?" Drake asked.

"We got a tip and believe me, I'm pleased we came. You have to learn to choose your weekend's entertainment more wisely. We don't need you making a mistake like this."

"You need to leave. I'm not doing anything wrong."

"Your daughter is in here."

Much to Pru's embarrassment, her parents walked into the room. They looked pale, annoyed, and again, disappointed.

"I'm so sorry," her father said, looking at Drake's mother. "It won't happen again."

"Be sure that it does. My son doesn't need to mingle with the likes of your slutty daughter. If I see her near my boy again, there will be consequences."

Pru felt sick to her stomach. She'd never been in the same room as Drake's mom and now, she was even happier she hadn't before. This was so embarrassing and humiliating.

"Get your clothes on, boy. We're taking you home."

"Everyone get the fuck out," Drake said. He took a step back and Pru kept the blanket wrapped around herself in the hope of trying to protect herself. She was shaking so badly. No woman should ever have to go through this. Not with her parents to see, or anyone to see. She couldn't believe this was happening to her.

She'd lost her virginity, and this had to be the worst experience of all.

"Drake, watch your language and how you speak to me. We're only doing what is best for you. One day, you will see that," his father said.

"What will I see? I didn't invite you here." Drake stepped up to her side, taking her hand. He wasn't shaking or nervous.

She wished she could say the same. Her nerves were getting the better of her. She wanted the floor to open up and swallow her whole. It would certainly make life a little easier.

"It's a good thing as well. Do you really think we want you mingling with these … these people?" his mother asked. "It's bad enough we have to put up with your damn parties and those boys you call friends."

"Without them, you couldn't keep an eye on me. They're not my friends."

"Yes, look what good it has done us. We should've known something like this was going on. You may leave," his father said, looking at her.

Drake held her hand a little tighter. It would seem she wasn't going anywhere, not unless Drake said so. "She's not leaving. You all need to leave, now."

"Son, need I remind you, this place is mine. It has our name on it, not yours."

"I'm still your son and last time I checked, your public image meant more to you than a place near the ocean. A place you rarely visit since it's too secluded to have your image in the paper with all the bullshit you like to pretend you do."

Her heart was pounding. She couldn't believe this was happening to them.

"Take your daughter and leave before I call the cops for trespassing," his mother said to her parents.

"Shut the fuck up, Mom. No one gives a shit about what you've got to say."

"Well, young man, they better because if you think I'm going to let this little tryst slide, you've got another thing coming."

"You're not going to stop us from being together." Drake squeezed her hand, and rather than show any weakness, Pru stood beside him even as she glanced at her parents. She saw the fear in their eyes. They were afraid of Drake's parents, and she knew it wasn't without cause.

She didn't know what to say or do to make this any easier for them. She loved Drake and had been willing to just let this all slide and not have a life with him once graduation came around. But now? What was she going to do? It seemed impossible.

His mother laughed. "Oh, you stupid, darling boy. You have no idea how ridiculous you sound."

"I don't know why the whore and those ... people are still here. Take your daughter and leave," his father said.

"She's not going anywhere," Drake said.

"Look, son, you think you've got the upper hand here, but you don't. You're nothing in the scheme of things." His father turned to look at her. "If you think for even a second you had a chance of getting our money and our name, we would never stoop so low as to give in to scum like you."

"I didn't," Pru said. She hated how wobbly her voice sounded. This was so unfair. Why couldn't she have the strength and confidence to stand at his side and to tell them all to fuck off?

His mother burst out laughing again. "Oh please. I recognize a slut whenever I see one. I bet you've been spreading your legs for all the rich kids. It won't do you any good. Rich men don't go for fat little tramps who'll have any dick."

Pru couldn't believe her parents weren't even standing up for her. They weren't defending her. Looking at them again, she felt so alone and lost. They were her parents. They should be on her side, and yet, they were just there, waiting. They didn't want to be here with her.

Were they embarrassed?

Ashamed?

She couldn't believe it, and yet, looking at them, she didn't know why she would think they would love her unconditionally. She was eighteen years old and could have sex now, and do a lot of other things, and yet they were treating her like a disgrace.

"You won't talk about her like that," Drake said. "She's not you. She's not either of you. You don't know what a good person looks like because you surround yourself with the vilest of people. Pru, she's better than you."

The only person willing to defend her was Drake.

She felt the tears well up, but she wouldn't let them fall. Not here, not now.

His mother sighed and his father chuckled. "Okay, it looks like we're going to have to teach our boy a lesson." His mother looked at Pru. "You really think this girl will ever fit into our world?"

"I don't want her to fit into our world. I want her for myself," Drake said. "She's a good person. I love her."

She smiled up at Drake and they shared a moment, but it was so brief. "You should let me go," Pru said.

"Finally, at least one of you sees sense," his father said.

"I'm not going to let you go. We can do this together."

"My parents are afraid, Drake. I can't do this to them. Your parents run everything in town. They fund the shops, the mall, everything. They have created jobs with their factories, and have sway at the bank. My parents can't afford their debts, not if they make them pay."

"Yes, I would listen to her. You see, Drake, if you don't let your slut go, I will make sure that not only is her little family run out of town, but she also won't finish school. She won't have any future, and well, when no one can get a job, they always end up on the streets. And I can tell you that's exactly where your little family is heading, Prudence," his mother said with a smile.

She had never met anyone so cruel in all of her life. They didn't even pretend to be any different.

Drake had bullied her, but this was a whole new level of mean. His parents would ruin her life and her family's just because they could. She didn't even know if she could stand to be in the same room as them.

"Don't let them win," Drake said to her.

Then to his dad, he said, "I'm not giving her up. If you do what you say you do, I'll make sure everyone in the world knows what monsters you really are. Let's face it, the only reason you're still relevant is because they believe all the lies you manipulate the papers with."

His parents looked at each other and smiled. "Son, you're not exactly in your right mind. You do well at school, but you've always been a troubled young man."

Before her eyes, Pru watched the couple go from looking all-powerful and in control, to seemingly filled with sadness and at a loss. Their performance was outstanding, and if anyone else had been watching them, they would feel for them.

She couldn't believe what she was seeing but it was the Connors, and they didn't care enough about her or her parents to even pretend what they were doing. They meant nothing to them.

"No one would believe you, son," his father said. "Just do as we tell you, and stop this."

****

How could this have happened so quickly? His parents didn't even know where he was half of the time and yet, here they were, telling him what to do. Drake held Pru's hand like it was a lifeline and in truth, it was.

He didn't want to let her go. His parents were wrong for making him do this.

Even a quick glance at her parents told him there was no chance of them helping. They turned a blind eye to his parents' manipulations.

Running a hand down his face, he still kept a hold of Pru. Once again, his parents had all the power while he didn't. If he went against them, he had no doubt this would be bad for Pru and her family.

"They're right," Pru said.

"What's that?" his father asked.

"You're both right."

Even as he fought to keep hold of her hand, Pru broke away from him. "I mean, come on. Why would I really want to date him?"

Drake frowned. "Pru, what the fuck are you doing?"

"I'm being real, for once. I mean, don't get me wrong, it wasn't easy being fake. I'm not a fake person, but you were so easy to fool. It's almost too funny how quickly you fell for it. I'm kind of shocked, really. You were always this big deal at school. All the girls practically falling over themselves to be with you. I figured I wanted a piece of the pie and what better way than making you fall for me. I have to admit though, you're not worth this effort. Sorry, you're not." She pulled away from him and looked at him. She shrugged. "I'm sure you'll get over it."

He stared at her, knowing she was faking this. She had to be.

"You were just so easy. Always looking for love rather than just accepting the fact it's not going to be coming to you. No one will ever love you, Drake."

"Now, I think you've made your point," his father said.

Pru pulled away from him and turned on her heel to leave.

Drake watched her go, knowing deep in his heart this was a performance for his parents. He had to believe that, even as a part of him had to wonder if what she said was true.

Don't be a dick.

She's trying to help.

Don't fuck this up.

He turned back to look at his parents who had smug grins on their faces that he wanted to wipe off. They were happy to see him suffer and it pissed him off. They were going to find out one day that taking him on would be their biggest mistake.

All of his life, he'd hated his parents, but those feelings, they didn't even begin to come close to how much he despised them at this very moment. He wanted to hurt them, to make them pay for what they had done. To watch them suffer, to hear them scream and beg him for forgiveness.

"You see, son, love is just a fucked-up mess. You've got to learn to keep women for one thing and one thing only, fucking." His father snorted, shook his head, and left the room.

"Drake, as soon as she's gone, get your ass home," his mother said. "I don't want to have to deal with taking the trash out anymore."

Pru's parents were still waiting.

He stared at them, and for some reason, he was so incredibly disappointed in them.

"You didn't fight for her," he said.

"You shouldn't have brought her out here," her father said.

"Neither of you gave a fuck about what my parents said." He couldn't believe he was looking at her parents. "Get the fuck out." He turned on his heel and went toward where Pru was.

"We would advise you against talking to our daughter."

"She's not your daughter. No parent would let another speak about their child like that." With that, he slammed into the bathroom.

Pru was nearly dressed. She pulled up her jeans

and he saw the tears in her eyes. He pushed the door closed, he didn't have to wait long before she threw herself into his arms.

"I'm so sorry." She whispered the words against his ear.

"It's okay."

"It's not, though. It's really not. I saw they were being serious and I panicked. I shouldn't have said the stuff I did, but hearing them, seeing what they were doing to you, knowing they wouldn't back down, I had to."

"It's okay." He ran his hands down her back just basking in holding her. His parents were wrong about her, about him.

"It's really not okay. I shouldn't have had to say or do any of those things." She pulled away, cupping his face. "What are we going to do?"

"We're going to keep on doing what we do best. Seeing each other without them knowing."

"Someone knew we were here, Drake. Someone told them. I don't know who. We've been so careful."

"It could have been someone in town. My father's not exactly a faithful man."

"What if it's not? What if someone back home knows and this is their way of getting payback?"

"Then they're in for a world of pain when I find them. No one messes with what I've got. Your parents are still waiting outside." He scowled, hating the fact he'd done nothing. His parents came, ruined everything, and left, and he'd let them.

"What are we going to do?" she asked.

He didn't like how helpless she looked. "I'm going to deal with this."

"How?" She pressed her hands to her face and groaned. "We should have known this wasn't possible."

"Don't say that."

"It's the truth. Look what's happening here. My parents are outside waiting to take me home, and yours, they didn't even stick around to see you leave. I don't know what's happening right now and it's kind of freaking me out. What do we do? I have no answers."

Drake didn't know what to say to her. He felt the panic rise up.

They both froze as there was a knock on the door.

"Come on, you two. We can't let you stay in there forever. Hurry up," her father said.

His anger once again rose to the surface. He couldn't protect either of them from inside a bathroom. "How can they even call themselves your parents?"

"Drake, they can't do anything."

"Don't justify their actions. Not to me. Not right now."

"I'm not trying to. I'm really not. This is so hard, watching them as your parents talked to me like that. Other than you, no one has ever treated me like that. I…" She stopped talking and he watched her return to crying.

It broke his heart to see her like this. "Please don't cry."

"We've got no way of winning this. No way at all. I don't know what we're going to do," she said.

"You keep repeating that."

"Because it's the truth. What *can* we do?" She rubbed at her chest. "I feel like all of this is hopeless. We're on our own. No one is ever going to help us."

He couldn't bear to have her like this. It hurt him to see her sound so helpless.

What can you really do?

Your parents are going to destroy every single kind of happiness you have.

He pulled her to him, kissing the top of her head

and just breathing her in.

"You know there's nothing we can do. We're all alone," she said. "I can't believe they called me a slut."

"You don't listen to them. Not ever." He pulled away, cupping her face. "Look at me. What I did to you before, I want you to forget all of that. My parents, they don't know what they're talking about. They're fucking idiots."

"But…"

"No buts. Don't listen to them. They want to get inside your head and destroy who you are but we're not going to let that happen. You and me, we're going to stay strong."

"You were right, Drake. We can't win this. You've got to let me go."

His parents had taken everything away from him, and it seemed they weren't done with ruining him even more. Any kind of happiness, no matter the size, they were always there, set to ruin it for him, and he couldn't handle that. Not anymore.

Gritting his teeth, he shook his head. "No, I'm not going to let you go. Not now, not ever."

"Drake, we both know there's no use in fighting this. They're the ones who will win in the end."

"Not if we fight back." He didn't know why he was having such a huge change of heart over this, only that he had to do something now.

"Drake, there's no point," she said. "It's fine. We both knew this was going to happen in the end. It only stopped now, rather than later. It's fine."

"It's not fine," he said.

Her parents were still waiting, and he couldn't think with them close, willing to take Pru away.

"This isn't over," he said. "Tell me you don't want to leave me, leave us."

Tears fell down her face and he tried to wipe them away but they just kept falling.

"Please, don't cry."

"I can't help it. I don't want this to end between us but I don't know how we can save this. It's so hopeless."

"I don't believe that."

"What?"

"I don't believe what we have is hopeless. Do you trust me?" he asked.

She frowned at him. "What are you going to do?"

"I need to know if you trust me."

"Yes, of course I do."

"Good. I'm going to make this work. I promise you. I just needed to know you trust me and that you're with me."

"Always. I love you, Drake."

"And I love you." He pressed a kiss to her lips. "Always. Never forget that."

Chapter Twenty
What is the plan?

Driving home with her parents was the worst thing Pru could ever think of doing. They were silent and even in their refusal to speak, she knew they were judging her. She couldn't blame them for being angry. They had always asked her to stay away from Drake, but she hadn't heeded the warning, and now look where they were.

Soon, she was back her home with parents who wouldn't speak to her, and she hadn't heard from Drake, which scared her. She didn't want him to be punished.

Her birthday weekend had gone from fun to crap within minutes. How did they know they were there? Who knew? She hadn't told a soul about her relationship with Drake, so how did anyone know? None of this made any sense to her.

They'd been so careful.

She stared at her cell phone.

Her parents were downstairs, talking in whispered tones. Running a hand down her face, she tried to clear her mind, but it wasn't happening. She had to confront her parents so she knew exactly what was going on.

Climbing off her bed, she threw her cell phone on top of the covers and headed down into the lion's den. She'd never been afraid to see her parents, but right now, she couldn't help but feel a little sick and at a loss for words.

"What do you think we should do?" her father said.

"I don't think there's anything we can do. I hope they're both not stupid enough to just see this is about them. It's not. It's about all of us."

"Why couldn't she have been with Sean? It

would have been a whole lot easier."

She closed her eyes. She hated hearing the disappointment in their voices but nothing was going to change what they saw and were part of. She didn't mean to fall in love with Drake, it just happened. For the most part, she couldn't even believe it. They had started out hating each other and now, well, she'd do anything for him.

Entering the dining room, she clenched her hands into fists and looked at her parents.

"Hey, Mom, Dad," she said.

They turned to look at her. Neither of them said a word.

"Is this how it's going to be? You're going to ignore me?"

"We expected better from you," her father said. "For the longest time, you've hated that boy and now we find out you were sneaking around with him."

"We both knew our relationship wouldn't be taken well. Look at the way you acted around his parents. Neither of us had done anything wrong and yet you couldn't even look at me or defend me."

"Do you have any idea the kind of power they hold? Do you know what they do to people who stand in their way? Before we came along, a young family lived here. The man was a worker and he wanted an increase in pay. He tried to rally the workers, and what did he get, his mortgage came due? He was run out of town for drug smuggling, and his wife, she ended up in prison for fraud. This is the kind of people we're dealing with. You make waves, a debt is called, or your job is on the fucking line, or maybe some old warrant appears for your arrest. Something is always there on their side! This isn't just some family who'll look the other way. They will destroy any kind of happiness we hope to have. Is that what you want? To destroy all of our chances here?"

They were treating her like the enemy.

Pain sliced through her.

"All you can think about is yourselves. You don't care about me or what I want. Just what you guys want." Pru couldn't believe what she was hearing and yet, it didn't seem to matter. "I've got to go," she said.

"You're not leaving this house. You're not going anywhere near that boy again. Do you understand me?" Now it was her mother standing up, glaring at her.

"You're telling me I'm grounded?"

"Yes."

"You've never grounded me."

"You've never acted so recklessly before. This isn't about you. You won't see that boy again. I mean it, Pru. We're finally in a good place in this town, and you're not going to ruin it for us. For any of us." Her mother slapped her hand down on the table. "Go to your room. I'll bring you dinner. I can't even look at you right now."

She hated this. As she glanced at the door, the temptation to run was so strong, but she knew it would only prove how childishly she was reacting. She had to bide her time. To know when to pick the right battles, and today wasn't the right time. Turning on her heel, she made her way back up to her room. Rather than slam the door, she closed it quietly.

Her cell phone buzzed on her bed, letting her know someone was calling. She saw it was Drake and quickly answered.

"Hey," she said. "Did you make it back okay?"

"Yeah. What about you? Anything with your parents?"

"They're treating me like I'm the enemy," she said. "Do you have any idea who could have known about us? I don't know how they were able to find us."

"I don't know, but I will find out. I promise you. I wish I was with you now. You know, holding you," he said.

She smiled. "I do as well. We'll be able to have that again. I know we will." She was lying, but Drake didn't call her out on it. "What do you think we should do tomorrow? It's a school day. Do you think anyone will know?"

"No one will. My parents will make sure of it. Whoever told on us, they'd be paid to keep quiet."

"You did warn me about how bad they can be. I had no idea it would be like this, Drake."

"I know. They're used to getting their own way."

And Drake had to keep in line. All of his anger over the past ten-plus years made a lot of sense to her now. She wasn't going to make excuses for his behavior, but it did make sense. No one could blame him for acting out.

Compared to him, she probably had the most ideal life between the two of them.

"What are you doing right now?" he asked.

"I'm in my room." She paused as she heard someone coming. "I've got to go. Someone's coming. I'll call you back."

She ended the call, pocketing her cell phone as her dad opened her bedroom door. Behind him was Sean.

Her best friend offered her a smile. She couldn't bring herself to smile back.

"I heard you talking. Give me your phone," her father said.

"You can't be serious."

"I know who you were talking to. Give it to me." He growled the words at her and she felt sick to her stomach.

Pulling out the cell phone, she handed it to her father. He placed it in his pocket.

"When will I get that back?"

"When you finally learn your lesson. We've told you to ignore that boy, and look what happened. Sean, talk some sense into her."

"Wait a minute. Why are you talking about this in front of Sean?" she asked, looking from her dad to her best friend.

Sean stepped into the bedroom. "I think we should talk."

"I don't know if I want to talk to you." There was no way Sean could have known. She and Drake were so freaking careful.

"You should be thanking Sean for not letting you screw up your life, or our family's. He's a good kid."

Her dad had left the tray of food on the bed but Pru wasn't interested in eating. She was more focused on the guy in front of her.

"You're the one who told?"

Sean sighed. "Don't look at me like that. I didn't want to."

"Wait, you're admitting you ruined my birthday by telling my and Drake's parents we were seeing each other? How did you even know? What right do you have to go telling people's secrets like that?"

"You were making a mistake."

"What? By your standards?" she asked. "You don't think I'm good enough for Drake?"

"Not good enough?" Sean burst out laughing. "Oh, please. I know you're good enough for Drake. You're too good for him. He had no right to you. Never had a right to you. You're better than him and his fucked-up family."

Pru pulled away from him, not really recognizing

the boy before her.

"This is ... you did this? You really knew? How?"

"Out of everything I just said to you, this is what you're picking up on?"

"How can I not pick up on this? You're my best friend and rather than ask me, you assumed and just ... how could you do this? Why didn't you come to me?" she asked.

"And have you lie to me, like you've been lying every time you've been with him. You and Drake, you were so full of each other you didn't even realize you were being watched. He's not worth your time. I did you a favor."

She laughed. "You think you've done me a favor? My family hates me. I had to take all of his parents' insults. I'm not a slut. I love Drake and he loves me."

"He's using you."

"You're wrong, Sean. If he was using me, we wouldn't have ever been caught and he would've made sure my humiliation was complete." She shook her head. "You're wrong about him. I was wrong about him."

Sean stepped closer and she pulled back, wrapping her arms around her waist and wanting nothing to do with him. She didn't want him anywhere near her.

"You can't be serious right now. Do you even remember what he did to you? Not his friends, him. Drake, he can't be trusted."

She lifted her head, staring at her best friend. "You've always been my best friend. Stood by me. Why didn't you come to me? Why did you have to go behind my back?"

Sean lowered his hands and released a sigh. "You weren't thinking straight."

"And you thought you could think for me, is that

it?"

"Pru."

"No!" She turned and glared at him. "I don't want to hear you speak. I don't want to hear you say anything. I'm done listening to you."

"Pru, don't do this," Sean said.

"Do what, Sean? Don't listen to you? Do you have any idea what you've done? Any idea at all? Do you even care?"

"Of course I care."

She snorted. "You could have fooled me. You told my parents. You told Drake's parents rather than come to me. Do you see the way they're treating me now? Like I'm some kind of troubled kid."

"Aren't you?" Sean asked.

"What?" She couldn't believe she was hearing this from him.

Sean picked up one of her fries from off her plate and shoved it into his mouth. "I don't mean to be a pain in the ass and state the obvious, but come on, Pru. You've been secretly dating Drake. Surely that has to come from some lapse in judgment. I'm sorry, but you're seriously troubled."

"I'm not joking around right now, Sean. I'm being serious."

"So am I!" He stood up and Pru glared at him. She was so freaking pissed at him. Not once did he even ask her about what she was doing or what her plans were. He just threw out assumptions. She was done playing this kind of game with him, with anyone. No one had any right to tell her what to do or how to live her life. She wasn't a horrible person.

He advanced toward her, grabbing her arms. His strength took her by surprise and she let out a gasp. "Let go of me."

"No. I'm not going to let go until you realize how fucking stupid you're being. Drake is a grade-A asshole, and you can't even see it. You're so blinded by your own hormones, you're being ridiculous."

"You're crazy." She tried to push him away.

"Think about this, Pru. What happened? You've been acting strangely since the night Ree called you to go to his party. Where I had to wait outside. What happened in there? Does he have something on you? Is he blackmailing you?"

"No one is blackmailing me."

"Could have fooled me."

"You don't know what you're talking about."

"I don't know what I'm talking about? Pru, you had sex with Drake. The guy who has been bullying you for as long as I can remember. You don't think there's something weird about that? I sure as fuck do."

"It doesn't matter. You're not my boss. You're supposed to be my friend and what you did, you should have come to me first." She stared down at his arms, which were still gripping her tightly. He sighed, releasing his tight hold, but he still held her. Pru didn't know if she even wanted his touch anymore. For as long as she'd known Sean, he'd been a caring, considerate person. She loved him but only as a friend. Never as anything more.

"He bullied you. Made your life miserable. Your parents couldn't do anything to protect you, and yet, you're still here fighting for him, why?"

"Because I care about him, and that's never going to change," she said. "Drake's not who I thought he was, but then, neither are you."

"Don't, Pru. Don't say stuff like that."

"How do you expect me to react after everything I've just found out?" She couldn't believe how close to tears she actually was. Sean's betrayal hurt so much.

More than she ever thought it could.

"Pru," he said, running his hands up and down her arms. They didn't offer her comfort, not anymore. She pulled out of his arms and shook her head.

"Seriously? You're going to let that asshole come between us after everything we've been through?"

"What exactly have we been through? Nothing. Not really. Whenever he has bullied you, I stepped in. You rarely stepped in to help me, and now, rather than come to me, you went to my parents." She shook her head. Her emotions were driving her crazy. "I want nothing to do with you."

"You don't know what you're saying."

"Why? Because I'm not thanking you for seeing the light? There is no way I'd ever thank you for what you've put me through. I want nothing to do with you. Get out of my room." She pushed him, not hard, but enough to make him take a step back.

"You have no idea what you're saying."

"That's where you're wrong. So fucking wrong."

"You swear now?"

"I do a hell of a lot more than that. Get out!" She screamed the words and pushed him out the door. The sooner he got out of her life, the better she'd feel.

When he was past the threshold, she glared at him. "You're not my friend." She slammed the door in his face and leaned against it, her head falling back on the wood. This wasn't how she wanted her life to be. There was no way she should be feeling hatred for him. In all the years she'd known Sean, she never once thought he'd betray her, and yet that was exactly what he did.

Glancing around her room, she hated it. Not only was it really small, but it reminded her of a life she no longer wanted to be part of.

There was a slight knock on her bedroom window. Walking over to it, she lifted it up and was shocked to see Drake hanging near her window, having climbed the tree just outside her room.

"Are you crazy?" she asked.

"Anyone in your room?"

"No."

"I saw the asshole leave," he said.

"What are you doing here?"

"You wouldn't answer any of my calls, so I wanted to make sure you were okay. The last thing I wanted was for my parents to send you away."

"They took my phone. Wait. Hold up. How would they send me away?"

"They have power everywhere. I know they've used their power with the cops to plant evidence. Drugs, money. I don't know what they will use but something that will get you taken away. I wouldn't be surprised if they didn't know I was here now, or not. They assume I do as I'm told."

"You've got to be quiet," she said as he climbed through her window. "My parents could walk in at any moment."

"I'll be quiet."

She closed the window and glanced at her door. "Did Sean leave my house?"

"I don't know. He's probably talking with your parents and saying how you'll get over the betrayal and he'll marry you. You'll have lots of Sean babies."

"Don't. I don't even want to talk about this right now."

"I was only joking around. You really think I'd let that fucker have what's mine?" He cupped her face, stroking her cheeks with his thumb. "I don't share."

"This isn't a joke. Sean found out about us."

"Because he's a perv. I recall telling you he wasn't a good guy."

"Yeah, and now he's even more of an asshole. Ugh, I hate this. How can you stand this?" she asked, pulling out of his arms and walking back to her bed. She sat on the edge and looked at him. "They could be watching you."

"And if they are, we'll give them a show."

"I'm being serious."

"So am I. My parents aren't watching me. If they were, I wouldn't have even been able to come here now. They've assumed I've followed their orders but they need to realize no one tells me what to do."

"No one?"

"No one." He pulled her in close. His face pressed against her neck and she closed her eyes, enjoying their closeness. "I've missed this with you. Missed it so freaking much."

"We've only been apart a couple of hours."

"Those hours have felt way too long." He kissed her neck and pulled back. "How are you?"

"I'm fine."

"No, I mean really, not just because of the sex but everything else."

"Everything else?"

"My parents."

She nibbled her lip and sighed. "I don't know what to say about them. It was intense."

"It was more than intense. Don't listen or even for a second doubt what is going on. You're amazing. I want you to always remember that."

"You're worried?"

"Of course, I am. Why wouldn't I be? The last thing I want is for you to run off and be with someone else," he said. He stepped away from her, cursing.

"I hate to break this to you, Drake, but I'm not going anywhere. If I can still be friends with you, and us have this fun, then you've got me for a lot longer. A parent calling me a slut or whore, or whatever it was they called me—it's gone a little fuzzy—I can handle it. After all, I did handle your bullying for a long time. Don't forget that." She stepped up close to him, wrapping her arms around his waist.

"You're a lot stronger than I give you credit for," he said.

"Don't underestimate me. I'll surprise you."

"You always fucking surprise me." He stroked her cheek.

"You're going to have to go again, aren't you? You can't stay here."

"I bet your parents would allow Sean."

"I know. I'm sorry he ruined everything. You were right about him the whole time."

"I did warn you."

"And I didn't listen because I'd never seen that side to him. I messed up. I'm sorry. I hope you can forgive me." She rested her head against his chest again, listening to his heartbeat. She smiled, loving the erratic sound.

He stroked her hair and for a few short seconds, she truly felt happy. Pushing all of their problems to the back of her mind, she closed her eyes and enjoyed the feel of him surrounding her.

"I loved every single second of our weekend together."

"You have no regrets?"

"None. I wish your parents hadn't come, obviously, but there's nothing I can do to change that." She tilted her head back and offered him another smile. He cupped her cheek and she pressed her face against his hand. "You're going to have to go soon."

"I will. I just needed to see you, to know you're still okay, and you're alive, and well, that you're safe."

"It kind of scares me how worried you are about your parents."

"You have no idea what they're capable of."

"I'm starting to get an idea. You think they can kill me?" she asked, joking around. One look at his face, and she knew this wasn't a joking matter. "I was kidding."

"I wish I was. You know, I didn't care about them for a long time, or worry. I lived my life and I knew they already had a plan, then you came along, and now, I can't stand them. I want nothing to do with them, and there's nothing I can do to stop them."

"We can."

"I doubt it." He pressed a kiss to her lips.

"Don't be so negative." She couldn't deny how afraid she was that he was right, but there was no way she was going to believe they couldn't be together because of his parents' say-so. There had to be a way for them.

She heard movement downstairs and she groaned. "You're going to have to go."

"Or I could stay here. Do you think they're going to let Sean leave? It's late and I can already see them pushing the two of you together."

"I will never love Sean or be with him. He was my best friend."

"Was?"

"I don't know how I can be his friend after what he's done. It's not fair."

"I hate to break this to you, sweetheart, but life isn't fair." He pushed some of her hair back.

"I know but friends shouldn't do that to each

other." She put her hands on his chest, feeling his heartbeat. "I don't think you'd understand."

"I have friends."

"Friends don't sleep with each other's friends, and they don't step out on you like that. There is a code."

"Ree's not your friend then."

"I don't want to know what happened between you and Ree."

"Nothing happened because she wasn't important to me. You are. You matter to me." He pressed a kiss to her lips. "I love being with you and I had no idea I could feel this way. To think I could have fucked this all up with how much I've been mean to you."

She smiled. "You don't have to go. Sean's not coming in here. I don't want you to leave."

"I don't want to go."

She wrapped her arms around him, holding him close, and he pushed off his shoes.

He removed his jacket and she put it in her closet in case her parents walked in. She doubted they would.

Chapter Twenty-One
Never wanted to leave

Drake knew deep down this thing he had with Pru would be coming to an end. All his life, he'd bullied her. Pushed her around, and for what? To fall in love with her and to lose her just as fast. He'd been a complete dick to her, and there was no turning back from what he'd done.

Stroking back her hair, he watched her sleep, knowing there was no way he was ever going to stop loving her. She was everything he had ever wanted in his life and only realized it recently.

"I want to love you for the rest of my life," he said. She was fast asleep and wouldn't be waking any time soon.

When she did wake, he'd need to leave. Her parents had already gone to bed. He'd been frozen in place as one of them had lingered outside her door, but they had clearly thought better of entering. They had left her alone and he didn't know if it pissed him off more to know they weren't even going to try to make things right. No one had a right to speak to their daughter like his parents had, but they'd been too cowardly to speak up.

This was all his fault. If he hadn't taken her away, or if he'd been even more careful in seeing her, she would still be in his world now.

He held a piece of her hair, running it back and forth through his fingers.

"I never thought I could care for anyone the way I do you."

She let out a sigh and snuggled up closer to him. He pressed his lips against her head and knew he couldn't fall asleep. Not yet. After another hour of holding her, he finally eased out of bed. He got dressed, all the while watching her as she slept through his movements. He didn't want to wake her up.

With his clothes back on, he walked over to the window, lifted it up, and climbed out. He had to find a way to get his parents off his back and away from Pru. They could run away, but it wouldn't work. They would find some way to manipulate all the people around them, and have Pru pay the price. He wouldn't allow her to be hurt any more than she already had.

Dropping to his feet at the bottom of the tree, he then walked off her property and headed home. Once he arrived at the gates of his house, he stared at the large building, hating it on sight.

People always admired the large mansion, but it was all lies. His life wasn't easy in this place. It was a fucking nightmare, and it was only now he realized how much he hated it. Shoving his hands into his pockets, he entered his home.

No one was waiting and he listened. There were no cars parked out on the driveaway. His parents weren't home. They'd given him an instruction and expected him to abide by their rules. He would never do as he was told again. Instead of going to his room, and as there was no way he could sleep, he went straight to his father's office.

Entering the room, he glanced around at all the traditional décor. His father had always been a little bit of a traditionalist. It hadn't stopped him from screwing the women in charge of decorating, though.

The large mahogany desk spread out near the windows. The black chair was more suited to being in a company as a CEO's chair or something like that. He'd watched his father sitting at the desk, looking like he was king of the world when it was the furthest thing from the truth. His father got off on hurting those in his way, of crushing them.

Both of his parents did.

Moving behind the desk, he took a seat and put his hands flat to the surface, staring across the room. Sitting back, he looked at the drawers and started to try to open them. None of them would open. A little lock on each corner kept him out.

He'd never taken the time to think of his father as a person, or where he'd hide keys. Getting to his feet, he looked around the room.

There were several large pieces of artwork. His father was a bit of a collector, but again, he didn't see the appeal. He touched one piece and it didn't move. With the next, it tilted forward and the keys spilled out of the bottom, dropping onto the floor.

It all seemed a little … easy. There was no way these were the keys to the desk, but as he tried one key and gave it a turn, it didn't move. He checked the other five drawers, and it was the last one at the bottom of the opposite side that sprang open.

It was empty.

Using the other keys, he opened up the desk. There was nothing in most of the drawers. Papers and pens in another. No letters. No evidence of the monster in control.

Sitting back, he tapped his fingers on the desk.

Maybe the evidence he needed to hurt his parents wouldn't be lying around in the office as it was the most obvious place to look. Getting to his feet, he left, heading upstairs to his parents' suit. They didn't share a room and hadn't for as long as Drake could remember.

The first room had to belong to his mother. It was too floral and perfect to be his father's. The moment he entered the right room, he knew it was his father's. It had a brand-new bachelor feel, which would have been exactly what he organized to have.

His father liked the idea of being a free man, but he wasn't, not really. Like his father before him, they were all trapped.

He didn't sit down but spun around, wondering if this would be where any delicate information would be stored. He had no doubt there had to be evidence here of some kind. His father was too paranoid to not have something close by.

Drake knew there would be information in safety deposit boxes, offices, with lawyers, and trusted assets, but it wouldn't all be in one place. The darkest shit had to be closest to him.

There was only one way to truly find out, and he moved toward the closet, opening it. The suits were all neatly lined up. It looked like a true, modern-day businessman's wardrobe. All pristine, orderly, and perfect.

Drake didn't know when it happened, but he had grown to hate perfection. Being surrounded by it for all of his life, he only saw how toxic it was.

Pushing the pants to one side, he knew there was no point in checking them. His father would never be so foolish as to leave pants lying around for anyone to see. No matter where he turned. There didn't appear to be a single clue to help him or Pru.

After leaving his father's bedroom, he entered his mother's. He never came to this room. The last time he did hadn't been pretty. His parents liked to present to the world a united front but behind closed doors, they despised each other. It often surprised Drake how they were able to have a child in the first place. Their hatred for one another knew no bounds.

The heavy scent of perfume hung in the air, and it was almost too strong to even stand.

Where his father wouldn't be stupid enough to

leave evidence lying around, he hoped his mother was too … trusting and conceited to even think of hiding her true self. He would love to see her face when the world saw her.

If only she kept video proof of her indiscretions.

He walked over to her vanity table and looked over the contents. Perfumes, makeup, hairbrushes, and combs all were placed on the surface. He didn't dare move one, in case she suspected someone was snooping.

Drake sat down at the table and slowly opened each drawer, finding underwear. He moved it gently to one side, hoping to find something, anything to use on them so he wouldn't have to abandon Pru.

The vanity table was clear. Next, he moved toward the closet. Unlike his father's pristine display of clothes, his mother was messy. Clothes were strewn all over. She never wore the same outfit twice, so why would she even need to keep anything neat and tidy? In the far corner, he noticed a couple of plain cardboard boxes. They didn't appear to be anything important and he pushed some of her clothes to one side to get a better look. Opening the boxes, he saw some old letters and photos. He pushed them to one side and found a locked safe. Lifting it, he inspected the box and frowned. It didn't look like something his mother would own. It even looked a little cheap, which got his suspicions rising.

In order to have complete control over his own life, he needed to know what was in the box. It could be nothing, but he couldn't allow his parents to know he'd even been snooping.

Pissed off that he'd hit a dead end, he glanced around the closet. With the size of the thing, it was almost another room. It certainly was big enough for a bed and someone to live here. Before he took his time getting to know Pru, he was exactly like his parents.

Always wanting the best and looking down on those who had so little.

Pru had opened his eyes a great deal, and he didn't want to lose her or what he'd gained in the process. His parents and their ideals were the monsters, not him. He'd changed and there was no way he was going to live the rest of his life bowing down to their needs when they weren't his own. He would fight them at every single turn. He wasn't afraid of them. What he needed to be was smart so his parents wouldn't know what he was up to.

At the bottom of the box, he saw a single key. He couldn't believe his mother would leave a key in plain sight. It wasn't like her.

Sliding the key into the lock, he flicked it open.

There was no way it could have worked. Opening the lid, he stared inside. At first, he wasn't sure what he saw. There was a single folder. Plain cream and it had his name written on it. He pulled it out of the safe and glanced over it. Turning over the front cover, he saw files and pictures pinned to the back. He removed the metal clasp, looking up and flicking through the paperwork.

He didn't understand it.

His name was on the form and so was his father's. Sitting down on the floor, he read through the official medical letter, nibbling on his lip as he read the letter.

Regret to inform you you're unable to father children. The words were right there in black and white.

"I should have known you would try to look for something."

Drake turned his head to see his mother sitting on the bed. He hadn't heard her come back inside. She hadn't tried to kill him and she didn't look angry.

"What is this?" he asked.

"You know exactly what it is. As you've been trying to tell us for some time, you're not stupid."

Right at that moment, he wanted to be stupid. "This doesn't make any sense."

"Oh, come on, Drake. It's not hard to see. Your father can't have children. He's fucking useless. Can bang as many bitches as he sees fit but will never be a father."

"But, how is that possible? I thought he'd ... fathered children."

His mother burst out laughing. "He hasn't fathered anything. Can't do anything with a bunch of blanks and that is exactly what he has to offer. Blanks. He's useless. There's no way he can continue his bloodline."

"If what this document says is true then why are you still with him? You're thirsty for money, power, all of it. Why do you still continue to stay married to him?" He didn't get it. There was no way his mother would marry a man she couldn't stand or stay with him. It just wasn't possible. Something wasn't adding up.

"Your father and I got married long before we realized he was hopeless in that department. Believe me, there's no way I would have stuck around if there wasn't an option."

"How can there be an option? Without another heir, his fortune gets passed on."

"To what? To a bastard child?"

"None of that matters to anyone," he said.

"Oh, please, you fickle child. It still matters. No one wants a bastard."

"But if I'm not my dad's, it's exactly who I am."

"Please, you're your father's child, just not completely," his mother said.

"What the fuck does that mean?" He didn't want

to play riddles, but it would appear his mother did. None of this made any sense. If he wasn't his father's son, then the fortune had to go to the next person in line. He didn't recall any living uncles or aunts. There was no way his mother would allow for that kind of power.

Think, brain, fucking think.

His mother just sat there on the edge of the bed, looking at her nails as if this was all just a boring show. He hated her on sight.

"Are you done trying to scrabble your brains and pretending you care?"

"Who am I?" he asked.

"Your grandfather was a frisky devil. Did you know that?"

"What?" His grandfather had died a couple of years ago, but whenever he took the time to visit, he was always ... around, smiling at him. Wanting to know about his life and who he was with.

"So you don't get confused, I will try to dumb it down. When your grandfather discovered your father couldn't have kids, there was no way he would allow his empire to pass on to no one. So he intended to do anything to make sure his pathetic waste of a son didn't screw this up."

Drake didn't know if he should trust what she was saying. "What does this mean?"

His mother laughed. "It means, my sweet little boy. Your father is not your father. He's your brother."

Drake couldn't believe it but why would she have any reason to lie to him? "No, it's not true."

"Oh, it is. I couldn't divorce your father. We're a powerful couple and hearing the unfortunate news of his inability to father a child, well, your grandfather wasn't going to stand for that. So we made sure this company wouldn't be in the hands of just anyone. No, it would be a son of his, and he'd be around as long as he could to guide that son, but he did have a heart attack, and well, die. Your father has been doing the best he could ever since."

"There's no way you could have kept this secret. Not from prying eyes. You had to have known the mistake you were making."

"I didn't have to deal with anything other than giving birth to you. It was my only job to do. Last I heard, the doctor who knew the truth met a very sad ending. He ate rat poison or something like that. Died painfully. There was nothing that could be done. No one could help him and he was all alone when it happened. He did die a rich man, though. So sad."

"You killed him."

"I didn't do anything of the sort. Your grandfather took care of everything. You were snooping for a reason. There's nothing to stop us. No proof. You, dear boy, are turning into a pain. Do you know what we do with pains?"

Drake got to his feet. "I don't care what you do. There's nothing you can do to me. You both need me more than I need you."

His mother snorted. "You really believe that?"

"Yes, otherwise you'd have gotten rid of me long ago and thought of the payout long before now."

"Okay. You do have a valid point. You're right. For the most part, you are safe and sound. You see, the thing is, Drake, you have a weakness and it's that weakness you show off that will get you killed."

"I don't have a weakness."

"Your poor girl who lives not too far from here. You really think we need to hurt you, when all it will take is striking out at her and her parents? They have no way of protecting themselves. No money and so much debt. We could make their lives even worse."

He wanted to slap her. To lash out and strike her face, to scare her. To do anything so she would be afraid of him. "What do you want?"

"You see? That wasn't so hard now was it? One day you'll see it's going to be easier to just do as you're told. I did."

"I never want to be part of this, or you."

"Son, you're already part of it. There is no getting away from who you are, or what one day you're going to be capable of. You think we're bad, but believe me, there are far worse people out there, willing to do far worse than us. We're like little puppies in the market."

"I doubt that. Stop dawdling. Tell me what you want."

"It's simple. Turn your back on her and never look at her again. It's not hard to do."

"I love her." He didn't beg or plead. Simply stated a fact. His feelings for Pru were love.

"Aw, it's so cute. How you think you've got feelings. There will be plenty of cunts along the way to keep you occupied, some who actually have experience in sucking a cock. Now, stop being a dick, get yourself together, and get the fuck out of my room. You're never going to find anything. Not here, not anywhere, so stop snooping."

Chapter Twenty-Two
Hopeless

Pru stayed home for the rest of the week. Her parents refused to talk to her and she was fine with that. The more she allowed herself to think of their intervention at the beach house, the angrier she got with them.

She was supposed to be their daughter, and rather than protect her, they were more than happy to step aside while those vile people spread their hatred at her. Sean came to visit her, but she ignored him. He brought her homework, which she always did when he was watching her.

He tried to talk to her, and after a couple of hours each night, he would finally get the picture and leave. Without her cell phone, she wasn't able to call Drake, and he still hadn't come to see her. No late-night visits. She stared out the window, looking across the street, but saw no signs of him waiting for her.

With her bag on her shoulder, she walked downstairs, ignoring her parents, just like they were doing with her. Two could play that game. She grabbed a couple of slices of toast with no butter or jam and left.

Sean rolled his car toward her, and she ignored him, biting into her toast.

"You can't keep doing this, Pru. It's not like you."

She took a bite of her toast. She could do whatever the hell she wanted to.

"Do you really think you and Drake had any kind of future? You're wrong. I can't even believe you thought about being with him when I'm standing right here in fucking front of you."

She finished off her toast without giving him a

SAM CRESCENT

look.

"To the likes of him, you're never going to be good enough. How can you even allow yourself to be with someone who only sees you as a means to an end?"

She kept on ignoring him, not wanting anything to do with him. They came to a crossroads and Sean swung his car around, blocking up her path.

She paused, watching him as he climbed out of his car and grabbed her arms. "Will you stop this? It doesn't make you look tough."

Pru couldn't believe it. She laughed at him. "You think I'm doing this to make myself look tough? Are you freaking kidding me right now?"

"I don't get you, Pru. I don't know what the hell is going on with you."

"There isn't anything going on with me right now, Sean."

"I'm your best friend."

She shook her head. "No."

"Don't do this."

"You know what a best friend does?" she asked.

"Pru, I don—"

"They don't go trying to hurt them by taking away one of the people they love. That's right, Sean. What I had with Drake wasn't us messing around. I love him. I know he feels the same way about me, and because you didn't come to me, you could have ruined that for the two of us."

"You never told me."

"Because I knew you'd act like this, and I didn't know if I could trust you. Actually, I wanted to tell you. Drake said you wouldn't understand and so I agreed with him. Do you really think this is easy for me? Having feelings for a guy who has spent every single day I've been here bullying me? No, it wasn't, but I got over it.

You know what? I don't want to talk to you. Not here. Not now. I need to be alone." She pushed his hands away and started walking away.

"I'm going to always be here for you, Pru. I'm not going anywhere."

She didn't stop but kept on moving forward. It was all she could do. Her family didn't understand her. Sean kept on following her in his car, and she didn't acknowledge him. Not even as he kept on talking to her, trying to reason with her. She didn't want to be reasoned with.

All she cared about was being left alone so she could deal with her own problems. Walking across the high school parking lot, she felt like everyone was staring at her. Sean finally pulled away, parking his car, and she went straight toward her locker.

Spinning in the combination, she looked inside and gathered the books she'd need for her first class.

"We need to talk," Drake said, grabbing her arm. He slammed her locker closed and before she knew what was going on, they were inside the boys' bathroom.

"Drake, what's going on?"

He pushed her up against the door. His fingers sank into her hair as he claimed her lips. The kiss was passionate and everything she ever wanted, but something was off.

Pulling away from him, she stared into his eyes, seeing something was wrong.

"What's wrong?"

"Nothing."

"Don't lie to me."

"We've got to go back to pretending."

"Why?"

"I can't risk my parents hurting you."

"Drake, we can't let them win. We can't let

anyone win."

"We're not letting them win. I've got to figure this out."

"There's nothing to figure out."

"Nothing is what I thought it would be. You have no idea what they're capable of."

"Then tell me," she said.

He pulled away and started to pace. He let out a breath and stopped in front of her. "My dad isn't my dad."

"What?"

"I don't even know if I can tell you."

"I don't understand," she said.

"I don't want to give you up. I never want to do that, but I don't know how I'm going to be able to keep this going. Not with my parents knowing. Everything is so fucked up."

"Sean is always around as well. My parents allow him to visit me. I can't believe he was the one to tell them."

"Do you want to be with him?"

"No. I only want to be with you."

"Then we've got to pretend. I can't stop my parents from hurting you, and they will."

"How can they hurt me? I mean, really?"

"You like having a roof over your head, right? Food to eat?"

"Drake, this is ridiculous."

"No, it's not," he said. "You have no idea how bad they can be. I do. I've lived with them. They only know how to cause pain and I can't allow them to hurt you."

"You're scaring me."

"Good," he said. "You have to be scared to know the truth. They're not good people. Do you really think they got into this position for fun? Hell no. They got here because they're fucking assholes." He slammed his fist against the wall, making her jump from the force of it.

"Drake?"

"I'm sorry. I hate this."

She put her hand on his back, trying to comfort him.

He pushed her hand away. "No."

"Drake?"

"I don't want to even consider this between the two of us."

"I don't understand." She frowned.

"This is hopeless."

"If it's so hopeless, why are you we talking about this now? You can't just give up."

"But I want to!" He slammed his foot down.

Pru didn't know what the hell to do. She laughed, then stopped before laughing again. "Okay, so you drag me into the boys' bathroom to tell me we have no hope. Just because your parents have threatened mine." She shook her head. "You know what, Drake? If you got what you wanted, fine. Just tell me."

"What the hell?"

"I mean it. You got me to sleep with you. Congratulations, I fell for you, and I fell hard, but don't try to make me think that your parents have this amazing hold on you that will force your hand to let me go. I know you. I've been your enemy for a long time, and you don't allow anyone to stand in your way or to take from you!" She couldn't stop the tears from falling. This was all a little too much for her right now. She'd been hoping to see him, to know the truth so they could work together, but he was too scared to even take a chance with her. She didn't know how there was even a way or any possible chance for them to be together if he was too determined to fight it.

"You don't understand."

"Yeah, I do."

"My parents will hurt you."

"So what?" she yelled and Drake jerked back. "Do you think this is easy for me? After everything that went down with your disgusting parents. The way they treated me. Do you really think I want this for myself?" She shook her head. "Of course, I don't, but I took it because I knew I wanted you. Now you're saying I'm not good enough to fight when all of our lives, all we've been doing is fighting. Just admit the truth. Tell me you used me to get my virginity. To push me aside."

He stared at her without saying a word.

She wiped at the tears.

Still … nothing.

She didn't know how much more she could take.

"Pru," he said.

She waited.

They could be interrupted at any moment, and still, he said nothing.

"Being with you was the best thing of my life. You've made me realize what a bastard I've been, and that's exactly what I am," he said.

"What?"

"A bastard."

"No, you're not."

"No, you don't understand and I can't tell you the truth."

She watched as he repeatedly ran his fingers through his hair.

"Drake, what's going on? Really?"

He shook his head. "It's over, Pru. That's what is going on. I'm done with this. I don't want to feel guilty about what's going to happen, and you and I, we're done."

"Like that?"

"Exactly like that."

Neither of them spoke. She stared at him, waiting. Again, he did nothing. Just watched her, and she knew it was over between them.

"I can't be with you and we're fooling ourselves. You and I, we're done. I don't want you."

She nodded and wiped at the tears again. "Okay. You're going to let them win."

"It's not about letting them win, Pru. It's about doing what is right."

"Really? And you're doing what is right?"

"Yes."

"If that's the way you feel."

He nodded.

She did the same, nibbling on her lip. "Fine. Then you can stop pulling me into the bathroom. I don't want to see you again or have anything to do with you. You and I are done." She walked past him.

Drake didn't stop her from leaving.

Once outside the bathroom, she didn't know what else to do. People stood outside their lockers and all of them looked happy. She shouldn't care. She should have expected something like this to happen, but she couldn't have known this would. How could she have ever planned for something like this?

Drake didn't want her. She had to move on.

She heard the door open and glanced behind her to see Drake standing there. He had this cocky look on his face, and she wanted to hate him, but she knew what kind of man he really was, and he was giving up.

There was no way she was staying in school. Not today. Not after what just happened. She had to get away from the school, from him. Without looking back, she walked right out of the main doors just as Sean entered.

"Pru, what's going on?"

"Nothing."

"Where are you going?" Sean asked, following her.

"Leave me alone."

"I know you're pissed at me. You can't keep on walking away from me."

She was aware of people watching her but she had to get away. How could she spend the day walking around school with Drake there?

Girls would be all over him and after being with him, she couldn't see that. She wanted to hate him more than anything. To go back to the way she once felt about him. "I'm not staying in school. I'm not going to classes today."

"You can't just quit school."

"Watch me."

"Pru, come on. Don't be like this."

"Why don't you go and tell my parents I'm not sticking around? Isn't that what you like to do? Go and tell someone I'm not being a good girl. I'm not being exactly how you want me to be?" She stopped to glare at him.

"That's not fair."

"No, you know what isn't fair? Your best friend going out of his way to hurt you. That's not fair, which is exactly what you've done. Why didn't you come to me? Why did you have to go to them?" she asked. Tears filled her eyes, she was so angry at him.

He didn't say anything.

She shook her head. "You know what, I don't want to talk to you. We've got nothing to say to each other."

"Don't walk away." He grabbed her arm and she

pushed him away.

"No, you don't get to pretend anymore. I know who you really are, Sean, and guess what, I don't like him." She turned on her heel and walked away.

There was no reason for her to stick around. What was the point? Seeing Drake every single day would kill her. Especially if he started to date other girls and she didn't know if she could handle him being with anyone else. She swiped away her tears, wishing this day could have gone better but knowing there was nothing she could do to change it.

Sean had messed it up and Drake wasn't willing to fight for them. She wasn't going to waste her time when no one else wanted to. She had to move on. Only, she didn't know what to do next. Nothing was keeping her in town.

Sure, she had to graduate, but she could do that in a different town. Pru's mind was made up. There was no way she was going to allow Drake's parents to control her. Without looking back at the school, she walked the short distance home. It wasn't too far, not when she needed to clear her mind.

Entering her home, she held onto the door handle and looked into the room. Nothing had changed since the morning, but she felt different now. Drake had ended things, and she accepted it.

"Who is it?" her mother said, shouting from downstairs.

Rather than answering, Pru closed the door and headed for her room, only to stop when she saw her mother sitting on her bed.

"Mom?"

"Pru, it's you." Her mother sniffled. "I was just making your bed. You know, making sure everything is fine."

"Were you snooping?"

"No. I wasn't. I know this looks bad. I wanted to come and make sure everything was fine. You know, do the motherly thing."

Pru snorted. "Yeah, sure you did. I'm sure you'd have no problem snooping in my things if Drake's parents asked you to. You let them talk to me like I was trash. Why not make me feel like it as well?"

She didn't know what she expected but her mother broke down in tears. She dropped down to the bed and covered her face with her hands. Pru paused, not knowing what to do. She couldn't recall a time her mother was like this. It seemed a little surreal to see her broken, sad.

"Mom?"

"Don't, okay? It's fine. Honestly. I shouldn't be surprised." Her mother sniffled. "I hate this."

"I don't understand."

"You know, when I had you, I was the happiest woman in the world. I had this little baby and she was the most precious thing to me."

"Was?"

"You still are, Pru. Your father and I, we didn't have a lot. We've never had a lot but here, we have to fight for everything. We live paycheck to paycheck and we can't give you the life that boy has. His parents can come and go. No one controls them." Her mother growled. "I hate them so much. I hated every second of when I stood in that room. My little girl was in love, but his parents, they're monsters."

Tears filled Pru's eyes. She didn't know what to say, not as her mother groaned. "You must think I'm a coward for letting them do what they did."

"I don't want to talk about it."

"I know. I can't say I blame you. Who'd want to

talk to her parents who meekly stood by while they called their daughter a slut and a whore?" Her mother groaned again. "I can't believe I did nothing. I just stood there like it meant nothing. I'm so sorry, Pru. So, so sorry."

Pru stepped back as her mother reached out as if to touch her. She didn't know what to do. She had every intention of leaving. Why was she making this so difficult now?

"I've got to go," Pru said.

"I know what you're thinking of doing. I can't say I blame you for wanting to run."

"I didn't say anything about running."

"You don't need to. You're home when it's a school day. After the way we treated you, I would have run myself as well." Her mother cried. "I'm sorry. I have to be strong."

"Shouldn't you be at work?"

"Yeah, I should. Your father is going to be pissed. I'll only get half pay but I couldn't go to work. Not after everything that's happened."

"I don't understand what the problem is. You were able to go to work every other day. What makes today so different?" Pru asked.

"You think this has been easy for me?"

"Yeah, I do."

"You're wrong. I've hated this so much." She stopped and Pru watched her grit her teeth. "You're my little girl. When I had you, I promised myself I would do everything in my power to protect you, and look what happened."

"Mom, I don't want to talk about this. I had sex. I didn't do anything wrong. Everyone's treating me as if I've done some big country disaster. I haven't. I fell in love." She swiped at the tears again. She hated crying but knowing she and Drake weren't going to be together again hurt. Her mother wouldn't understand.

She was all alone. "I don't want to talk about this."

"Sweetheart," her mother said. "I know you feel all alone but I can promise you you're not. I know you've finally had sex and with that boy. It's not your fault he was the wrong guy."

"No, he wasn't. I loved him. I know you and Dad want me to be with Sean, but he's just a friend. Well, he was a friend. He's nothing now."

"You fell in love with Drake, and now you're home crying. You can't love him. His parents are too powerful. They have already set out a map for his life and it's never going to include you."

"I know."

"Then why are you even giving it a chance? Why do you even feel any hope?" her mother asked.

"Because I love him. I love him even after everything we've been through. I thought it would be enough, but it's not. Like everything, it's fucked!" She growled out the last word. "Will you get out of my bedroom?"

"I love your father. Always have. He's the love of my life and always will be. There have been so many times we've been such a huge disappointment to each other." Her mother sniffled. "We never expected it to be like this for us. We had so many plans."

"Mom, what do you want?"

"I get that you want to leave. I know the feeling. You think I haven't thought about packing up my life, moving away, and getting as far away from everyone and everything as I could? I have. So many times I've wanted to do it. It would be easy to do. Just throw everything in a case and not look back."

"Why haven't you?" Pru didn't want to care about what her mother did or didn't do. She only cared about getting out of town as soon as possible.

"Because … I'm not a coward."

"You're saying I'm a coward?"

"I'm saying a coward runs away. They don't stick around to fight. They run at the first sign of trouble."

"So I'm a coward then. I don't want to be having this conversation."

"I have to admit, it's not exactly the kind of conversation I hoped to have either. I never imagined I'd have to consider my daughter wanting to run away from me, but then, I didn't see us working from paycheck to paycheck. I know you want to run. I know right now you don't see any other way for yourself, or for anyone, and I respect that, but sweetheart, running is not the answer. It will never be the answer. All you will do is live with a bunch of regrets. I don't want you to live with that."

"You think you know me?"

"I do know you, honey. I know you a great deal and you're not a quitter. If you run now, you'll look back in years to come and know you should have stayed." Her mother stood up. "You think running away means you win. It doesn't. They win. This guy, he wins because he doesn't have to see you for the rest of the school year. Winning is showing up. Not letting them see you're in pain."

"Even though I am?"

"Let it drive you to succeed. Don't let them win. Be the one who decides when you leave or not." Her mother stepped toward her but Pru moved away. "One day, I hope you can trust me again. I do love you, sweetheart, no matter what you decide."

Her mother stepped out of her room.

She immediately grabbed the suitcase, put it on

top of her bed, grabbed a whole heap of clothes, and threw them inside. She didn't stop until the case was full. After she zipped it up and made her way across her room, she stopped. Her reflection in the mirror caught her attention. There was nothing great about looking at herself. She was still the same old person. Still Pru. Only this time, when she looked at herself, she didn't see a fighter. She saw someone who quit.

Glancing down at the case in her hand, she then looked back up and the view didn't change.

She was running away.

This was her plan. To run away, not look back.

This wasn't the kind of person she was. Not ever.

Putting the case down beside herself, she looked in the mirror and she really didn't like what she saw. Someone scared. Someone sad. Broken.

This wasn't how she planned her life. Not even close.

****

Drake didn't see Pru for the rest of the day. He looked for her and she was nowhere to be found. His boys were around him and of course they were curious as to what had been happening to him for the past couple of months, but he brushed it off. Told them to get a life and to stop gossiping like a couple of girls.

By the end of the day, there was still no sign of Pru. He didn't like it.

She shouldn't be on her own.

When he found Sean standing by his car, scrolling through his phone, he reacted.

Grabbing him by the jacket, he shoved him hard against the car, spinning him around so the bastard knew who he was dealing with.

"You remember me?" he asked, putting his arm across the guy's neck. He didn't put too much pressure.

The last thing he wanted to do was to hurt Pru's best friend if she'd forgiven him, even though it would give him a sick sense of satisfaction to harm him, to really make it hurt in ways he never had before.

"What do you want?"

"Where is she?" he asked.

"What?"

"You know who. Don't play the thick card with me. It doesn't work."

"You mean the girl you've been using these past few months?" Sean laughed. "How did that work for you?"

Pulling him close so his lips were against his ear, Drake made his threat. "If you think you've got some kind of leverage over me, you don't. The moment you told my parents and they came, all leverage you could have had to stop me hurting you was gone. For all of your intelligence, you're not too bright. I'd be careful how you talk to me." He shoved him once again up against the car and it gave him a great deal of satisfaction to see him in pain.

"What do you want?"

"I want to know where she is."

"I don't know. Okay? She ran out of here after she spoke to you. I don't know where she went or what she's doing. I don't know," Sean said.

Staring at him, he saw the bastard spoke the truth. He didn't know how he knew, only that he did. "You made a big fucking mistake in telling my parents," he said.

"And you think you're the one who's supposed to end up with Pru? She's far too good for you. I don't even know why the fuck she went with you. You're a first-class asshole. Look what you did to Ree. She's been begging for your attention ever since she went to that party."

Drake was growing increasingly bored with the conversation. Wrapping his fingers around his neck, he wondered what it would feel like to see the life zap right out of him. He'd gladly do it. To see an end to this boy. He wasn't a man. A man wouldn't go behind his back but face him.

"Do it. I know you want to. I know you want to kill me," Sean said. "You'll probably get away with it as well. Hide my body."

"You're being dramatic." He let Sean go. "When you see Pru, tell her I'm looking for her."

"She won't talk to me," Sean said. "She hates me just as much as you do."

"I doubt that."

"Believe me, it's the truth."

"You don't know what you did. We were happy," Drake said. "You ruined that."

"Please, you never would've been together for a long time. You don't have what it takes to handle Pru."

"And you do?"

"I've been her friend for a hell of a lot longer than you. I know what she needs. You don't have a clue."

Drake wanted to pummel the bastard but that was what Sean wanted.

"Go on, Drake, hit me."

"I don't believe in hitting girls," he said. He stepped back. "If you see Pru, tell her I'm looking for her."

"Not going to happen. I'm not going to encourage her to forgive you. You may as well get that out of your thick fucking skull."

Drake walked away. There was no reason for him to listen to him.

Why do you want to see her? You've got to let her

go.

He had to make sure she was okay. He didn't like not seeing her for the rest of the day at school. He'd be able to let her go just so long as she stuck around and he got a chance to just look at her, even for only a second, maybe a little more.

You're going insane.

After walking to his car, he climbed behind the wheel, watching Sean. He didn't like the bastard but right now, he was his only chance of finding out if Pru was okay.

Just go and see her.

He didn't care what his parents said. He had to go and talk to her.

Turning his key in the ignition, he started his car, pulled out of the school parking lot, and headed toward Pru's house. It didn't take him long and most of the journey was a blur. He parked in front of her house. There was no car in the driveway. He went up to her house and knocked on the front door.

No one answered, so he knocked again.

When he was about to knock for a third time, Pru's mother opened the door.

"Why are you here?" she asked.

"Is Pru home?"

"You've got a lot of nerve showing up here. You've got to leave," she said.

"Not going to happen. I need to know Pru's okay. I know you don't like me and I accept that, but I need to see her." He looked at her mother, hoping his pleading didn't fall on deaf ears. He wasn't used to begging. Everyone jumped when he gave an order and he missed that right now.

"If Pru wants to talk to you, she will. Come in. I don't want the neighbors getting any ideas, and you better tell your parents that I didn't want you here," she said.

He stepped into the house., surrounded by warmth, which was the complete opposite of his own home.

"Pru, someone's here to see you."

He waited at the bottom of the stairs and when she arrived, she paused. At first, she didn't make a move, then slowly, she walked downstairs until she was at the bottom.

"What are you doing here?" she asked, arms folded.

"I wanted to see you. You weren't in school."

"Drake, you have no right to care. Not anymore."

"I know. I know. There's no way for me to make this up to you, and I'm sorry about that."

"Drake, go home," she said.

He captured her arm as she went to walk away. He didn't want her to turn her back on him, not now. "I know right now you're hating me, and I accept that, but you have to know I don't want to do this."

She looked down at his arm and he let her go. "I know, but this is the way it's going to have to be. I'm not going to mope after you. I'm moving on. There's no point in us dwelling on what could be."

She wasn't crying or upset. She looked bored.

"What's going on right now, Pru?"

She laughed. "Seriously? I agree with you and you don't like it? A girl cannot win with you, Drake. Don't you have like an entire flock of girls waiting to please you?"

Drake didn't know what to say. "I didn't want to hurt you."

"And you didn't hurt me. Honestly, I'm fine. There's nothing for you to worry about. I'm not going anywhere. There's no reason for me to." She clapped her hands together. "Is that it? Is that all you came here to do? To see if I was fine?"

He wanted to shake her. "You were upset today after I said it was over."

"I was, but now I see so clearly now. You can leave."

"Pru, be real with me."

She rolled her eyes. "What do you want me to do here, Drake? You want me to scream at you? Tell you how wrong you are for pushing me away?"

"I don't know what I want."

"Well, maybe it's time you figured out what it is you do want. It can't be me, remember? I'm not good enough in your parents' eyes and to be frank, I don't want to be good enough for them. I was never with you because of your position or your wealth. I couldn't give a damn about either of them. Money makes the world go round but it's not what life is about. You made your choice. Stick with it, and I'll stick with what I know." She moved toward the door. "You really should go. I don't know who's watching us and I don't want to be called a whore again."

"You and I both know you're not a whore."

She sighed. "What is this, exactly? Do you feel guilty for how you ended it? I thought the old Drake was back?"

"Pru?"

"No, you need to leave. I'm not going anywhere and I'm not going to be some punching bag for you or for anyone. Please, leave."

He didn't want to go. Staring at her, he wanted nothing more than to take her in his arms, hold her, and tell her it would be all right, but what was the point? She wouldn't believe him. "I'll go."

"That would be really good."

He stepped out of the house and when she started to shut the door in his face, he put his arm out, stopping her.

"What?"

He didn't say anything, merely looked at her one final time. It was all he wanted to do. To memorize what she looked like so he would never forget her. With that, he let go of the door so she could throw it in his face.

Chapter Twenty-Three
Time to get over it

The days blended together. Pru got up each morning. She had breakfast with her family. Since her mother didn't go to work, they argued when her father arrived, but she wouldn't feel guilty. If it hadn't been for her mom, she'd have run. It would have been all too easy for her to do exactly that. To try to escape the hell she felt she was living, but that wasn't the case. She couldn't win by turning her back on those who would do her harm.

It was no way for her to live and she certainly wasn't going to let those bastards think they'd won. They had humiliated her in the worst possible way and she wasn't going to let them get away with it.

Sean still visited but she continued to ignore him. Her parents often took the time to chat with him, but she couldn't do it. Friends didn't do that to each other. He should have come to her, and even though she knew she had to forgive him at some point, he'd still betrayed her trust, after everything they'd been through. Sean was convinced they could make it and she'd get over her *issues*. As long as she saw Drake, it was going to be impossible to remember why she was ever friends with Sean.

Now, Drake, that was a whole new story.

He'd gone back to being the guy he'd always been. Mean, nasty, and he took it out on whoever walked in front of him. It was like the past couple of months hadn't mattered to him. The only difference she saw was that none of his anger or hatred came at her.

She merely didn't exist to him. Whenever they crossed paths, she ignored him. They were nothing to each other.

Like now, she stood at her locker and he was just a few feet away. There was a kid in the year below him. The boy had a serious case of acne, but Drake wasn't letting the kid go. He kept on poking fun at him.

Just ignore it.

You don't want to start this.

She reached into her locker and in the back were a couple of pictures they'd taken together. Selfies of their time. The smiles, the happiness. It seemed so foreign to her. There was no way she could have fallen for the bully in her life, but she had.

"Hey," Sean said, making her jump. She put the pictures down, hoping he hadn't seen them, not wanting him to know what she missed most. She didn't say anything.

Glancing back at Drake and his group, she saw he was looking in her direction and quickly averted her gaze.

The last thing she wanted was to draw attention to herself. So far, since they had completely broken up and severed all contact, she'd been able to avoid him. She didn't know what would happen if his friends were to bring her into any conflict. She liked to think nothing would happen, but she doubted it. All she wanted to do was get through the school year.

"I'm sorry," Sean said.

"For what, exactly? For hurting my feelings? For getting caught?"

"For not coming to you. For being a giant dick about everything."

She slammed the locker closed. "It doesn't matter now, though, does it? Everything is back to the way it was."

"They're not hurting you. At least there's that."

She laughed. "I don't know if you're trying to be

funny or not. They'd stopped hurting me before." She shook her head. "I don't want to talk about it."

"You can talk with me about anything."

"I can't, Sean. If I could, this wouldn't have happened in the first place."

"I'm sorry."

"I know, and I'm sorry too. You have no idea how sorry I am, but I can't change what happened and neither can you." She looked over at the guys and it hurt.

She wanted to stop Drake from doing something he'd regret but it would only draw her back to him. They were nothing to each other and she had to accept it.

Sean touched her arm and she wanted him to stop, but she didn't say anything. "I really am sorry."

"Me too."

He pulled his hand away and she breathed out a sigh of relief.

"Well, well, well, if it's not the two losers together," Ree said.

After Drake had slept with her and tossed her aside, she'd stopped being friends with them. Now, since she and Drake had broken up, she'd seen Ree wrapped around him. Pru tried not to be jealous but it was hard. Ree flicked her hair off her shoulder and sneered at the two of them.

Folding her arms, Pru stared at her former friend. No one else had befriended this girl. It was her and Sean, but from the start, she'd always wanted more. She hadn't been content to just be their friend.

"What do you want?" Pru asked.

"What do I want? First, I'd love to rid the school of freaks like you."

Pru sighed. "Really. Without freaks like me, you wouldn't be where you are today."

Some of Ree's friends laughed and snorted. There

was a time Pru would have played nice. She'd be in her own little corner of space, ignoring everyone. Content to be by herself or with Sean.

"Oh, please. You think I wouldn't be where I am now if it wasn't for you. You have no idea who you're talking to."

"I'm talking to the girl who couldn't get into Drake's party and needed me for him to even look in your direction," Pru said.

"Pru, this isn't like you," Sean said.

Yeah, well, maybe it was. She was tired of people hurting her and others taking advantage. Hands on her hips, she stepped up to Ree. She could take this girl. It wouldn't be hard.

Ree laughed. "I could have gotten into that party."

"You called me like a little girl needing mommy's help. Drake didn't want you at that party. You were nothing but a pest. You don't have enough money to even be in his league. Believe me, I know."

"And you think you do? You're nothing but a poor little bitch," Ree said.

"Yeah, I am, but I'm not trying to belong to him. I never wanted to. We were your friends, Ree, but this right here is your loss. When it's over and no one wants to be around you, you'll come crawling back. No one likes a bitch, and you're behaving like one, first-class."

Ree slapped her hard and Pru took it. She didn't mind the pain of the slap. She loved it, in fact. At least she knew she was alive still. The only person she'd ever been in a fight with was Drake. They had never gotten along and each of them had always hurt each other in one form or another. Looking at Ree right now, she wanted to hurt her.

Ree lifted her hand and Pru didn't even think

about it, she pushed her hard, making her stumble back. As Ree came back for more, Pru didn't try to end the fight. In the back of her mind, she knew this wasn't about today. This was because she had to see Ree with Drake. She had to witness the other girl touching him, being able to be with him when she couldn't, and it pissed her off so much.

Within seconds, they were on the floor. Ree straddled her and the open slap turned into a fist. It hurt, but Pru shoved her off, rolling her to the ground and this time, she got three punches in.

Before she could land a fourth blow, she was grabbed from behind, her arm held out.

"Yeah, you better fucking get her off me before I hurt her," Ree said.

"Get off me. Let me go. She needs to fucking pay."

Whoever held her didn't let her go. She suddenly pushed into a classroom. The door shoved closed as she was pressed up against the door.

She stared into Drake's eyes.

He'd gotten between them.

He'd stopped her from fighting. Glaring at him, she tried to shake him off, but he held on to her. "Let me the fuck go."

The rage was unlike anything she'd ever experienced. She didn't even know where it had come from. Why was she suddenly so angry? It wasn't like she was jealous of Ree or even cared what the other girl had.

"No. You're going to hurt yourself if you don't stop."

"This isn't your fight."

"It is, Pru. You're not the fighting kind and you have to stop." He captured her hands, pressing them above her head, and she wanted to scream at him some more.

Taking several deep breaths, she waited. The moment he let his guard down, she intended to claw his eyes out and show him who he was really messing with. She pressed against his hands, but he was much stronger than her. Even with all the adrenaline and rage consuming her. "Let me go."

"Pru, she's not worth it."

"Is that what you say to her every night when you're done with her? That she's not worth it?"

"You think I spend my nights with her?"

"Why not? It's not like you need to worry about commitment. You can do whatever the hell you want, right? You don't have to care about anyone. Your parents have your future mapped out for you." She took a deep breath, hating how mean she sounded.

Finally, when she couldn't take staring into his eyes another moment, she looked away.

"Are you done yet?" he asked.

She didn't say anything. *What is wrong with me?* "Yes. You can let me go."

"I'm not letting you go. The principal was heading our way and I don't want you to get in trouble."

"I can handle myself."

"Pru, stop being a bitch and just accept you can't handle everything."

"You have no right to interfere with my life." She stared into his eyes, letting him see all the pain he didn't think he was causing. "Remember? You told me we were over, that we were through, and any right you had was gone."

"Pru, I didn't want it to be like this."

"Neither do I. I wonder how you'd like it if Sean was all over me. Do you think you'd be happy about it? Do you think you'd be happy for me to hold you back, telling you not to hurt him?"

"I don't want Sean anywhere near you."

"We never get what we want, and you're just going to have to deal with what happened. You're not the boss of me, and you never will be."

He slammed his hand beside her head but she wasn't afraid.

All their lives, he'd hurt her, but in the past few months, she'd seen a side to him she knew no one else saw.

"Stop trying to win this. You won't like where it goes."

She smiled. "I'm not trying to win anything, Drake. You think people are going to talk because you pulled me off your fuck buddy? What will your parents think?" This time when she shoved him back, he didn't put up a fight and backed off.

Brushing down her body, she pushed some hair off her shoulder and opened the door.

Everyone had disappeared from the corridor and while Drake had been holding her back, class had already reconvened.

"If you go to class, there will be questions," he said.

Ignoring him, she walked out of the school. She still didn't have access to a car, but she had no problem with walking. What she didn't expect was for Drake to keep on following her.

"Your parents will probably see you being all naughty," she said.

"Don't care."

"Oh, please, you care and we both know it bothers you." She stopped and whirled around to glare at him. "I have to say I'm surprised, though. Doesn't it get you all hot and bothered to know a couple of chicks are fighting? It must be really hard for you to contain yourself."

"Why are you being a fucking bitch!" Drake didn't back down from her taunting. He stepped right up into her face. "Is this what you want? You want me to get into your face? Growl at you? Scream a little? What exactly is it you want from me?"

"I want fuck all from you." She tried to leave but he grabbed her arm. "Will you stop doing that? I don't want you touching me." She raised her hand as if to slap him across the face but he stopped her. She couldn't do anything, and she hated him for it. "Ugh! Let me go."

"You seem to think I'll just accept this kind of behavior from you."

"I really don't care what you think you want or don't want from me. I just want you to leave me alone."

"You see, I'm trying to do that. For your own safety, I'm fucking trying. I know shit now that makes all of this impossible."

Drake wasn't hurting her hand but he also wasn't letting her go.

"What do you mean?"

He glanced back at the school. "Are you willing to go for a drive with me?"

"No, I don't think that's a good idea." *Why are you suddenly nervous? Don't you trust him? Don't you want to go with him? Why is it so hard to give in?*

Was it really hard?

When Drake started to lead his way back into the parking lot, she didn't stop him, not even when he pushed her into the passenger seat. She went willingly. Even as she put her seat belt on, she knew this was a really bad idea. Nothing good could come from her going with him. Yet, she knew there was nowhere else she wanted to be. This wasn't about hurting each other or annoying one another, this was about so much more and there were times she truly was tired of fighting with him. It seemed to be all they did.

Relationships shouldn't be this hard.

"Are you dating Ree?" Pru asked.

"No."

"Then why do you have her wrapped around you like a second skin?"

"It's all part of the act. Surely you know what it means to have someone who wants to see everything and know everything. My parents, they've got eyes and ears everywhere. I've got no choice but to act the part in order to keep them off my back." He shrugged. "So it's what I do."

"You really think they're going to have someone watching you from inside the school?"

"Yep."

"Isn't that a little creepy?"

"You've met my parents. I didn't say it wasn't creepy. I know what my parents want."

"But Ree's not made of money either."

"Exactly. For them, I'm just using Ree and they're happy for that."

"You know that's weird, right? Why didn't they accept it with me?"

"Because with you, I kept it a secret and we both know it was a hell of a lot more than some party fling. I … hid you from my parents. Not because I was embarrassed but because I didn't want them to hurt you or ruin what we had. You are so important to me and have been for the longest time. I can't stand to have you hurt."

She couldn't believe what he was hearing.

"I thought … I don't know what I thought."

"I know what you thought and it's not true. None

of it. You think I want to give up what we had? Not after everything we went through." He shook his head. "I'm sorry I made you feel that way."

"Drake, you've got nothing to be sorry about. Not really."

He laughed. "Please, don't make this easy for me. We both know I can be a prick of the biggest kind."

"Well, I don't know about that, but yeah, okay. But I also haven't made things easy for you." She didn't pull away from him when he took her hand or locked their fingers together.

"I haven't been with Ree, not since that one time, and I never will."

"We've talked about this, Drake. One day you're going to get married."

"I don't want to and I've got a plan."

"If it's killing your parents, it's not going to work." There were a lot of things she was willing to do for him but going down as a murderer wasn't one of them.

"You're no fun." He glanced over at her. "No, I'm not going to kill my parents. One of them is dead, anyway."

"Huh? I didn't read anything in the news about it. What do you mean one of them is dead anyway?"

He chuckled. "Do I have you confused?"

"A little, why?"

"Good."

He was silent.

She kept waiting for him to spill whatever secrets he had.

He didn't say a word.

"Drake, come on. Seriously? You're not going to tell me anything?"

"Nope. You don't need to know, at least not yet."

"This is so unfair."

"Life, my darling, is unfair."

She scrunched up her nose. "You do know that was weird, right?"

"Yeah, on a scale of one to ten, that was right up there on the weird factor, I agree."

She laughed. It was good to laugh with him and to have him holding her hand.

Leaning back against the headrest, she sighed. "Do you think Ree reported me?"

"If she knows what's good for her, she'll leave you alone."

"You know, she used to be friends with me and Sean."

He squeezed her hand a little tighter.

"Don't worry. There's nothing going on with Sean and me. We're ... I don't know what we are."

"You haven't forgiven him?"

"No. I want to. I mean, I should. He's my best friend."

"He's still the bastard that ruined our fun for us, Pru. You don't have to forgive him for me."

"I know, but he's always been my best friend."

"A best friend who wants more from you. Don't forget that. You can pretend all you want, but it's not going to work. He wants something from you, which is why he's always around you."

"It doesn't have to be sex or even a relationship. Some guys aren't wired to think with their dick."

"You do know how stupid you sound right now, right?"

"Hey!"

"I'm a guy. I know what a guy is thinking and feeling and believe me, it's not about hanging out in a chick's room and doing homework. I'm surprised you haven't caught Sean staring at you in the bathroom or something like that. The guy is a creep."

"I've never caught him, so he clearly is the perfect gentleman." Again, why was she defending Sean after everything he'd done? It wasn't like she was on his side and yet, she was acting like she was. None of this made any sense. None at all.

"Are we done arguing about this?" Drake asked. "We will always disagree about that asshole. He's not good enough for you. In fact, I'm not good enough for you."

"Don't say that," she said. "Let's not talk about Sean."

Drake didn't agree.

"He's not here with us. Don't let him get to you, Drake. I'm here with you, not back at school with him."

"Do you really think it makes it any easier for me? Especially knowing he's going to get to hold you one day. You can't stay angry with him forever. It's not who you are."

She sighed. "You keep pretending you know me, and the truth is, you don't really know me at all."

"I do, trust me, I do."

She wasn't going to argue. What was the point?

"You know, one day you will thank me for not letting you beat down on Ree."

She snorted. "Don't hold your breath."

"I said one day, not today. I know right now you're pissed at me. You're probably hating my guts and you know what, you've got a right to that." He shrugged. "I can't stop you."

"Good, because I don't hate your guts, Drake. I'm just pissed at you for a lot of reasons."

****

Drake could handle pissed.

He hadn't wanted to pull Pru off Ree, but he knew deep down she wouldn't have wanted to hurt the other girl.

Ree wasn't where her anger was No, it was at him and his parents, and he had to learn to accept that she was going to hate him for a time. He'd dragged her to his car, threw her inside, and took off, leaving the school.

This was nice, though. At least he got to spend time with her while he told her the truth of what he learned. He would do anything to extend their time together, but he wouldn't push it. This was for them, for one last moment together.

"How have you been?" she asked.

"Do you really want to know?"

She sighed. "Sure, why not?"

"I've been better." He may as well be honest with her. There was nothing about what they were going through that he liked or even agreed with.

"Me too," she said. "I'm trying to get over it."

"I know."

They were both hurting.

"Sometimes I wish I hadn't gone to that party."

"I know."

"It would have been so much easier if I'd stayed away. If we'd hated each other. You know, you being your mean self, and me, well, just fighting against you."

He laughed. "It wouldn't have made life easier, Pru. I think we can both admit neither of us truly hated each other."

"I don't know. I think if I said it enough times, I'd start to believe it."

He looked over at her and saw she smiled at him. "I've missed this."

"Yeah, and you're going to have to get your fill for now. Are you going to tell me what it is you wanted to say?"

"Soon. I want to … prolong this for a little while longer."

"Okay. I don't mind."

He stared at her hand resting in her lap.

They hadn't been apart that long, but for him, it was too much. Reaching out, for this day only, he took her hand.

"Drake, do you think this is wise?" she asked.

"Yes, it is."

She tried to tug her hand away.

"Pru, please, you're with me now. We may as well do this properly. I'm going to hold your hand and then I'm going to tell you the truth of what I learned, and together, we're going to figure this out."

"But we both know there's no way we can work. We're only prolonging the inevitable."

"Or we can both come up with a way to be together."

She groaned. "We've been through this. There's no way."

"You don't know all the facts yet," he said. "Don't start thinking we're over until we know more."

"We're yo-yoing back and forth and I don't get it, Drake. Why can't we just accept that this is it for us?" she asked.

Drake gripped the steering wheel even tighter. He knew he'd fucked up by trying to push her away and he saw the error of what he'd done. Now, he had a way to fix it, or at least he thought he did.

"Can we just hold off all conversation of us being completely over? At least until I tell you the truth about everything?" he asked.

"Sure, I don't mind."

He nodded. He drove for another half an hour,

coming to a stop at a diner. He took a deep breath, wanting to feel like this was it. This was their chance to finally be together. He hoped Pru would know what to do.

"Drake, are you okay?" she asked.

"I'm fine. I just … you know, I have to deal with everything." He released a breath and stepped out of the car. He didn't want to tell her straightaway how much hope he had that she would be able to find a solution for both of them.

When he was at Pru's side, he took her hand, and together, they walked hand-in-hand toward the diner. He took the lead, finding them a nice quiet booth to eat in.

They were served within seconds but it wasn't a very busy diner.

"What are you having?" the waitress asked.

They both ordered burgers with extra fries.

Pru tucked her hair behind her ear and he was caught by how beautiful she looked. "This is a nice place."

"I guess." He glanced around, not really paying attention to the diner.

"Are you going to tell me what all of this is about?" she asked.

"Fine. Fine. It's a little hard to wrap your head around."

"Try me."

"You remember my dad?" he asked.

"Yeah, it's kind of hard not to. I seem to recall he didn't have a whole lot of nice things to say to me." She shrugged.

"I'm so sorry about that."

"It's not your fault and you shouldn't, you know, be worried about him."

"You don't have to defend him to me."

"This is all a little out of my comfort zone."

He took hold of her hands. "He's not my dad," he said.

"What? But isn't that the whole point of you being you?"

"I know. My dad can't have kids. I only found it out recently. He's firing blanks."

"Firing blanks? You mean he can't have kids?"

"None. Not one. I'm not his son."

"But, wait. You look so much alike. How can this be possible? Are you sure they're not lying to you? This could be another of their tricks."

"They're not lying."

"How do you know?"

"My dad is, in fact, my brother. My grandfather slept with my mother as he knew without a doubt he was not firing blanks."

Drake waited for his words to sink in and when they did, the look of shock on her face was priceless.

"Wow," she said.

"Yeah."

"What does this mean?"

"I don't know. I was hoping you could tell me."

"I don't understand. How can I tell you anything? I don't have a clue what this all means."

They stopped talking as the waitress placed their food in front of them.

Pru said thank you to the woman and Drake immediately did the same. There were times he forgot about simple manners.

"What are you thinking right now?" Drake asked.

"I don't know. How are you feeling? I mean, that's a lot to take in for anyone. How are you handling it? Are you even handling it at all?"

Drake loved her concern, craved it even. He'd

been without anyone caring for a very long time.

Neither of them reached for their food. He wasn't hungry, not yet.

"I don't know how to handle it, in all honesty. I mean, I know my parents weren't the best kind of role models, you know? They were shady as fuck, but I don't know what to think of what they're doing now. I mean, how am I supposed to deal with this shit?" He sat back, staring at his food that was now going cold.

"What do you want to do?"

"I honestly don't fucking know. What am I supposed to do?"

"I don't understand. If you don't know what to do, why did you bring me here?"

He looked across the table at her. He smiled but it didn't reach his eyes. "I don't know. I guess I hoped that … you'd be able to find something that meant we could use it against them."

"Oh," she said.

"Yeah, I'm not a good kid. Never have been."

"Drake, you're far from a kid." She rubbed at her temples.

"Can you do anything with the information I've given you? Anything at all?"

"I'm trying to figure it out. I'm not a genius. I mean, what is it you're hoping to achieve?" she asked.

He picked up a fry, stuck it in his mouth, and chewed on it. "Finding some way for us to be together. Don't you see that?"

She released a breath but didn't eat any food. "I don't know how finding out your dad is your brother and not really your dad is going to work. By law, he's the one in charge of the company, unless something happens to him. But wouldn't it go to your mom?"

"No, it has to go to the male line. It's in the will."

"But if he gives it to her in the will, wouldn't that change the entire will?"

Drake sat back. "No, he can't do that."

"Why?"

"There are terms and conditions when it comes to passing the business and the entire wealth onto a woman."

"Am I going to be pissed when I hear them?"

"I don't know. Do you want to hear them?"

"May as well." She finally picked up a fry and started to eat it.

"Okay, the only way any of the fortune or inheritance could be passed onto a woman was if the only child they had was a female. They have to keep on trying to get a son, a male heir."

"Wow, your family is very sexist. Why don't they want women to have the inheritance? Do they not think a woman can handle a good company?"

"They can't keep the name."

"Huh?"

"When men and women marry. The title changes."

"But they can hyphen the name, or they don't even have to take it at all. Men can take a woman's name now, I'm sure of it. Your family has some very outdated views."

"They'd have to find a man willing enough to take a woman's name."

"You think love won't do it?" she asked.

"Clearly love has never been tested and then you've got to worry about gold diggers."

"I see your point. If love won't get them to change their name, a cushy lifestyle will. I see." She shrugged. "I don't know if this will help you at all, Drake. In the eyes of the law, they're still in charge, and will be for a long time."

"And you don't want me to kill them?"

She rolled her eyes and he laughed. "You're not going to kill them. It wouldn't work, and you know it. There's nothing you can do but wait it out. I'm sorry."

"What about if I show them to be incompetent? Is there a way for me to get away from them?"

"Emancipation is a real deal, Drake. I'm not a lawyer and I don't know how it all works." She took his hand, locking their fingers together. "We're not going to win this. We're not going to be together." She pulled his hand close, pressing a kiss to his knuckles. "And we've got to accept it."

"I don't want to."

"I know, but it doesn't change the fact we have to." She pulled away and he made no move to hold her hand again.

There was no point.

He'd been grasping at straws.

There was no future for them.

Chapter Twenty-Four
Everything happens for a reason

Graduation wasn't far off, and with it, studying, college applications, and just life. Pru spent all of her available time trying to make a decision between staying in town or leaving for good.

There was nothing but her parents to hold her back.

They loved her, she knew that without a doubt, but … she wanted more. Her mother had told her not to make a decision based on staying with them, but for herself.

At a fast food restaurant, she took a huge bite out of her burger, closing her eyes as she tried to think. Every time she looked at the two applications, the college in town, and one out of state, she always hesitated, and it wasn't a good feeling.

What did Drake want to do? Did he have any plans for his future, or was it to follow in his parents' path rather than his own?

Chewing her food, she stared across the mall and watched as people passed by. She'd finished her shift an hour ago, and now she was bored. The only place to go was to head home.

"I have to say, I figured my son would have more class than to go for a girl like you, but I guess there's no accounting for taste."

She paused, looking up to see Drake's father standing beside her. He stood out like a sore thumb. He wore an expensive-looking suit and sneered at everyone around him. She didn't know why he'd come to a place he clearly despised.

"Mr. Connor, what are you doing here?" she asked, sitting up. She didn't want to be alone with this man.

"You and I both have our reasons for what we do, and well, they kind of mesh right now."

"I don't understand."

"I don't know what kind of hold you have on my son, but I want you to let him go."

She stared at him, confused. "I don't have any hold on him."

The older man raised an eyebrow.

She looked around the dinner hall but no one was paying any attention to them.

"I'll make this simple." He pulled out an envelope and slid it across the table. "I want you gone. Your family as well. I've already paid a visit to them. They made the right choice."

"What is this?"

"A new start. A chance to find a way for yourself without anyone present," he said.

She lifted up the envelope and sure enough, there was a check inside, along with some cash. She didn't bother to count the money.

Closing the envelope, she looked at him.

"You can go to any college you want. I'll pay for it."

She stared at him, not really sure what to say. The check was for a huge amount. More than she would ever need. "You'd be willing to send me to college, pay for it, and all this money as well?"

"I knew the temptation would be too good for you to resist."

"I didn't say I was going to take this."

"If you know what is good for you, you'll take it." The threat was very clear in his voice.

She looked around the mall again. No one paid them any attention and she couldn't believe no one was watching.

"Your parents have already accepted their deal. This is for you, and there is a time limit on it, so you might want to consider what it is you want out of life."

"You're trying to pay me off," she said. "I'm not my parents."

"Your parents know some sense. This thing between you and Drake, it's not going to work out. I don't even have to be here right now, offering you money and a chance at a life. I could be doing a hell of a lot of other things to occupy my time."

"Then why aren't you?" she asked. She was growing tired of people telling her what she should do with her life. This was her life and she'd do whatever the hell she wanted.

"Why aren't I what?"

"Why are you wasting your time on me if I'm not important? What could I possibly do to you? You've proven your worth time and time again." She sighed, staring down at the envelope.

"Because you and I both know Drake isn't going to give up without a fight and I'm hoping you've got more sense than him."

"He wants what he wants. You can't be annoyed with him because of that." She stared at his father and wondered what else she could say to make him see reason. Sitting back, she folded her arms, waiting.

"Drake's life is planned out. We have a woman picked out for him already. You don't belong in it but in order for you to accept that money, I need you, we need you, to break his heart."

"What happens if he walks away?" she asked.

He stared at her without saying a word.

"I know you'd set out to destroy your son, making it impossible for him to have a life of his own, but what will really happen?" She was growing tired of all the secrets and lies. It was boring keeping up with them. What happened to living like normal kids when things didn't happen or confuse people? Why couldn't they go back to that?

She rubbed at her temples before giving his father her undivided attention.

"You know the truth of his heritage. You know I'm not able to father children," he said.

"How do you know that I know that?" she asked.

"I may not have fathered Drake but I have raised him. In a fashion. I'm guessing there is nothing that boy hasn't done that he hasn't told you. Anyway, if Drake walks away from the family, if he cuts himself out, then there is no longer an heir to pass the wealth onto. The will has stipulations, Prudence. In order for the next available heir to inherit, he must be part of the company in some way. They have to have a direct link."

"But if Drake has no direct link, it doesn't stop you and your wife living in comfort." She didn't see the big deal.

"I want you out of the picture."

"Why? You've got everything you could ever need. I don't see why you need anything from me." She stared at his father—no, brother. "Unless ... as your brother, Drake is entitled to half of the company already."

"You have no idea what you're talking about."

She saw how uncomfortable he was and knew instantly she had hit on something. "That's it, isn't it?"

"You would be wise to take my offer." He got to his feet. "I suggest you think about what kind of a future you want. One where you're the boss of it, or one where you're having to take orders."

Within a matter of seconds, he was gone and she

stared at the envelope. Could it be possible that all this time Drake had assumed he was set to inherit when the real truth was he could already be entitled to half of the company, which was why his parents—or brother and mother—were trying to control him? Could it really be that simple?

She didn't want to think about it as being so easy.

Could it be easy?

Licking her dry lips, she picked up the envelope and grabbed her cell phone. The only way to deal with this problem now was to call Drake and have him meet her, so they could both figure this out."

"Hello, I was hoping you'd call."

"Who are you with right now?" she asked.

"The guys."

"I need to meet you at a private place. Do you know someplace?" She looked around the mall, hoping no one was paying her attention.

The last thing she wanted was to draw attention from a spy. This was all too much right now. She felt sick to her stomach. Taking a deep breath, she tried to calm herself, but she felt excited, giddy, and so many other emotions she couldn't even begin to describe.

Leaving the mall, she made her way out toward the cabs, hailing one down and giving him the directions to where Drake said to meet him. It was off the beaten track, and the driver wouldn't go down the forest-lined driveway when they got to it.

Climbing out of the car, she paid the driver and after he advised her to give up, because the house up ahead could be haunted, he left. She walked up the long driveway. It really did look like it had come straight out of a Halloween movie.

When she got closer to the clearing, she saw Drake's car and started to run. He sat on the porch steps of the house in question, which looked like it was falling apart. The moment he saw her, he got up and rushed toward her.

She threw her arms around him and smiled.

"Not that I don't appreciate your call, but I didn't think we were going to do this," he said.

"I have so much to tell you." She caught him up to speed on his father's visit including the payment he'd given her, which she handed him back to him. "You're going to need this."

"Why?"

"You need to have someone check out your father's will. If your father wanted the company to remain in the Connor name, and he was willing to sleep with your mother to achieve it, don't you think he would have taken all the extra measures to keep it secure?" she asked. "Like, giving half of the company to you?"

"But wouldn't I have been … told about this?"

"Drake, you only knew a little while ago that you were his brother. He could have it worded that it could be divided equally between his son or son*s*."

"But, why wouldn't anyone tell me?"

"Because no one knew. It's why your parents are so determined to keep you in their own little world. To control you."

"You think it could be as simple as getting the will read again?"

"I honestly don't know. I could be wrong, but why else would they be trying to buy me off? It makes no sense. I'm not important. I lost count of the number of times they told me that. Remember? I mean nothing to them." She shrugged. "What do you have to lose?"

She shoved her hands into her jeans, waiting. Glancing behind him, she looked at the house. It really needed a lot of work.

"What is this place?" she asked when he still hadn't said anything.

"It belonged to my uncle."

"Your uncle?"

"On my mother's side. She had a brother. One she tried to disown. He was a great guy. He didn't want the money or the prestige, the title that came with his wealth. Before he was cut out of the inheritance, he got this place. There was a time it was amazing. Everything in pristine condition."

"What happened to it?" she asked. The house looked like it needed to be condemned.

"Age. My uncle got sick and rather than reach out and ask for help, he was stubborn. Tried to deal with cancer and fix this damn house."

"I'm so sorry. You never said anything about this before."

"Not a lot to say, to be honest." He looked behind him.

"Is it yours?"

"Yeah. He gave all of his money to me and this place."

"Why don't you use the money to invest back into this place?" she asked. She walked up the steps, being careful not to step on any of the damaged ones. "I mean, this is your life as well, and if you love it, why give it up?"

"I guess I haven't really thought about this place. My uncle loved it and from what I remember of him, he was really proud of it. He'd take the time to fix everything and he always said the best kind of things in life, the ones you treasure, are always worth fighting for or taking the time to hold close to you. You know, sentimental stuff like that."

"He sounds nice."

"He was. As you know, my mother is nothing like him. She's always been about material things and getting more. Greed runs heavily in my family."

She stood at the door. The glass in one piece of the window had been broken.

Drake got the key out of his pocket, slid it into the lock, and flicked the door open. The heavy scent of mold and dust was in the air. There were also lots of cobwebs.

"There's so much work that needs to be done. I doubt I'll ever get it finished."

"Not with that kind of attitude. I'm a great believer of if you want something and are willing to work hard to get it, you will. Isn't there a part of you in there somewhere who believes in seeing the true potential, even out of a dump? Look at us. We were enemies and now look at us."

"Is this the same woman who told me not too long ago that we should give up?"

"I wasn't the first person to feel that way. You were, remember? I guess we've both made a lot of mistakes," she said.

They stepped into the main room. Some of the walls were missing and the ceiling had a hole. She could look straight up into the roof.

"Were you tempted?" Drake asked.

"Was I tempted with what?"

"The money."

"You're really asking me this?"

"I … I don't know what I'm asking. I just, I'm curious."

"I don't want this money, Drake. Your father came to me and I found it so odd for him to be so determined to get me away from you. You can't deny this could be your shot. Your way of finally getting away from them." She looked around the house. "Do you still have the money to repair this?"

"I can't believe you didn't take the money," Drake said.

She sighed. "Do you want to fight about it some more? Not everything is about money. I don't want it."

****

Drake held the envelope in his hand and was still a little taken aback that she hadn't given in to temptation. His father had offered her an easy life, and even though she still held the envelope, he knew for a fact it didn't mean she'd taken it. Just the opposite.

"My parents took the money, but I didn't. I don't want any part of his blackmail money. Do you think that's what he does with all the girls you want to date?" she asked.

"Probably. I don't know of anyone who has turned him down, or to be honest, anyone he's actually bought off, not of my girlfriends. I know he does it all the time with the women he fucks."

"Your parents have hurt you a lot, haven't they?"

"More than I care to think about. They're not going to keep getting the chance though."

The house they stood in was a wreck. It needed to have a lot of work done. So much, in fact, he'd have to get many professionals in. His uncle had told him that even though it looked like a crumbling wreck, there was still so much more to it, and he believed it. He thought back to the eyesore in town. When he saw the true potential in even a wreck. He wasn't the kind of guy to give up and he wasn't going to start now.

At the time, he hadn't seen the truth, though. He'd only seen the house as a burden.

One he'd pushed to one side while he got on with his life, which didn't include working on crumbling buildings.

"Is it safe to go and look upstairs?" she asked.

"No, it's not."

"That sucks. I think this place could look amazing." She walked toward the back of the house and he still held the envelope within his grasp.

This was crazy.

Could it be as simple as getting the will read again? He didn't want to think it was so easy.

Pru came back to him. "Are you okay? You seem to be in a bit of shock."

"I just … are you sure?"

"Am I sure of what?"

"The will? It couldn't be that easy."

"Why not?"

"Because nothing comes to me like that. My parents have held a great deal over my head and I haven't been able to get out of any of it. I don't believe for a second it will be that easy."

She grabbed his shoulders and smiled. "I haven't said it's going to be easy. First, you need to find someone who can get a copy of the will. I don't know if your family's lawyers will read anything to you without alerting your mom and your brother. That is still a little weird to me."

"Yeah, me too."

"Use that money. Find someone we can trust. I don't know of anyone. Did your uncle know anyone?"

"I don't have a clue."

She cupped his face. "If you don't want to look, then you don't have to. I'm not taking the money, Drake. I'm not leaving. I'm going to fight for this and I'll wait until you're ready." She pressed a kiss to his lips and when she pulled away as if to leave, he let go of the envelope and grabbed her arm, not wanting to let her go.

"Drake?"

He gripped the back of her neck, tilting her head and slamming his lips down on hers, silencing any protest with a kiss. He'd missed her so much, missed this.

She let out a little moan and he swallowed it down. "Drake, Drake, we can't do this."

"And why the hell not?" he asked.

Her lips were already swollen and he didn't want to deny himself for another moment. He'd already had to wait for her, and this was just too much torture.

"I came to help you."

"Tell me you don't want this. You don't want me and I'll stop right now."

"Drake, we're in a house that could fall down on us."

"It's structurally stable. Believe me, nothing is going to hurt you." He had to have her. He cupped her face, staring into her eyes. "Please, Pru, I need you."

He wasn't lying to her. He was fucking desperate for her, ached for her.

She nibbled her lip and nodded. "I want you too." She put her hands on his shirt, sliding them up to wrap around the back of his neck.

He pulled her close, running his hands down her back and cupping her ass before going back up again, kissing her hard. He didn't want to let her go.

Pru started to unfasten the buttons of his shirt, and he didn't fight her. He helped her by gripping her shirt and tearing it open. The buttons keeping her away from him pinged in all directions but he didn't care.

The moment they were almost naked, he pulled her close, feeling her nakedness against his own. He closed his eyes, basking in the feel of her. "I've missed you so much."

"It hasn't been all that long since we were together," she said.

"It feels like a lifetime." He kissed her lips and slowly began to trail kisses down her body.

They got their shirts off and he took care of her bra. They were both completely naked in his uncle's rundown house and Drake kissed her hard. She whimpered and he had to stop.

"Wait," he said, and he couldn't believe he'd put a stop to their makeout session.

"What is it?" she asked. "Are you okay?"

"I'm fine. More than fine, but are you?"

"What do you mean?" she asked.

"What is this?" *What the hell are you doing? You've got the girl and you're kissing her. There could be a solution to all your problems.*

"What do you mean?" she asked.

"You're kissing me back."

"Don't you want me to kiss you back?"

"Yes."

"Drake, I'm really confused. You want me to kiss you but you want to stop kissing?"

"I do want to keep on kissing." He ran his fingers through his hair. "Unless this is goodbye."

"Why would it be goodbye?" she asked. "That doesn't make any sense."

"Look at what we've had to live through so far. Tell me this isn't goodbye?"

"It's not goodbye."

"You're not lying."

"I hate to say this, Drake, but you're really sounding like a girl." She stepped toward him, cupping his face. "Look at me. I'm naked. I'm here with you. I think I've found a way for us to be together and I'm not going anywhere. This isn't a goodbye kiss. I'm making out with my boyfriend. Is that a little hard for you to believe?"

He stroked her cheek. "Yeah, it is. Not your reasons behind it, but after everything we've gone through so far, it's hard for me. I've missed you, and spending any time away from you kills me."

"I hated being away from you as well. I hate your parents and your brother. It's hard to know what to call them." She giggled. "I'm sorry. I shouldn't laugh."

"I'm right there with you."

"I don't know if this will be our last time together. I don't know what the future is going to be like for us. I don't even know if we've found a solution. It could all be crap, but I do know that I want this. That I want you. I'm not kissing you and I'm not about to sleep with you because I'm going to leave. I'm here because I want to be here. There's no one else I could ever want to be with. I know it's hard for you to see the truth here, but it is. I don't want that money. I don't want anything but you. I'm sorry my parents took the money, but I'm not them. I'm my own person."

He'd heard enough. Kissing her hard, he silenced all of her reasons, no longer needing them. He believed her, trusted her, and there had never been a single reason to doubt her.

He'd opened up his jacket and spread it on the floor. Taking her down to it, he broke the kiss. "I should be doing this on a real bed. In a good house."

"Drake, there's nothing wrong with this house. It just needs a little loving and it'll be good as new. I can help you, if you'd like."

"This is what I love about you. Nothing is ever too much for you. You're always willing to be with me."

"I bet this was something out five-year-old selves couldn't imagine, right? You and me, dating, falling in love, finding ways against all the odds to be together."

"Damn, to think how much I hated you." He smiled down at her. "I can tell you I don't hate you. Far from it."

"I don't hate you either. I didn't hate you back then, but I've got to know, why did you push me away every single chance you got?" she asked. "I don't get it."

"I … I don't know. You were new and I think you were happy. It seems like a lifetime ago."

"It wasn't so long ago for either of us." She touched his cheek. "Why was my being happy a problem for you? I was never mean to you. In fact, I always tried to be nice to you."

"I know. I hated you for that. Nothing I did ever affected you, not really. You always rose above it. Then of course, you fought back, and it made me mad you would do something like that."

She giggled. "So no matter what, you were going to hate me and I was going to react the wrong way."

"I never told you my feelings were normal or even justified. I know I'm an asshole."

"You're not an asshole. You're a pain, sure, but, not an asshole, not anymore. Unless you push me away again. I'm not going to let you do it. You've got to stop letting them win, Drake. It's just you and me now."

He wasn't used to having anyone on his side. Even his best friends had their own agendas. He'd push them to see how far they were willing to go, but he knew they were there at his parents' request. Paid to be his friends.

Not once had he been given a chance to be normal. His whole life had been about control in one form or another. Each time with his parents playing in the background.

"You know you're the first one who has been real

to me. Who hasn't used me, who has given me the truth."

"There's nothing more I want from you, Drake, than you. I know you've spent a great deal of your life having to work with your parents, but you don't need to worry about them."

"What if they try to take you away from me? They will know you've helped me," he said.

His parents weren't above removing a problem.

She cupped his face. "I'm right here. I'll stay by your side. I don't have to go back home. I've realized I don't want or have a future unless it's with you, and I can't lose you." She pulled him close, kissing him. "Now, will you make love to me?"

"Are you horny?"

She laughed. "How old are you?"

"I'm old enough to know I'm horny." Even realizing all his life he'd been alone, and Pru was the only real person, he was still turned on by her. Nothing could ever take away his need to fuck. Moving between her spread thighs, he kissed her hard.

"You do realize, of we find out the truth and I get half of the money, I'm totally marrying your ass."

She rolled her eyes. "You haven't asked me, and I'm a traditional kind of gal. I need to be asked before I could even think of accepting."

"We're going to have a problem," he said.

"Why?"

"I don't ask. I never ask."

She giggled. "Then you're going to need to learn to give a little. I accept in a lot of things you don't ask. You're stubborn and you're used to getting what you want on a silver platter, but…"

"You better be careful of your *but*," he said. "It could get you in trouble."

"It sounds dangerous."

"Oh, it is. It'll mean a lot of kissing. A lot of sex."

"I can handle the sex, so long as you're up to the challenge. Do you really think you can handle me?" she asked.

He ran his hand down the curve of her ass, gripping the flesh. "There's not a single part on you I can't handle." He took possession of her lips again and she opened up to his touch.

She moaned his name in between kisses, and he could easily get used to the sound.

"I want you, Pru," he said.

"Then take me. Don't hold back."

He trailed his lips down to her neck, sucking on her pulse. He wanted to mark her so everyone knew who she belonged to. No matter what the will said, or his parents, he was done being their lap dog. He was going to find a way out of this for both of them. There was no way he was going to give her up.

After trailing kisses down her neck, he hovered over her breasts, staring at the beauty of each. She had nice, large tits, and as he flicked the tips with his tongue, she gasped.

"Sensitive?"

"Yes."

Taking one into his mouth, he bit down and her scream echoed around the house.

"That feels good."

He did the same to the second nipple, flicking the bud back and forth before biting down. Sliding down her body, he placed kisses over her stomach, following the path to just above her pussy. "Spread your legs."

"Drake?"

"I want to taste you. We're in this together. You're my girl, and I want to taste you."

She spread her thighs wide and he stared down at perfection. She was so pretty and it wasn't like him to think of a woman's pussy as sexy, but Pru's was. He'd been the only guy inside her.

He was never going to allow another man to take his place. Pru was his, would always be his, and he wasn't going to let her go, not ever.

Sliding his hands beneath her ass, he gripped her flesh and pressed his face against her pussy. He glided his tongue between her wet slit then plunged inside her, feeling her cunt tighten around his tongue. But he didn't stop there. Drawing his tongue up, he teased over her clit, circling the bud then delving back down to fuck her. Her taste was exquisite.

"Please, Drake," she said.

"Tell me what you want." He tongued her clit and listened as she begged him to let her come. He loved hearing her voice, and as he worked her pussy, he knew this time he wasn't going to let her go.

When she came, he didn't stop. He continued to stroke her until she screamed his name, and when she was poised and on the brink of a second orgasm, he moved up her body. Her orgasm coated his mouth as he kissed her lips.

Gripping his cock, he slid between her slick folds, found her entrance, and slowly began to fill her. Every single inch of her, swallowing him, consuming him. Setting him on fire for more, and he gave it to her. He plunged to the hilt, staring into her eyes as he began to rock back and forth, riding her.

She wrapped her legs around his waist. He gripped her hip and plunged in, fucking her, slowing down, and then speeding up.

"You feel so fucking good," he said.

"I love you, Drake. I love you so much."

"And I love you." He'd take on the world for her and he didn't think he'd ever felt such strong emotions in his life. He couldn't believe the person responsible for his mood change was Pru, but he didn't care. He loved her, and this was the reason he was willing to fight for as long as it took to keep her.

He'd grown tired of being his parents' puppet. All his life, he'd done what he'd been told, only rebelling in some stupid way to try to hurt them. He was a child then, but he wouldn't allow them to win against him again. He was going to fight them.

Kissing her hard as he fucked her, he knew this was the woman he was going to stay with for the rest of his life, and no one was going to take her from him. He'd fight to keep her. It would be the only thing he'd ever want and it would be worth fighting for.

Chapter Twenty-Five
We won

"You know, I don't like it when they charge me a fucking fortune for going against my parents," Drake said.

"Can you blame them? It took us two weeks to find the lawyer who'd be willing to go through the necessary channels, quietly so as not to alert anyone who may want to know if your real father's will was attempting to be located. We got that and it did cost a fortune, but you now have your answer."

"I do." He squeezed Pru's hand a little tighter as they walked down the main street toward his home. He didn't want to drive up to his parents' place, not when he finally had the means of being his own man. His lawyer and their private investigator had been able to find he was entitled to fifty percent of his father's wealth as well as shares within the company. He'd made a copy of the birth certificate citing his real father's name, and a simple blood test had helped to prove that his supposed father was, in fact, his brother and he was entitled to half of everything. The press had a field day as it had been brought to light who the new heir was who would inherit half of the fortune.

His parents, they tried to fight him, but the will was ironclad, all thanks to his real father. The one he never really got to know. The one who wanted to keep his fortune within his family.

He was now a wealthy man. Not only was he wealthy but he was also without any parents. Along with the will and getting half of the fortune, his lawyer had also set up an emancipation order for him. He had proven time and time again that he didn't need his parents and so the judge had ruled him free. His parents had to deal with the fallout but he didn't care.

"I couldn't believe it was this easy," he said.

"This easy? Drake, most of our senior year was fighting this. I'm taking a gap year so I don't have to go hunting for colleges so I can be by your side to help you. None of this, not a single part was easy. It was, in fact, really hard."

He pulled her close, kissing her lips. "Marry me," he said.

Pru pulled away. "What?"

"You heard me. I want you to marry me. I don't care about anything else right now. My parents can't hurt me. If they do, well, the press will have a field day with that information." When he was asked by one reporter what made him seek the emancipation order and the truth of the will, he'd told the woman straight—that his parents had told him to stop seeing the woman he loved.

To the press, it had made him a hero. The kind authors wrote about. He and Pru had also been approached as they hoped to tell their story. They believed many people would love to read about how they were once enemies and came together against all the odds, to live their happy ending.

"I expected a yes," Drake said.

"I know and I … wow. I mean, I expected it, but I guess this is all a little new for me." She laughed. "I can't believe how nervous I am. Does that make me crazy?"

"You're not crazy. Actually, that's a lie. You are fucking crazy.

"Drake?"

"What? You stuck around with me. You didn't give when many people would have. I know I would have. I've never stuck out for anything before in my life."

"You're a lot stronger than you give yourself

credit for," she said.

"Or you see something in me that I don't see."

"You're a good guy, Drake."

"It still doesn't answer my question, Pru. I love you more than anything in the world. I don't care about the company or the money, or anything else. The only person I want, the only love I have, is you. I'll give it all up to be with you."

Tears filled her eyes and he hated to see her cry. She didn't deserve those tears. "Please, please, don't cry. Don't do that. You know I can't stand it when you cry."

"I know." She sniffled. "I love you, and I know I shouldn't." She stopped to chuckle. "But I can't remember when it happened that I fell in love with you."

"And this makes you cry? Finding out you're in love should be a happy, joyous occasion."

"Oh, it is. I just … I can't believe it's finally over. It is over now, isn't it?"

Drake sighed. "I believe so. The will is ironclad. It was probably one of the reasons they never wanted me to find out the truth. I would've been able to contest it long ago if I knew the truth. Their hold on me was based on my inheritance. They did it all to keep me in place."

"And now that you're free, how do you feel?"

"Like I can take on the world."

She chuckled. "Do you want to take on the world?"

"No."

"Okay, Drake Connor, tell me. What is it you'd like to do? Not what is expected of you and not what you think I want you to do. I want to know your thoughts. Your feelings. No one else's."

He ran his hands down her back. "I want to make love to you."

"Get your mind out of the bedroom for one

second."

"Fine, I want to marry you, Pru. I want to make you mine and for the rest of the world to know who you belong to."

She opened her mouth, closed it, and smiled.

"Shocked?"

"A little."

"Why? You knew this is what I wanted."

"I guess I knew. I just didn't think it would be what you wanted. I mean, I'd hoped you'd still want me."

He cupped her cheeks, tilting her head back, and ran his thumb across her full lip. "There is no one else I want or could ever wish to be with. You're the love of my life, Pru. The money, I'd give it up in a heartbeat."

"Really? This coming from the guy who wanted to keep me as his dirty little secret so he could keep his money."

"Okay, fine. I didn't mean it like that. I knew what my parents would do, and they would go out of their way to hurt you and your family. Do you think I could ever live with myself if something was to happen to you?" He pushed some hair off her shoulder, stroking her cheek. All he wanted to do was kiss her, to hold her, and to convince himself he didn't need to put on a show. He'd won. His parents had lost and now, there was nothing holding him back. "I would always do everything I could to protect you."

"Pinch me."

"I'm not going to hurt you. Ever."

"Oh, I don't want you to hurt me. I want to know this isn't a dream."

He kissed her lips and heard her moan. "It's not a dream. You and me, Pru. You're mine now and I'm not letting you go."

She wrapped her arms around his neck and he ran his hands down her back, gripping her ass.

"Wait," he said to which she groaned. "I don't have an answer."

"An answer?"

"Will you marry me?" he asked. He let her go and slid down to one knee.

"Drake, you really don't need to do that."

He took her hand in his. He knew he didn't have to do anything but he was going to. "Pru, I love you so damn much. I love you more than anything. I want to see you every single morning and night. I want to hold you and the only way for me to do that is if you agree to marry me. Please, marry me, and make me the happiest man on the planet. Don't cry."

"When did you get so romantic?" she asked. "I don't expect you to be romantic at all, and here you are saying the right things. Stuff I really want to hear."

"I guess when I nearly lost you. It started all of this. I never expected to fall in love with you, Pru. I didn't see any of this happening. I always figured my life would be like my parents'. I'd find the woman they wanted me to marry, have a few kids, cheat with other women. Work myself into making more money."

"And now?"

"Now, I want to have a life with you. Just you. I don't want to play their games. I'm a free man. They will always be part of my life, I accept that, but they're under investigation now. The company, it falls to me, I want to do what I can to keep it going. Thousands of people rely on me to make the right decisions so they can stay in a job. All I want though, is you. You're my life, Pru. I want to grow old with you. Have a life where I wake up seeing you."

"You're making me cry."

"Please tell me for a good reason."

"Yes, it's all for a good reason."

"Is that a yes, you'll marry me?"

She nodded her head. "Yes, I'll marry you."

He pulled the ring from the box and slid it onto her finger. "I'm not going to give you the chance to back out now. You know this is you and me for life."

"I know."

He got to his feet and pulled her into his arms. "I love you, Pru."

"And I love you and I don't care what is thrown at us. No matter what people say, we will always fight them together, yes?"

"Yes." He pushed some of her hair off her shoulders and stared into her eyes.

"What is it?" she asked.

"I never thought I could be this happy." He'd watch his parents and saw how much they hated each other, and he believed that was how life was supposed to be. There was no way he could have ever thought to have these deep feelings for anyone, at least not for the girl he'd tried to hurt so many times. All of his anger and hatred had been wasted. There was no point to his feelings. Pru never deserved his anger or his scorn. He'd watched her and hated her on sight, seeing the happiness she felt with her family. Even when her family hadn't been rich, she'd been new and he'd been jealous of her. That was on him, not on her.

"What are you thinking?" she asked.

"I'm thinking about the first time I saw you."

"When you hated me?"

"I hated how your parents seemed to love you. They were there with you that first day, kissing you. Telling you it would all be okay."

"I was five."

"My parents were never there."

"I'm sure other kids' parents were there. Why didn't you hate them?" she asked.

"You were new and I don't know. I was a kid and I just wanted to hate someone. I don't hate you, Pru. I could never hate you. Can we forget the past?"

She tilted her head to the side and smiled at him. "I don't know. I think I'd like to keep on remembering the past. Without it, we wouldn't be here." She took his hand and locked their fingers together. "Besides, it's not how a story starts that matters. It's how it ends."

Epilogue Part One

Five years later

"So, what are your plans now?" Pru asked.

She looked up from where she'd been reading her book to see her husband of five years walking toward her. Water dripped down his body from where he'd been swimming in the ocean. This was their first-ever honeymoon.

They'd gotten married in Vegas the moment he'd been granted half of his inheritance, including his position on the board. He'd started renovating his uncle's house, and he'd flown her to Vegas to put a ring on her finger. From there onward, her life had been a whirlwind. With his parents being investigated for murder and other business offenses including fraud, and even child entrapment, the board had turned to Drake for guidance. Being only eighteen, he had no choice but to go to college and work his ass off as fast as he could for a business degree while also taking the advice of his real father's most trusted advisers and associates. During that time, she had also taken a business degree to help him where she could. She'd become his PA, and between the two of them, they were able to keep the Connor company up and running.

There were a lot of decisions they struggled with. Drake really felt the overwhelming pressure of being responsible for a lot of people's livelihoods. It meant a lot of sleepless nights, studying as long and as hard as they could. They had each other.

Which was why it had taken them over five years to finally get a honeymoon together. They'd been living in married … bliss, for a long time. They argued all the time, but it was their thing. She didn't hate him, not one bit, and after each argument, they always made it up to each other.

"Right now, I'm going to get some sunscreen and make sure my beautiful wife is completely safe from all these UV rays. I can't have her getting ill on me now, can I?"

"It sounds very protective," she said. "I was wondering what your plans are after our honeymoon."

"Are you in such a rush to be done with our honeymoon already?" he asked.

She let out a moan as he massaged the sunscreen into her body. "No, I'm not done yet."

"Good, because we took a long time to get here." He leaned forward and kissed her cheek.

She turned her head and smiled at him. "Can I let you in on a little secret?"

"You can let me in on anything."

"I don't want to leave. I'd love to stay here forever."

She closed her eyes as he rubbed a spot on her back. He was doing a lot more than rubbing sunscreen. He was massaging her back and making her ache for more.

"You know I could make that happen. We could get a place on the beach. All we'd have to do is fly out a couple of times a week to go to the office, but we could stay here."

"Nah, I know I don't want to leave, but we've got a life back home. It took us forever to get your uncle's place perfect." She rolled over and his fingertips stroked over her stomach. "I want us to live there, raise a family. Don't you want that?"

"I want to be wherever you are." He ran his fingers up, stroking beneath her breast.

She released a little gasp. "There are people here."

"I know. People can't see us right now. You should know and trust me. I would never do anything to hurt you, or let anyone see what belongs to me. You know how important you are and I will never give you up." He leaned down and kissed her.

"Pinch me," she said.

"Now, why would I do that when I've just told you I don't want to hurt you?"

"I don't know if I can handle all of this," she said. "I'm so happy, and I didn't think it was possible to be this level of happy." She cupped his cheek. "Look at us. Happily married."

"And in business together. Let's not forget that." His fingers moved down to her stomach.

"What's going on in that head of yours?" she asked. "You think I don't know when you've got something going on? I do and I know you're thinking about something. Let me hear it."

Drake didn't speak immediately and she sat up, giving him her full attention.

"What is it, Drake?"

"You know I love you, right?"

"Yes, and I love you too. You know that?"

"Yes, of course."

"Drake, you're worrying me now. I don't know what to do."

He laughed. "I … we've shared a lot together. You know about my family. My past. You've stayed by my side when I've fought my parents, and of course when I got rid of my friends."

Yes, his three friends who'd only been there because his family had paid them to keep an eye on him. Pru didn't like to think about them as they weren't even worth worrying about.

"Then of course there was Sean."

She'd pushed him out of her life as well. They only had each other. Everyone else, they'd left them in some form or another. There was no reason to keep people near them when they only seemed intent on destroying them. Pru had also found it easy to do the same with her parents. They had all been too toxic in their lives. She and Drake, they wanted a clean start, and the only way to get it was to cut off everyone else. They had successfully done it. Now, they were living their life.

"I haven't seen or heard from him in a long time," she said.

"He's doing okay. I hear he got married to his college girlfriend," Drake said.

"Good for him." She sat up and pushed Drake to the ground. "Now it's my turn to put sunscreen on you. Tell me more about this family you're wanting to have."

"I'd like a little boy or girl. Any kid to be honest. I want us to start a family, Pru. I'm ready. Are you?"

She looked down at the man she loved and smiled. Putting her hands on his body, she nodded. "Then, Drake, you better start putting a baby inside me."

Epilogue Part Two

Another five years later

"Come on, baby, push," Drake said.

"I'm pushing. Ow!"

"I know. I know." He held on to his wife's hand. This was the hardest part and he fucking hated it. The sex was always fun and he always made sure his woman was taken care of in the bedroom, but watching her suffer, this was the worst kind of torture he knew. Seeing her in pain was never a good feeling to him.

He hated this.

Their third baby in five years. They were only going to have one. No, he only wanted to have one. Their first baby was … torture.

He'd hurt and bullied Pru for years, but nothing had prepared him for seeing the pain in her eyes during birth. When she held their first-born daughter, Katie, he still hadn't wanted any more kids, but his wife, the love of his life, she had wanted more. The pain, she had told him, meant nothing.

Pru was one of the strongest women he'd ever known, and watching her give birth, not once, not twice, but now a third time, he didn't know how she survived.

After another push, she collapsed to the bed, and she didn't let go of his hands. He kissed her wet cheek. She was crying and sweating. "I don't know if I can do this," she said.

"You can, baby. He's being a little bastard, I know, but when this is done, you can rest. I'm here with you." He gripped her fingers tightly even though his had no feeling. "I love you."

"I love you too," she said, sobbing.

"Are you ready?" the doctor asked.

Pru nodded and Drake tensed up as she started to

push again.

She let out a scream, giving another push, and it was exactly what was needed. He heard his baby boy cry out as Pru collapsed to the bed, gasping for breath. "I can't do it again."

"It's okay. I've got you," he said.

"Well done. You have a beautiful baby boy," the doctor said, putting their latest addition into her arms.

Drake knew this feeling. The overwhelming love and contentment.

"Hello, Liam," she said. "I'm your mommy."

Their son opened his eyes.

"Your sisters are going to love you."

Drake kissed his wife, and then his new son's head.

Katie, Amy, and now Liam. His children.

"He's perfect," she said.

"The best," Drake said. "This will be our last."

"You keep on saying that, but we'll see." She lifted her hand for him to take. "I love you."

"I love you. More than you could ever know."

Epilogue Part Three

Ten more years later

    "And she still fell in love with you?" Liam asked.

    "Yes. You need to understand, though, I wasn't a good man. I was an awful man. Your mother deserved someone far better than me."

    Pru smiled at her husband as he told the kids the story of how they came to be. He left out all the gory details of his parents, but he made sure his kids knew that he hadn't been a good guy to start off with.

    "But, Mom, how could have you ever loved a bully? I mean, you tell me not to allow Adam at school to even bother me. You encourage me to stick up for myself," Katie said.

    "I stuck up for myself against your father all the time."

    "She's right," Drake said. "Not a moment went by when your mother didn't make me pay for what I did to her. I'm so pleased she never walked away."

    The alarm on the oven beeped and she got to her feet. "That's dinner. Go and set the table, kids. Wash your hands, you know the drill."

    She waited for the chaos of their five kids to run off. Their last baby, another boy, had been their final. She'd been too ill to have anymore, and even though she would have loved for them to have a big family, she knew she wanted to be around to see them all grow up. The doctor had warned her about the damage more children would do and her body wasn't strong enough. There was too high of a risk.

    Drake and she had talked long and hard about what it meant to them to have no more kids. They had come to the decision together.

    Drake grabbed her hand and pulled her down into

his lap.

"What are you doing?" she asked, giggling.

"Do you realize we've been married twenty years now?"

"That we have. Does this mean you're not going to be forgetting our anniversary this year?" she asked, teasing him.

"I never forget our anniversary. I seem to recall you going into labor and spoiling my big surprises."

She laughed. "I'm such a horrible, bad person, right? Giving birth to our babies."

"I love you," he said.

"I love you too."

"No, I was thinking about our past, what we went through. Thank you for never giving up on me. For giving me a chance."

She touched his cheek. "Drake, you own my heart. There is nowhere else in the world I'd rather be than right here, right now."

"Does that mean you've got a kiss for this old man?" he asked.

"Hey, you can't be that old. Unless you're calling me old?"

"I'm not doing anything of the sort." He pulled her in close and kissed her hard. "I love you so damn much."

"I love you too," she said. "More than anything in the world. In fact, I hope you don't have plans for the next twenty years because I intend to drive you crazy."

"I look forward to it."

The End

www.samcrescent.com

SAM CRESCENT

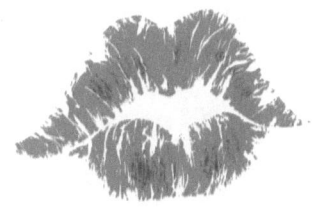

EVERNIGHT PUBLISHING ®

www.evernightpublishing.com

www.ingramcontent.com/pod-product-compliance
Lightning Source LLC
Chambersburg PA
CBHW021440240626
47153CB00001B/226